WOODS GIRL

WOODS GIRL

A novel by

JACK BOONE

Edited by

JOHN E. TALBOTT

BRAYBREE
Publishing

Published by BrayBree Publishing Company LLC

FIRST EDITION

ISBN-13: 978-1-940127-23-1

Printed in the United States of America

BB
BRAY
BREE
BrayBree Publishing Company LLC
P.O. Box 1204
Dickson, Tennessee 37056-1204

Visit our website at www.braybreepublishing.com

This reclaimed and completed novel is dedicated to the man who banged out the words on an old typewriter as the ideas and words poured from his heart and head. His words, thoughts, and ideas in this novel could have easily been lost to time and almost were. Indeed, both the author and the reading public have waited as long as 80 years for this—or any—dedication to be written.

And so, here's to you, Jack Happel Boone, and although it seems awfully presumptive and arrogant of me to dedicate your own work to you, still I congratulate you on your achievement.

ACKNOWLEDGEMENTS

I wish to acknowledge the assistance of several individuals whose efforts were integral to the successful publication of this long-lost work. My friend Dr. Shawn Pitts offered his thorough and critical reading of this manuscript and gave constructive comments. I am especially thankful to Wade E. Osburn for his very helpful and thoughtful assistance and cooperation, as well as that of my friend Karen Hobbs. The staff of Freed-Hardeman University's Hope Barber Shull Academic Resource Center provided assistance in my research. I am thankful to the late Fred Robertson for his gift of Jack Boone manuscripts and papers to me many years ago, from which part of this work was possible. Finally, I wish to thank Kevin McCann for his work in putting this work into such a presentable fashion that would make Jack

Boone himself proud. There are many whose efforts and patience allowed me to dedicate myself to this task and to them I am very grateful.

INTRODUCTION

THE PUBLISHING FIRM of Frederick A. Stokes published Jack Happel Boone's novel *Dossie Bell Is Dead* in 1939. Set in the Tolby Nation, it was a fictionalized version of West Tennessee's Hurst Nation. It told the sordid story of characters such as Luster Holder, Dossie Bell Holder, Heber Kiler, Birdie Kiler, Buck Humphries, Brother Winnie Lazenby, Sudie Lazenby, Granny Murdie Blackburn, and a host of others. It was the saga of a 48-hour period in which death and dark times were visited upon the Nation. The novel was well-received by critics and Boone was under contract with Stokes to publish two more novels, including a sequel to *Dossie Bell Is Dead*.

Jack Boone had published several successful short stories in nationwide and regional magazines and journals during the 1930s. He had professional and personal friendships with men such as Donald Davidson and Merle Constiner. His work was gaining attention and his subject matter was quite relevant to the times. His academic career seemed on the rise and his literary career seemed to be taking form. Boone's prospects never seemed brighter.

Mysteriously, it never happened. There were no more novels and no sequel. The once bright and promising literary career faded along with the academic career. By the end of the Second World War, he could no longer get anything published. By 1950, his academic career had reached its zenith and steady employment as an academic finally eluded him. Eventually, Jack Boone drifted into literary and historical obscurity. It all seemed to end and simply fade away. With his death in 1966, it seemed his career and literary legacy had died with him.

With the exception of a very few people in and around Chester County, Tennessee, no one remembered him or his writing. *Dossie Bell Is Dead* was accepted as his one and only novel-length work. With each passing decade, the dim mist of history slowly engulfed Jack Boone and the facts of his life slipped further away from the world.

My first interest in the man and the writer began in 1994. For more than a quarter of a century, I studied this local literary figure. His life was and remains a mystery. Then in the summer of 2019, the pursuit of the man and the career seemed to come together. It began with the publication of the 80th Anniversary

Edition of *Dossie Bell Is Dead*. This edition was published originally to expose another generation to the novel that many compared to *Tobacco Road*, setting up Boone as the next Faulkner. I also wanted to present an unpublished novel called *The Dean's Secret*, a satire about state universities and their concentration on athletic programs. The subject matter had little broad appeal, but it was Boone's answer to his own personal conflicts with university administrators during his academic career.

Then the unexpected happened. I realized, quite by accident, that the keys to the mystery lay only a block away from my office. Jack had died in 1966 and his brother Vernon a year later. At the time of their deaths, they were living in a small garage apartment on Cason Street in Henderson, Tennessee, the town in which I practice law. Their lives were spartan at best, a sort of enlightened poverty. The brothers drank heavily but were generally quiet-natured in their older years. Their mother was dead and they had no relatives in Henderson. The little garage apartment became a dilapidated time capsule. Their personal effects and stacks of papers, writings, and battered furniture gathered dust for several years. In the mid-1970s, Freed-Hardeman College (now Freed-Hardeman University) purchased the lot and the little garage apartment.

Fortunately, for the sake of posterity, someone saw fit to box up the papers scattered around the little apartment and store them in the college's archives.

There they have remained with no fanfare, no publicity, and no apparent interest for over forty years. As I searched through the boxes of material, I was overwhelmed. I had never expected to find them and yet there they were. They were of special interest to me because I already had a large collection of Boone's letters, writings, short stories, portions of manuscripts, and the unpublished manuscript for *The Dean's Secret*. With this newfound collection, suddenly the story became more complete and things began to make more sense as I tried to understand Jack Boone.

As I poured back through my own Boone papers and those at the university, I began to assemble pieces of a mysterious puzzle. I had long wondered why the sequel to *Dossie Bell Is Dead* had never been written despite Jack being under contract to do so. In fact, as I discovered through bits and pieces contained in both collections, he had indeed written that sequel. It was entitled *Woods Girl* and told the story of what happened to the major characters of *Dossie Bell Is Dead*, including Luster Holder, Heber Kiler, Birdie Kiler, Buck Humphries, Brother Winnie Lazenby, Sudie Lazenby, and Granny Murdie Blackburn. It also chronicled the conflicts between Luster Holder, the Greeber family, and Heber Kiler.

However, it was not a simple proposition or process. I discovered a number of interesting and perplexing facts about this hitherto unknown sequel. Jack had sat down and written the novel on three different occasions. His efforts began in and around 1939, the same year that *Dossie Bell Is Dead* was published. He worked on it for several years, producing two type-written manuscripts and a handwritten one between 1939 and 1945. Unfortunately, by 2019, only bits and pieces of these versions existed. Segments were intact but none in their entirety. In all, nineteen pieces of manuscripts were scattered among both collections and more than 450 pages of notes and manuscripts from which a discernible story could be extracted.

Over a period of three months and more than 400 hours of intense effort, an intelligible manuscript began to emerge. Slowly but surely, the pages, chapters, and story came together. Like pieces of a quilt, the pieces had to be sewn together. It became necessary to write transitional sentences and paragraphs in some cases. A few scenes were evidently incomplete. Using his notes and my own knowledge of Boone's writing style, I was able to mend and tie these loose literary ends together without altering the intent or style of his work.

I must confess that when I first encountered the pieces of long-forgotten manuscripts, I thought I had found the first drafts of *Dossie Bell Is Dead*. But as I continued to read them, I realized that it was a story that took place anywhere from three to five years after Dossie Bell Holder's death. I settled on four years ultimately, a nice middle ground. In the course of *Woods Girl*, there emerges a more thoughtful, more deliberate Luster Holder. We learn that Jack's characters have depth not explored in his first novel. The pieces of this sequel were sometime found on the back of other manuscripts, as Boone had reused these pages to type new manuscripts and new stories. Still, they were there.

I feel it imperative to give the reader an idea of the struggle it took to bring this long-lost novel to life. In the summer of 2019, no one knew a sequel existed except for Jack Boone and he had been dead for more than 53 years. That fact made the effort to extract the novel from the mist of time even more difficult. No one knew the storyline but Jack. No one knew the intent of the characters but him. It was all there, but it was a jumble of words, phrases, and pages. In some places, I found three complete versions of the same chapter though each was written slightly or significantly different. In some cases, only one version of a chapter existed, but it was scattered and the pages had to be carefully reassembled to pull together the completed chapter. In other cases, portions of three versions were pulled together to render a complete chapter. It was a daunting task, yet entirely worth the effort. A work that has been eighty years in the making, *Woods Girl* is now a reality.

There remains for me certain questions for which there are still no apparent answers. Why, when he was under contract, did Boone fail to submit a completed manuscript? Or did he? The answer is simple. We just do not know. Why did he write three different manuscripts and yet never make any apparent effort to publish it? Again, we do not know. There is no correspondence to indicate that the manuscript was ever submitted for publication. With the existence of five other novels, why was this one with three drafts so incomplete and apparently discarded by Boone? When did he abandon his effort to write this sequel? Once again, we simply have to venture an intelligent guess.

Despite these questions and the lack of discernible answers, there remains a fascinating tale that was thrice told. Indeed, *Woods Girl* is an interesting story. Not only does it expound upon the various characters introduced in *Dossie Bell Is Dead*, but it gives a clearer picture of the environs of the novel—the Tolby Nation, Firbank, and Sobby. The Nation and its people, in all their virtues and limitations, are portrayed perhaps more fully as a community than they were in *Dossie Bell Is Dead*. There is more depth to the characters. Their thoughts and attitudes are more fully explored. Boone makes what appears to be a far more deliberate effort to define his characters, an effort that greatly enhances the overall story.

Ultimately, Tiddy Greeber—a young girl of the Nation and a native of Missouri—is our woods girl though she is not particularly the main character or protagonist. Following a pattern that Boone used in *Dossie Bell Is Dead*, a series of events and story lines play out in each chapter as the novel progresses that all come together to provide an explosive and interesting climax. The harshest possible penalties must be paid by some and others finally get the rewards for which they have longed.

Buck Humphries emerges in *Woods Girl* as a young man taking on the responsibilities and burdens of an adult. He has choices to make and he makes them, for good or for bad. He is in a different position than four years earlier when he was a scared boy being sought by Squire Heber Kiler.

Luster Holder is once again presented as a man who has had his eyes on a goal for a long time and will now achieve it due to fortuitous circumstance. Yet he is also shown as a man who has tolerated insults and efforts that undermine his reputation within the Tolby Nation, yet he chooses to ignore such indignities and keep a cool head. He is portrayed in this work as far more complex than he was in *Dossie Bell Is Dead*. The first book depicted him in appearance psychologically not much better than an animal. He was a man who said little, apparently thought little, and showed no emotion when presented with the death of his woman, Dossie Bell. He sits and appears unmoved by scandalous confessions and is given little credit as a thinking being.

That changes in *Woods Girl*. In this work, Luster Holder appears as a man of emotion—calm and deliberative emotion, but still emotion. He is a weary man frustrated by his circumstances and by misunderstandings of his own nature. He doesn't understand why Sudie Lazenby doesn't just leave him and free them both from their frustrating existence. He doesn't quite understand why the Greebers believe he poses a threat to them or why they work so hard to bring harm to him. Luster, we learn, has been watching his enemies and is more than prepared to meet the death challenges they are going to pose to him. He is tired of people, including Birdie Kiler. He is tired of being misunderstood by folks who call him such names as the "half-blood Indian" or "the Cherokee." He is a weary man confronting the factors that have wearied him so much.

Then there are the antagonists who are constantly working toward self-serving goals. They include Squire Heber Kiler, his rebellious daughter Birdie Kiler, and the Greeber menfolk, especially Ard and Tank. These people, all in some form or another, pay the price for their sins and transgressions. Their ultimate individual fates change the course of Firbank and Tolby Nation history.

The cast of supporting characters are indeed characters. There are the gossipy old authorities on the care of the dead and the news of the living, among them being Granny Murdie Blackburn, Clemmie Bean, and Urfie Pearl Buckner, all ready to share the news of the Nation. There is the simpleton, Wurner Crouse, universally recognized as an "idiot" but also credited with being the best newscaster in the Nation. There are the children—Dink, Pistol, and Tadpole—all pitiful and crude beyond their tender years. Brother Winnie Lazenby, described by Squire Kiler as a woman in men's breeches, and his estranged wife, Sudie Lazenby, are seen as the hapless and sympathetic characters they are. Blanche Greeber finally appears in the midst of the action swirling around the Nation. Finally, we see the people of the Nation gathering to ensure they don't miss the biggest events in recent Nation history.

It also becomes evident that the Nation is a land full of historians. The people retain the memory and knowledge of big events and don't let go of them. This trait turns out to be a major irritant to Luster Holder but a great help to the reader. Events are happening at great speed and gravity. Who will prevail and who will fall? Who will thrive? Who will simply survive? Who will wind up in Sobby Cemetery? The story is finally before our eyes after 80 years of waiting. How does it measure up? Well, that is an individual judgment. It is hoped that the reader will enjoy it, take something away from it, and understand these characters and their ultimate fates.

It is important for the reader to understand that *Woods Girl* is a product of its time and the social mores of that time. Just as in *Dossie Bell is Dead*, the reader will be confronted with terminology and attitudes that may not be particularly comfortable. In fact, the reader will encounter racist terminology but no different than found in Mark Twain's *Adventures of Huckleberry Finn*. While we see it disdainfully today, we still must consider the times in which this work was written. As in his first novel, Boone provides a literary snapshot of his times. Those times, like ours, possess their virtues as well as their negative aspects. We do not have to agree with the attitudes and language of Boone's characters to understand and appreciate the story being presented on these pages.

Like most of Jack Boone's literary works, *Woods Girl* has waited decades to see the light of day. The lost career of this frustrated but creative man is reemerging. As each of his long-lost short stories and novels are edited and published, the hope is that Boone's voice will finally find an audience so long after he last pressed the key of a typewriter. There's no question that he never found his audience, perhaps largely due to the nature of the publishing industry in his day. This is a new era and publication options are far greater than they were when he was a writer in the twentieth century. The determination to give Boone an opportunity is strong. I am determined to see that his works are fully available.

Therefore, it is with pleasure and satisfaction that I present to the reading public *Woods Girl*, the long-lost and now found and reassembled sequel to *Dossie Bell Is Dead*. Perhaps somewhere on the ethereal plain, as Jack Boone himself called it, the author is pleased that his works will not be lost and forgotten after all. Maybe the wait and the suspense were worth it. Just maybe. Enjoy!

John E. Talbott, J.D.
Administrator
Jack Happel Boone Estate

WOODS
GIRL

1

A T THE CRACKLE OF LEAVES, the squatting hunch-backed man edged farther back in the bushes and away from the woods trail. The Nation woods were thick and dense. The undergrowth was perfect for hiding away and bushwhacking a man. It was the way it sometimes had to be. Folks in the Tolby Nation were accustomed to bushwhackings and sur-prise attack. That kind of thing had set them apart and was what birthed them as a community when the Civil War ended. And men like the squatting hidden hunchback could only exist in the confines of the Nation. They simply weren't made for the side-walks of Melburg or towns like it. And even in the Nation, Ard was an oddity.

As he squatted in the thick undergrowth, one huge strong brown hand tightened on the barrel of the shotgun across his lap. The old shotgun was well-oiled and clean. It had brought down many varmints from the trees, bushes and fields. It could do the job and do it well. That hunchback, Ard Greeber, thrust out his grizzly chin, eyes boring through an open space in the leaves and saw the tall figure emerge from the depth of trees and approach in long, easy strides. In fact, the tall Cherokee hillman, Luster Holder, always took easy strides.

Greeber saw the hard black eyes and above them the bangs-like cut of the dark straight hair, the shoulders which bulged beneath the khaki hunting coat. He now grabbed the gun with both hands. He didn't raise it and he was calm but inside he was shaking to his core. He didn't change his position even when the lithe figure came closer, closer, then stopped abruptly, sniffing the air like a wild animal. He held himself stone-still until the other resumed his silent way, then passed on, the sound of his retreat growing fainter and fainter and fainter before it was drunk up by the silent woods.

But Ard Greeber's heartbeat wasn't silent. He could almost hear the thump-thump of his excited, angry heart beating in his own chest. It beat in rhythm with his heavy, labored breathing. Fear, excitement and anger fueled him and pushed him along.

The stooping hunchback dug his long, claw-like fingers into the dark earth and crushed handfuls of dirt and leaves in his powerful hands. Those same powerful hands had a vice-grip-like strength. He seemed more animal than human. And so as Ard Greeber stared at the figure in the near distance and his hatred boiled and seethed, he remained quiet. His mind wandered to what he could do. The deformed man had, for the last year, heard story after story about Luster Holder and the entire Tolby Nation held the big Cherokee in a combination of respect, awe, fear and wonderment.

Sure, the deformed hunchback had heard the stories. Hell, they'd all heard how fearless Luster Holder was, how he ran the wildest portion of the Nation territory. They'd heard about his woman, how she'd died and the saga of her burial. They'd heard about the influence of Luster Holder in this remote and lawless portion of West Tennessee. It perturbed not only Ard, but the whole damn Greeber clan that the half-breed Indian was held in such awe and fear, which would likely amuse Luster Holder himself, who didn't think about such things generally.

"I could'a plugged the bastard easy," he thought, "but that ain't the way I'm wantin' it. I might coulda lept out and rode him to the ground if I hadn't minded what folks say about him. They say he's got ears like a blood hound and as fast as 'ere panther ever jumping from a low limb. And they say he always carries a 32-20 under his belt and has knucks and a frog-sticker and can use 'em so fast he'll leave a body full of holes so quick his victim don't even feel no pain a-tall. I can tell 'em at the house he sho' can't be bushwhackered. You can see it by his eyes that he don't miss nothin'. Hit'd take me and the whole durn family to do hit. But by God, I ain't wantin' it that way. Hit ain't just no family affair I thinkin' of now."

All this the hunchback silently contemplated as his breathing grew more and more normal and his nerves calmed and simmered.

He mulled it all over. His thoughts continued, "Hit's her, goddam her. That damn Birdie Kiler! Luster may of coldcocked Pap but she spurned me… spit and throwed 'hit in my face and said it was him she was cravin' because he was a man and no mon-stronony built like a spider and which 'orght to mate with a female river turkle. And that damn Cherokee loved Mammy Blanche. He didn't give an hoot-in-hell about Birdie! No, I ain't wantin' to bushwhacker him. I aim to meet him head on where folks can see. I'll break that durn gun barrel back of his head like it was a broken splinter. Then I'll show her whether I'm a man or a varmint."

That's what Ard Greeber was thinking…pure and simple. He got to his feet, pushing the holly leaves, stickers and all, aside and stepped out in the path, gun grasped in one hand. He didn't straighten up, for he couldn't. Standing, he was still squat to the ground, his insect-like legs folded beneath his stom-ach, which ballooned out like a bullfrog's. His feet, in split brogans, were daintily small for the huge torso, which barreled up to massive shoulders whose bulging muscles strained the seams of his thin rayon shirt. The shoulders tapered back to a small waist, tightly bound with a broad leather belt, and in the middle of his back was a mountainous hump which seemed to give him balance and keep him from toppling over. He was indeed a queer sight to behold.

The bare head was huge and moon-shaped, and a fine bristly stubble grew sparsely over the purplish scalp. His elongated chin was sharply thrust out from the prognathous jaws, and the full-lipped mouth beneath a splayed nose revealed the sharp yellow tips of his eye teeth. His porcine eyes were reddish and sunken deep in hollow sockets, the bushy brows meeting an inch below the hair line. He had no neck. The head was flush with his shoulders.

With one clawy hand, he worked a pint bottle from the pocket of his gray-cotton breeches and began gouging at the wedged cork with flat fingernails. He stopped and turned a bristly ear to the wind. He shook his head ponderously, then impatiently flipped off the neck of his bottle with his thumb and, thrusting the clean-cut opening into his mouth, drained the bottle. With a curse he tossed it into the bushes and wiped his hands on the front of his shirt and began shuffling up the path in the direction in which the other man had disappeared.

2

THERE HAD BEEN over four years of peace in the Nation—dreary, monotonous peace—which was enough to make a body long for the clammy feel of Death's cold hands. Then just as it seemed that Murdie Blackburn would have to go on to her grave without ever again experiencing the thrill of laying out another murdered corpse, fortune smiled on the cantankerous old soul. Only last year Tank Greeber, with his wife, six sons, one daughter and little Negro boy, had come to West Tennessee from Missouri and bought the Luke Tolby place on the edge of the Nation. Squire Heber Kiler, a brother-in-law of Luke Tolby's, had sold Tank the old three-hundred acre farm, although it really belonged to Birdie through her mother, she being Luke's sister. After the Greebers got settled, Tank surprised

Nationites by announcing that he was a first cousin of Luke Tolby and the last male descendent of the original Tolby clan. Yes, sir, Tank had big plans. He was going to run Luster Holder right out of the Nation and reclaim the thousand acres which John Holder had stolen...something Luke had had better sense than to even try.

Apparently, Tank Greeber lacked that better sense. To make matters worse, Tank and his sons set up a moonshine still down by the Forked Deer River and began selling liquor in competition with the half-breed...something else no one had ever dared to try. Luster could deal with competition as long as it was fair and above-board. But Tank wasn't fair or above-board. He was low-down and he aimed to destroy the big hillman. Still, threats and dirty tricks wouldn't draw out a man like Luster Holder.

Months passed while the Greeber threat echoed and re-echoed on hill and in hollow from the Seven Ridges to the Big Survey, all over the Nation. Folks talked in whispers about the Greebers being touched in the head at trying to provoke a killer like Luster Holder, and death struck again. Death was a neighbor the Nationites had come to know well. She didn't come to borrow sugar or flour, but souls and she kept them. She didn't return them or bring anything to replace them but grief and sorrow.

And this time, she came for a Greeber. Tank Greeber, sire of six sons and one daughter, was found drowned in a barrel of his own sour mash at his own

backwoods still. Finding him alone at the still, someone must have crept up on him while he was lean-
ing over testing a barrel and heaved him head over
into the thick alcoholic mash, for when Ard Greeber
discovered him, only his bare feet were visible. Even
Ard thought it an odd sight, a man drowned in his
own creation.

The Greebers settled on Luster Holder as the
murderer, but the law wasn't so sure nor were the
folks of Firbank, who knew the half-breed. "It wasn't
Luster's method," the law men said. He would have
shot or knifed or choked Tank, but it all would have
been done face to face with no sneaking. It looked
like the work of a bushwhacker. When the officers
refused to go back in the hills and question Luster,
the Greebers said they'd go themselves and drag him
out alive so they could beat him to death before the
eyes of all in the Nation. The law advised them to
be satisfied to just bury one of the family under the
cedars at Sobby graveyard. And, investigating stories
about Luster they'd heard and never believed, they
decided to wait until he came out of his own country
before tackling him. However, Ard, the hunchback,
who was affectionately called Spider by the brothers,
cursed all of them and set himself to get even with
the Cherokee in his own way.

Like some slimy creature which had crawled from
the green coating of a bottom slough, Ard scrabbled
over the outskirts of the Nation country firing his
challenges at Luster to show himself and be judged.

The monster showed no fear, for he'd made it plain he wanted the meeting with Luster to take place right in front of Goddard's Store any Saturday evening the Cherokee chose to appear. Two weeks had passed since Ard had hurled his dares, spreading the word in that bear-growl voice of his, a voice which was birthed in his huge belly and blown out at his throat, that Luster Holder was a yellow coward and didn't dare accept his challenge.

But Nationites knew better. Nobody ever knew what the giant hillman was really thinking. He never talked and he always acted unpredictably, biding his time until the right moment. Folks at Firbank knew he wasn't afraid of God, man or the Devil. They remembered how he had killed four revenuers at one sitting when they raided his still. They hadn't forgotten the two deputies sheriff who came out after him and whose bodies were never found. They recalled the thieves who were caught snaking out logs on his bottomland the morning that Dossie Bell lay cold in death, a white man and a Negro, the only evidence of whose disappearance were the circling buzzards over the old Chickasaw Mound on Luster's farm near the Forked Deer River. They remembered the fights at the store when the Cherokee had been ganged early in his career. They could still see the flashing knife, the crashing fists, the glint of the brass knucks, the heaving, the gouging and the stomping. They could still hear the snapping of ribs, the cracking of joints and see the blood dying the clay hitching lot at the

Firbank store. They could still read the epitaphs on the blackening headstones above the graves of those who had disputed the unwritten laws of John the grandfather, Nick the father and Luster the son, men who had lived their own lives and were never known to start trouble unless it was shoved off on them.

Ard Greeber was a fool, many said, and should be satisfied to mark his old pappy off as a total loss, one who'd got careless and messed with the wrong man. Even if Luster had tired of his new woman, Sudie Lazenby, and was horsing for Birdie, Ard had better forget that too. It was hard to live, easy as hell to die. Folks knew in their hearts just how easy Luster Holder could make it for a man to die.

But there were some who said that Ard Greeber wasn't human and that if ever he got those huge animal claws of hands on Luster's throat, the Cherokee's days in the Nation would be ended. Over in the stock-trading lot at Melburg, hadn't Nodey Simms seen Ard knock a young bull cold with one backhanded sweep of his broad hand? Hadn't Dermon Coates, that mule man from out of Missouri, seen Ard wrestle a grizzly bear at a county fair last fall? He'd gotten his long arms around the bear's middle and popped its back like a peppermint stick.*

Any way a body looked at it, Ard Greeber just wasn't human, and it'd pay Luster to be prepared to use every means to preserve his life when that

---

* Boone's short story "Out of Missouri" told how fierce a wrestler Ard "Spider" Greeber could be.

meeting took place. Wurner Crouse said he'd spied on Ard back in the woods and that he bayed at the moon like a hound when it shone full and silver down through the pines. Wurner said that Ard carried on everyday conversations with animals and one reason he couldn't be hurt was that he had a topa conjured into his belly by an old Negro voodoo woman in Missouri, a topa in the form of a black panther. But folks gave it the lie because Wurner was an idiot, was always seeing things himself and probably imagined all of it. No matter, Ard was dangerous without witch-stuff and it was rumored that even his own brothers were afraid of him, as had been his pappy before them. And everyone could believe that.

Murdie Blackburn, better known in the Nation and round about as Granny Blackburn, knew better. The idiot was speaking the truth. Yes, she had lived to meet another day of great promise. Tank Greeber's murder had been a good, sound primer and had rekindled the fire in her spirit. Never had she so enjoyed a sitting up so much as she did that one over the old Greeber sire. Everybody it seemed had been there, including Luster Holder, although the family had sent word for folks to stay away. Granny had called Urfie Pearl and Clemmie and they'd gone together. They heard the news and were there when the boys rode up with their father thrown across a mare mule like a long sack of wet meal.

In memory she could see those Greeber sons even now, the four grown ones...Code, Corbin, Seeby and

Sarl and the boy Clell, dark, slouched, and as unholy mean-looking as hungry wolves.

Granny Blackburn had put the grieving widow to bed and cleared the menfolk out of the house, including the little boy, Pistol, who didn't seem to know what had happened and cared less. She tried to chase out that girl Tiddy, the only daughter, but had given up and let her stay, after she'd threatened to set fire to the house. She'd never forget that young wench, slim and curved and wearing nothing but a thin cotton dress. The girl had arms and legs browned by the sun and the wind. Like a satisfied cat stalking a bird, saucer-big eyes like wet periwinkles in that impish brown face, she watched the three of them lay out her old pappy. She was just a little bitch to an old woman but enough to set boy and man to snorting like an aroused stud horse being led toward the standing stall. It was known far and wide that Tiddy ran wild like a wood-born creature and it was easy to believe she was chasing after poor Buck Humphries.

There had been glorious confusion attendant on such occasions. It had been another night of never-to-be-forgotten excitement. And while they'd raked the mash off the bloated old codger with a curry comb and scrubbed him with a horse brush before they ended up sending him off to the undertakers to be embalmed, the pet cat, Sylvester, and her brood of ten-week old kittens had squalled and meowed at the screens. Two hound dogs whimpered and mourned under the floor. The widow herself was stoic, quiet and seemingly unaffected but four of the brothers cursed, drank and fought on the verandah. That varmint Ard had bayed at the moon from a windswept hillside back of the house, his Godawful howls splitting the silver night like something gone stark mad.

At the wake proper, Blanche Greeber, the wife had appeared and, like folks said, she was the prettiest woman to live in the Nation since Dossie Bell Holder. A blonde with honey-gold hair and sky-blue eyes, she was Tank Greeber's second wife, the mother of Tiddy and Pistol, and seemed untouched by grief at his passing.

Granny Blackburn had seen enough to believe what she'd heard about Squire Kiler's being so interested in the Greeber widow, that he was planning to double-cross Ard on the trade for Birdie. It was funny that the hunchback hadn't sensed it himself. But the Squire wasn't the only one interested in Blanche Greeber. Even on that night, she had noticed how the men-folk kept eyeing her. And it hadn't escaped her that the widow kept staying in the room with the body of the man she surely couldn't have loved. Had Luster Holder's presence had anything to do with it? Was he the one she kept watching, like she was trying to settle it in her mind whether or not he was the murderer. If Luster was aware of her presence, no one knew for certain.

Granny Blackburn gave thought to so many things she'd seen up to now. When Luster's woman, Dossie Bell, had died, that was a time of real excitement, the kind Granny recalled with soft eyes. The very same day, Bode Holley's body was found with its throat cut just like Luke Tolby's in a drift of the Forked Deer. The deaths had been a puzzle. They'd been gunning for each other but they sure-God couldn't have cut each other's throats. Anyway, at that great and memorable time, Birdie had birthed a baby boy in a crib at Kiler's barn, even while the funeral of Dossie Bell was in progress up at the Sobby church house. It was also shortly before the body of her mother, Millie, was found in the woodlot, dead of a stroke, even while she was on the way to Luster's cabin to help out. Granny had found Birdie in the crib, bloody as any hog ever fresh shot and slaughtered, with the baby squalling in her lap.

Yes, those were two great days and nights, enough to make a body live a long life just to see it happen. The old Squire had dragged the unwilling Nazarene minister, Brother Winnie Lazenby, through the bottom in search of the boy, Buck Humphries. It was young Buck, whom the Squire said was the father of Birdie's baby. While all of this was happening, Sudie Lazenby went to Luster's cabin in the rain to sit up with Dossie Bell's corpse. Everybody knowed Luster laid Sudie that same night in the cabin while Dossie Bell was laid out in the next room with the storm roaring and the cats squalling trying to eat the corpse. Then there was the funeral, with the church crowded with men, women and children from every spot in the county and the Nation. Brother Lazenby had broken down and confessed his love for Dossie Bell and told how he'd caused her death by slipping out there to her cabin while Luster was away and how he'd tried to get Dossie Bell to leave Firbank with him. He had accused her of giving herself to the seventeen-year old Buck Humphries before she admitted that Buck was her own bastard son. Her heart was weak and she dropped dead.

Folks at the Sobby church house expected the big Cherokee to kill the preacher then and there. But after the services, Brother Lazenby didn't show up at the grave. He had left in a hurry for parts unknown and hadn't been heard of since. Luster had taken Sudie home with him back to those wild hills to take Dossie Bell's place as his woman, and she'd been seen by few people since.

That was four years ago, a wonderful, wonderful time. Buck Humphries hadn't been forced to marry Birdie, although the child, which at first looked kind of dark like the Tolbys, got to favoring Buck more and more. Birdie made peace with her father and he agreed for her to entertain the men of the Nation and round about if she'd make them pay and would split the earnings with him.

Yes, there'd been peace in the Nation and the territory for four years now but that was about to change. Now was the promise of the greatest day of Granny Blackburn's eighty-five odd years. The only thing not definite as of yet was whether her route would lead back to the Greeber home two miles the other side of Firbank or deep into the wilderness of the Nation hills to Luster's cabin where, according to the Bible, he lived a life of sin with the Nazarene minister's wife.

Whichever way the course lay, Granny Blackburn was ready.

She dipped in silence, beady little eyes sparkling with the fire of anticipation, as she waited for the inevitable, old but far from outworn and with the patience of a mangy old bitch hound.

But after a while, she got tired of sitting. She craved action. When she sat too long, her blood just stopped circulating and seemed to dry up and blot around in her veins. She pushed up slowly from the chair and crept just as slowly down the steps.

Pecking along with her hickory stick, she set out in the direction of Firbank, three miles away.

3

URFIE PEARL BUCKNER met the two old women at the steps. "Come on in and set, gals," she greeted them. "I was expecting you'uns."

Granny Blackburn and Clemmie Bean took seats in shuck-bottomed chairs in the open hallway between the cabin walls. Granny Blackburn gripped that knotty old hickory stick between her stilty legs, and the flaps of her black poke bonnet jiggered up and down as she worked her toothless gums together. She struggled to regulate her wheezing breath.

Urfie Pearl, a tall, rail-thin woman with watery blue eyes, continued to stand. "Wurner just left," she said, "he was in a hurry to git to the store, so I told him to leave off going by your places because I knowed you was on your way here. That idiot was out there last night and says that Luster'll sure show up at the set time."

"I was dead certain he'd come out this time," Clemmie said. She was a birdlike woman with parchment skin, and her phlegmy gray eyes, continuously shifting, darted from right to left ceaselessly, like at any moment she might leap up from her chair and flee in panic. She was indeed a gray, yellow-skinned little mousy woman who was constantly nervy, restless, whispery, and always listening.

Urfie Pearl sat down and lifted a dishpan of whippoorwill peas to her lap. The sun of mid-afternoon played cat-and-mouse on the broad floorboards as it sieved through the greenish-yellow leaves of a chinaberry tree at the end of the back porch.

"Like us gals have been figuring for a long time," Urfie Pearl continued, "things between Luster Holder and the Greebers are coming to a head, because Luster's at last got tired of havin' that spider critter lowrating how he's gonna crush ever' bone in his body and leave him for the buzzards to feast on. He's accepted Ard's dare and'll meet up at Goddard's store without no weapons except what they was borned with, I'm sure of that!"

"Is it all set for four o'clock?" Clemmie asked.

"Yes, but you and Granny'll have time to set a while and git your breath back before we start," Urfie Pearl told her.

Clemmie edged her chair closer to the other two.

"Wurner ain't got the sense of a bitch mink," she said in a thread-thin voice, "but he don't falsify none. I seen folks passing our place before sunrise on their way to Firbank, and I guessed the blow-off was really coming, so I hurried over to Granny's and we come over here as fast as we could make it."

Urfie Pearl reached for her snuff jar beside the chair.

"Accordin' to Wurner," she began, "they're piling in from all directions and are already so thick around the store and schoolhouse you can't stir 'em with no stick, and..."

"I'm thinking Luster's come out of them hills one time too many, for Ard won't be up there by hisself," Clemmie broke in, "if him and them brothers don't bushwhack him before he reaches Firbank, they'll sure gang him up there, for they aim to have revenge for their pappy's death."

Urfie Pearl drilled the smaller woman with glassy eyes, "Listen, Clemmie, Luster ain't afraid of all the Greebers put together, Code, Corbin, Clell, Seeby, and Sarl, with Tiddy and Pistol throwed in. And you know as well as me that it never was proved that Luster killed Tank Greeber no-ways. The law never found no solid facts."

Clemmie licked her snuff-cased lips and said weakly, "Them officers never ventured back in them hills to talk with Luster hisself. But that ain't the main reason Ard wants him out of the way. Although I don't believe it at all, Ard hisself thinks that report that Wurner knowrated all over the Nation earlier this week wasn't no false one, though it was plumb pesticatin' to git straight just what the idiot was saying, I gathered enough to know that troubles a-brewing in Firbank once again."

Clemmie Bean edged her chair forward yet again and confided to the others, "I knowed when Luster started going over to Kilers, they'd be new trouble...he's shore tard of Sudie in a hurry. I said at the time..."

"Tard of her?" Granny Blackburn broke in an explosive rattle, "He was tard of her atter that first time when she let him lay her, and his woman a stillwarm corpse in the next room!" Her bone-thin nose hooked sharply toward her hairy upturned chin, her palsied head vibrating in ceaseless and rhythmic negation. The other two women sat still, listening.

She continued, "Luster ought to of sent her on with that durned preacher wherever he takened out to Arkansas, parts unknown." She stretched her turtlish neck and spat a stream of amber colored snuff spit off the porch and it splattered like a contorted spider web on the hard-packed clay ground.

"Still and all, Granny, them Greebers mighta forgot about him if he hadn't went to Birdie," Urfie Pearl declared pulling out her underlip and putting a fresh dip of Rooster Dip between her lip and her gums. She continued, "She'd been after him for over five year now and he wouldn't pay her no mind. Then he musta heard that Ard Greeber was tryin' to break in and after all them threats from the Greebers, he come outta them Nation hills to bed up with her."

Clemmie tucked wisps of iron-gray hair under her pink bonnet and pontificated, "I figger he done hit for spite, not 'cause he liked Birdie. They say he never could stand her vulgar ways none and repulsed her real hard several times."

Granny Blackburn cackled and snorted, "Flitter! Luster's like every godburned man in Firbank. He was male-burnin' for her. The old Squire's boasted all over the Nation about hers being the best stuff ever laid on bleached domestic sheets. He drums up trade for her and by now every durned man old enough has been out to that old house in them cedars to have a crack at her. At first, she give it away free, and the old Squire beat her something terrible. Then she got to chargin' and he seen her side of it. They say she splits with him fifty-fifty."

"That don't exactly seem fair-like," Clemmie countered, "After all hit's her..."

"Oh, hit's all right for her and him to go in cahoots, he feeds and beds her," Urdie Pearl cut her off. "They say that Squire's arranged some right good trades, taking anything from a quart of likker to a shoat fer pay when the suitor don't have no ready cash money. Of course, if I was Birdie, I wouldn't trust to give him complete squatter's rights as the feller says."

Urfie Pearl kept on, "Why...you cain't trust the Squire no further'n you can throw a greased bull by the tail. I wouldn't be a might surprised if he don't tap her hisself, him durn well knowing that her Uncle Luke Tolby used to do the same hisself. Anybody that'd try to turn that Ard Greeber into her would do anything. That Squire's a low-down son of a..."

Granny slapped a clawy hand against her sharp knee and interrupted Urfie Pearl, "That's what's brung on this here brewing trouble. Ard Greeber, that durned hunchback, offered the Squire a fine brace of mules if he'd arrange a standing for him. Then he said he'd throw in forty acres of good bottom land and a whole run of likker if the Squire'd git Birdie to come and live with him as his wedded wife."

"When'd he do that 'ere, Granny?" Urfie Pearl asked unbelievably.

"Where you been keepin' yourself, Urf? Norey first got wind of hit on the party line early this morning. Then I rushed over to Goddard's as fast as my laigs would carry me. Freel Goddard larnt me more. Birdie...she balked when the Squire tole about the bargain. He taken his razor strap and commenced whoopering hell outen her with that bastard young'un of Buck Humphries a-bitin' and scratchin' at him 'fore he give hit a backhanded lick and laid hit out cold. Birdie...she fought back like a cornered coon and the fight ended in a draw. The Squire's gittin' old and rusty for such things."

Granny wheezed, caught her labored breath, and continued, "About that time that durned spider shuffled up and demanded to know if the bargain went through. Birdie...she stood there hipped and defiant and yelled, 'I'd ruther couple with a mud turkle than you, you squash-faced varmint. Luster Holder's the one I'm burnin' for. He's a real man and no varmint and if you fool with him he'll rip that durn hump off your back and stick it down your stinkin' throat!' And he lost his head and jumped up on that high porch like a bullfrog and made at her, sweeping the Squire to one side so hard he crashed through a front winder. Birdie...she dodged the critter and run for the upstairs with that durned spider springing after her. About that time, the Squire come out with his shotgun and said he'd blow Ard's guts out."

She caught her strained breath again and continued, "Ard seen he had him. He vaulted down them steps and off the porch in one big leap and off towards the woods. But he turned back and screamed like a mad panther, 'If you lay with Luster Holder tonight, hit'll be with a dead man!' He told her she'd done signed Luster Holder's death warrant. Then with them words he went to slinging words and threats and dared Luster to meet him Saturday. That was Monday and today's the big day! Then he started off to the store. About that time Wurner come by to say Luster had heard Ard's threat and was on his way to find him, and that ever'body and his dog figgered they'd meet at the store and was pouring out there."

"Who seen all this here, Granny?" Clemmie asked.

She cackled, "Who do you reckon? Wurner, of course! He trailed Ard from the store and hid behind a tree in the front yard and seen it all."

Urfie Pearl leaned over toward the older woman, "Granny, have you thought that maybe Squire Kiler's forgot all about that Birdie deal with Ard and is working behind his hunched back?"

"Make yourself clear, Urf." Granny demanded.

Urfie Pearl explained, "Well, I've heer'd by reliable sources that since Tank Greeber's murder, the old Squire hangs out a lot at the Greeber house and talks with them other brothers when Ard ain't there. I just can't understand it any other way. Like their Pappy before them, the Greeber sons are dead-set against Ard giving him that land but still and all, it may be...surely he's not trying to git a better bargain from one of them for Birdie?"

Granny Blackburn cackled, "Yore mind's quit working for you, Urf. You got it all wrong. Hit wouldn't have nothin' to do with that ere widder of Tank Greeber's, that ere Blanche, now would it? With that hair the color of egg yo'kes and eyes as blue as 'ere robin's egg ever hatched by no robin, she's the purtiest woman besides Luster's dead Dossie Bell which ever come to Firbank, and I 'low the Squire'd give his whole farm, with Birdie throwed in, to her stepsons if they'd git Blanche to come live with him."

"I don't believe that's what them secret trips are about, Granny. Anyways, she wouldn't wipe a runny nose on an old bastard like him," Urfie Pearl snorted.

Granny wiped her chin and answered, "I hain't sayin' she would or wouldn't but something keeps tellin' me that maybe he's bargaining for Blanche. They hain't nary a loose man in the whole Nation which wouldn't run to her if she'd just give the signal, Luster amongst them."

"You ain't meaning to..." Urfie Pearl started to ask incredulously.

Granny stopped her cold in mid-sentence. "I hain't meanin' nothin' except to say solid that she's just the soft woman type Luster'd crave if he was just rid of his present woman. And when he craves a woman, God Hisself cain't stop him."

With that declaration ringing in her ancient ears, Urfie Pearl reasoned, "But, Granny, Luster wouldn't want all of them young'uns of Blanche's. Let's see, there's that little feller, Pistol, and that young female, Tiddy, that's already sizzlin' for that boy Buck Humphries...and that little nigger, Tadpole, too."

"Shoot, Urf, them young'uns wouldn't be in Luster's way. They run nekkid in the woods like wild dogs anyways...so folks say," Granny laughed hard and sharp.

Urfie Pearl interrupted her and brought their discussion back to Birdie when Clemmie sniffed, "Still and all, as I've argued all along, she herself is responsible for laying herself down and wallowing

with the hogs. Nobody forced her to incesticate with
Luke Tolby...her Mammy's own blood brother...nor
to cut his throat with that razor neither when he got
tired of her, just like she done Bode Holley on the
same day. Wurner seen her in the river bottom and
everybody knows she wasn't down there gathering
hickory nuts in the middle of the summer."

As the other two women stared at her intently,
Clemmie continued, "If anything happens to Miss
Sudie, Birdie would be the one to woman up with
Luster."

She went on. "And anything I hear in this
Godforsaken country shouldn't orght to surprise
me none. All I got to say is Buck jest got hisself out
of that trouble with Birdie Kiler by the skin of his
teeth. This time he's playin' with death. They say
them Greeber menfolk jest mortal worship their little
sister. You shorely hain't forgot this early what Clell
done to that Ches Oldham up at the store?"

"Buck's got too much sense to fool with her," Urfie
Pearl said. "Birdie scared him so bad he'll never touch
another female as long as he lives."

"Maybe not, Urf, but if he's a real man I wouldn't
put no money on it," Clemmie replied.

"Why you want to restir up all that now,
Clemmie?" Urfie Pearl asked. "It was just idle talk.
Just like I said once, Wurner slipped up on that one,
him so usually reliable and all. There was so much
happening, anybody could have got mixed up...espe-
cially an idiot."

Urfie Pearl leaned closer to the older woman. "Are you going back to the store, Granny?" she asked anxiously. "Hit'll be the godawfulest fracas ever takened place in this here settlement!"

"I'll go along to keep you company, Urfie," Clemmie said eagerly. "I sorta..."

"Naw I hain't going," Granny said, her venous eyes dripping with distance, "you two go on and I'll wait here for yore story of hit. I'm gonna rest up so's I can git my strength back to he'p lay out the corpse. And I think I'm a-knowin' already what name hit's gonna be called by."

After the two other women had left for Goddard's Store at Firbank, Granny Blackburn remained in her chair in the run. The cooling August breeze made her drowsy. Her head nodded, but she didn't go to sleep. It was no time to sleep and miss a thing. New trouble had come to Firbank and the same ones were in the center of it again...Luster Holder, Birdie Kiler and the Squire. But the trouble between Luster and Ard Greeber wasn't over Birdie alone. Only a year ago the Greebers had come from Missouri and settled at Luke Tolby's place on the edge of the Nation, that section of wooded pine hills which had been controlled by Luster Holder ever since his grandfather, John Holder, a Cherokee Indian, had come from the East Tennessee mountains to gun out the Tolbys, who then owned most of the land. Old Tank Greeber and his six sons had left Missouri just ahead of the law and come to Tennessee to buy the Tolby place from Squire Kiler, who had claimed the place after Luke, the last of the Tolby men folks was killed. Yes, sir, almost everyone in the Nation knew their history well and new history was about to be made in unforgettable ways.

4

Buck humphries swam toward the sandbar in the center of the stream, and crawling out of the brown water, he lay flat on his back, his long legs spread wide, his head resting against clasped hands. The silence of the surrounding woods was only broken by the steady hum of bees in the blackberry bushes and the chatter of small birds in the willows. Occasionally a water bird darted above his face and in the distant blue of the sky, buzzards floated in graceful circles.

The boy felt at peace with everything now that he was away from Firbank and the gathering talk of impending trouble between Luster Holder and the Greebers. It was good too to be away from home for a little while too, away from Old Henley, his pappy, who, with his creeping years, talked more and more of the rapidly approaching time when he would, without the aid of a cane, walk the streets of New Jerusalem. And out here on the Forked Deer River, he was safe from that girl, Tiddy Greeber, who was dogging his footsteps with more regularity, even sneaking up through the cornfield near the house for a chance to whistle him out to be with her, seemingly unafraid of anything but the cracked voice of Old Henley, who warned Buck against the "horsin' little bitch in boy pants", just as he'd warned Buck against Birdie Kiler.

In the last four months, the thought of Tiddy Greeber sent his blood to circling madly in his veins and filled him with such an aching heat that he had to come to the river nearly every day to cool himself with a swim. His fear of her was not the fear he'd had for Birdie. This was the fear of real love, for he'd never known love before, even if he was nearly twenty and had lain with Birdie near the Firbank School House more than four years ago now. He'd never forget that moonlight night when she'd stopped his buggy at the crossroads and crawled in beside him. He'd first turned seventeen and, knowing her reputation, was almost scared into a night spasm. He recalled her flashing eyes and smile, the warm voluptuousness of her thighs, the mad pressure of her soft, yielding breasts and the sharpness of her teeth on his shoulder as she seemed trying to drain the last of life from him.

After the episode with Birdie, he'd been sick and ashamed and had stayed closely at home with his fanatical father until he heard that Birdie was pregnant. Then the old man had given him a shotgun and chased him to the woods, where he stayed for three days and nights, while the Squire searched for him, dragging Brother Lazenby with him to perform the ceremony.

The halfwit, Wurner Crouse, had found him to let him know of the tragic things which had happened during his absence. He told Buck of the death of the woman he worshipped like a mother, Dossie Bell, the beautiful brown-haired woman whom Luster had taken as his woman after she'd been abandoned by her own people, the woman whom Brother Lazenby had permitted to be turned out of the church because she'd lived with a man she'd never married. Feeling old, broken and lost eternally, he had listened to the idiot's weird description of the funeral at Sobby, of Brother Lazenby's confession of his love for Dossie Bell and of his part in her dying, of how he, Buck, was her blood son, her love child in sin. But far from being crushed by the latter revelation, he had known a spiritual and physical elation, and Dossie Bell's memory became heavenly sweet to him. Wurner concluded with a garbled account of the birth of a son to Birdie, who had been grannied by Murdie Blackburn herself at the crib in the Kiler barn. He gathered that it wasn't his, that it favored someone else, a dark swarthy brat unlike the fair, blue-eyed Humphries.

Still not at all sure of himself, he returned to his father and learned that the Squire was no longer looking for him. Millie, his wife, had been found dead of a heart misery and afterwards Wurner had run across the bloated bodies of Luke Tolby and Bode Holley, who'd been out gunning for each other because of a stolen keg of liquor and had met their ends. These events had taken the pressure off of Buck. The Firbank settlement was in a furor. Officers from Melburg had come out and questioned this one and that one and learning no more than they already knew before they'd left the county seat. There were more buryings under the cedars at Sobby church house and life resumed its usual course.

As the whole of that week of terror died away, he had heard that Birdie, with her mother gone, was wilder than ever and that the Old Squire was not only reconciled to her way of life but was urging her on and profiting by it. Buck tried to forget all about her. He was horrified when Wurner brought word that she wanted to see him. He never went. He knew too well what she wanted. He remembered her last words to him on that silver-sprinkled night, her laughter raucous and her husky voice booming when he'd cried to her, "I cain't see you no more, Birdie! I cain't! It's a sin again' God Almighty."

First, the laugh, then she'd said in a low, mean tone, "I ain't keerin' a goddam if you do or don't.

You're like a durn jackrabbit anyways and all I was wanting was to teach you to satisfy like a man 'cause you've sho-God got what hit takes as a starter and just don't know how to use hit, 'y God. And I cain't see in the Glorious Hell why God hangs such gifts on fools and idiots. I'm gonna have me a real man soon and he'll give me all I'm needin'.'"

Birdie's voice had been, like her ways, ugly and low, for Birdie never cared what she said or how she said it and always seemed to take a perfect delight in cheapening herself. Even now Buck's face burned, and he looked down at himself and was ashamed. Birdie had told the truth when she noised it about Firbank that "I durn nigh raped that scutter." Better than anyone else he knew she had done just that, for he was just a tapper who'd only passed through his period of puberty six months before. Everybody, including his pappy, had said he was sixteen at the time, and it'd worried him to know that he had reached adolescence so late. Then, after his woman's death, Luster had given him Dossie Bell's Bible because he knew she'd want him to have it. In the Bible, he found his name and the date of his birth written in her own delicate hand. He was but fourteen when Birdie had taken advantage of him. He guessed he'd just been large for his age, for now at nineteen, he wasn't much larger, just filled out more solidly.

Again, he felt the burning in his face. He wondered who her real man was. For months afterwards he had fought to erase the filthy experience from his mind. Even when he had read the Good Book while he was at home, his mind was on things lustful. He had spent most of his days in the woods hunting and fishing in a vain effort to escape himself. He was always longing and wishing to talk it over with someone, but not his father, not Old Henley, who thought he had forgotten, and was a pure little boy again. He couldn't mention his struggle to Luster, for the big hillman would set his steely and dark eyes upon him and say nothing, although in his mind he'd be thinking of what a fool, what a weakling, had come from the womb of the only woman he'd ever cared for. In the darkness of the night, the image of the squirming body would come to him, life-like, and he would again succumb to the vile temptation. Afterwards, he'd lie awake, restless, as he would be angrily hating himself until he cried himself to sleep. It was an every night experience, which drained and destroyed his very soul.

Then with him feeling that he'd never be able again to wash his soul and body clean, he had been caught in the barn loft by his father the evidence in hand. In all his life, his father had never laid a hand on him and the old man never whipped him even then, but the scalding and scathing words from the cracked old throat had been worse than a beating.

"Jest keep 'hit up," he screeched, his tobacco stained beard parted by the wind and foaming like soap suds over his scrawny chest, "and you'll be crazier than Wurner hisself. Hit's a worse sin even than a-layin' with a slut like Birdie Kiler. Hit drains out the brain hitself! Forget that loose bodied bitch and grow yourself into a man!"

That and the fear had saved him. With Brother Lazenby gone, he had started back to church at Sobby. In the teachings of the Good Book, he could forget his evil cravings. A year passed, then another, and again his body was washed whiter than snow.

Then the Greebers had moved to Firbank and brought with them troubles etched in black letters across the peaceful sky of the Nation country. Old Tank Greeber and his sons had settled in the old Tolby house a mile north of the Forked Deer River bottoms and begun operating a 500-gallon capacity still. They had announced openly that they intended to put Luster Holder out of business and run him out of the Nation, just like his grandfather had the Tolbys themselves, so they could operate back in that wild section without being pestered by the law. They spread the word that they were the only living remnants of the once powerful Tolby clan and that the land rightly belonged to them.

Not a word had been heard from the taciturn Cherokee and in their first year in the Firbank settlement, the Greebers hadn't come into contact with him, nor had they gone into the hills to search for him. Luster continued to live his own life and haul truckloads of liquor to the county seat. So far, the big Cherokee was still untouched and the powerful presence he'd always been.

But this hot August had brought things to a boil. Crip, Luster's Negro, had been beaten up and a carload of liquor highjacked. Then Tank Greeber was dead and the finger of murder was pointed to Luster, although Buck was sure the giant hillman would never have killed a man in such a underhanded way. After all, everyone knew that wasn't Luster Holder's way.

Anyhow the smell of death penetrated the Nation air once again. Some day soon the meeting of Luster and the Greebers would surely take place, and Buck cringed at the very thought. Only once had he seen the Greebers together at the store, tall, hard-bitten, powerful men...grizzly, cold, daring, dangerous, all except Ard Greeber, who didn't fit into any human description a body could summon out of all his knowledge, something between a wild man and a reptile. As he hobbled along, tapping the ground with his huge knuckles, he carried on his back a deformity that looked more like a pointed sandstone than anything else. One look at such an evil built creature was enough to make a strong man grow sickly weak and a child to run bawling for its mammy. Buck wondered if Luster had even seen him.

He would have stayed clear of the Greebers and left them to Luster's worry alone, but one Sunday in early spring he had seen Tiddy at the Sobby Church, the prettiest wisp of a girl he'd ever dreamed of. As she'd sat there in the choir, her golden voice high above the rest, she had seemed to melt into all of him and begin running around in his life blood.

Her large eyes were the color of cornflowers wet with the dew of an early morning, her hair the color of honey and in short ringlets around her ears and although she was a blonde, she was tanned to a velvety smoothness by the sun and wind. Her nose was slightly upturned to give it a sort of sauciness and her lips, slightly parted and seemingly puffed as if a little swollen, sent a sickly ache over his whole body. It was not such an ache as he'd known for Birdie, but something so deep that it stayed with him long after he'd left the church building.

It was a week after he'd first seen her that the ache in him became excruciating. He was in the Sobby Church once more. He was on a bench closer to the front and his eyes were on her again, entranced when she looked in his direction and stopped singing. The brown of her face deepened, her lips parted in a slow smile and her eyes widened in a surprise of discovery. He had been so flustered that he felt like leaving and fleeing through the woods. But he summoned all of his fading courage and decided to stay on, and he marked that decision as the beginning of the second period of worry and dismay in his young life.

As the benediction was given, he hurried from the church. He was almost to the woods when she called out to him. He had stopped dead in his tracks, not turning, as his heart pounded savagely beneath his thin cotton shirt. She had bounded up to him like a deer, faced him smiling so close to his face that he could feel the sweet warmth of her breath and get the smell of it, something so wondrous he could never describe.

Her eyes were round, bright and misty as she said, "I'd heard about you, Buck Humphries, and I'm not disappointed. You're a pretty boy and I want you for my feller."

Her laugh was like tinkling glass as she said, "You see, I'm sending you 'sweet hello' by myself and not waiting for nobody else to do it."

She didn't look much more than twelve but was young, so beautiful, so bold and there was nothing common and vulgar about her boldness. There was the innocence and honesty of a little girl who was used to having her own way and had now seen what she wanted more than anything else in the world and wasn't afraid to ask for it. Buck had tried to tear his eyes from her while tasting something sweet in his mouth and he kept having to swallow to keep from choking.

He looked at Tiddy and somewhat exasperatingly said, "You're just a flip of a girl and too young to be thinking of sweet-hearting."

She frowned and stamped a small foot, "I ain't neither no little flip of a girl, Buck. I'm….I'm sixteen year old going on seventeen."

"Don't lie to me, Tiddy. I know better than that," Buck challenged her.

She stomped her foot and, red in the face, stammered, "I…I ain't lying, Buck. Us…Us Greebers just grow slow and don't fill out in no great big hurry much."

Buck shook his head, "I heard Clell say you was fourteen that day he whipped the boy at the store."

"Clell just don't..." she chewed her lips, dropping her eyes.

She looked back up again, "I'm sorry I lied, Buck. Clell told the truth. But I'm going on fifteen and girls in these parts grow into women fast and marry real early. Anyways, Buck, if I'm just a little kid to you, it don't make no difference if we do something, just fer fun...like go swimming together."

He turned away from her, "I still cain't..."

His voice trailed off.

"I've got to go now," he said faltering.

"I'll just walk with you a piece of a ways," she said like she was positive he wanted her to and linking her arm into his tingling one. They had gone into the cool woods for over a mile before she stopped and stood back from him and explained, "I'll haft to be scootin' to dinner or Clell or Ard'll be out lookin' for me. What you doing later on?"

He didn't answer right away. For the first time he became aware of the fact that Tiddy's clothes made her look more like a boy than a young lady.

Finally, he rubbed his dry lips together, "I cain't rightly know, Tiddy. Pap, he wants me to stay close since his miseries keep him at the house. He's been having some troubles."

She grinned at him, "Cain't you tear loose and meet me here? We could go swimming in the river."

Flames had licked around his heart, "It just ain't Christian to go swimming with no girl, especially nekked," Buck said trying to beg off.

Tiddy raised her large eyes to Buck in a look of complete innocence and protested, "Why, Buck? 'Cause it wasn't meant for a boy to see a girl that way til they's married?"

She squeezed Buck's arm. "Shoot, Buck. I used to swim with boys a lot before we moved from Missouri."

A wistful look deepened the blue of her eyes and she said, "I cain't see no earthly harm in it. A boy's made one way and a girl another. What's bad about that? Anyways, I don't mind you seeing me that way and I sorter hanker to see all of you with no clothes on."

Then before he could move, she clasped her arms around his neck, pulled down his head and kissed him full on the lips. She snuggled close and his nostrils were filled with the soft, warm smell of woodsmoke fused with an intoxicating odor which was young and fresh like the woods. "You're mine, Buck. I knowed it when I seen you watching me in the church. You're my own sweetheart and I don't ever want nobody else. I love you so much I'd just like to melt into you below your hide and run around in your blood day and night."

Buck blushed, "You hadn't oughta say such things, Tiddy. It just ain't holy-like."

With shaking hands, he unclasped her arms from around his aching neck, delicately like she was a fragile piece of China.

"It ain't just right for you to talk that way, Tiddy," Buck said in a voice unlike his own, "We hadn't oughta be here alone in these woods. Folks would pass around bad talk that'd be hurtful to you. Your brothers would kill me."

She looked up at him, lips drooping like she was about to cry, "Ain't nothing bad in a boy and girl loving, Buck. I'm pure and you're pure and we're young and far from sin. Don't you love me?"

His breath almost stopped. "I just gotta go, Tiddy," he said and whirling from her, had run swiftly into the forest and never slacked his pace until he reached the old double-log cabin on the eastern ridge of the Nation. Only then did he have time to relive the moments in the woods and to realize what a fool he'd been. And with a jolt he knew he'd never be happy until their blood ran in one stream, that he loved her so much that he wanted her to hurt him and hurt him bad. He longed for her to put her soft mouth against his throat, then sink her teeth into it and draw the life fluid from him until he was cold in death. She was wrong in believing him pure. He still carried the dirt of that night with Birdie. He wasn't fit to associate with her. He didn't want to contaminate one who was pure and Christian as Tiddy.

So insanely did he crave her that he was now afraid of himself. He decided then and there to have nothing else to do with her. And although he learned to dodge her successfully, he lived in mortal fear of her brothers and that through some evil power they could read his hidden thoughts about her, even if she had never mentioned him to them they would find out.

He had violent nightmares in which he saw Ard Greeber scrabbling toward him. The hideous creature would clamp his tentacle-like arms about his body, sinking his sharp tusks into his throbbing throat and he'd awake with a piercing scream, while Old Henley yelled hoarsely for him to shut up and let an old man get his rest. The wild dreams became an obsession with him, even during the working hours, and he was positive that if any Greebers ever sucked out his life blood, it would be Ard. He was equally positive that he would meet certain death regardless if he ever got up the nerve to declare his love for Tiddy.

With chills climbing over him, he remembered what had happened to Ches Oldham, a young sharecropper boy who lived at Gum Hod over beyond the Nation. One Saturday Ches, slightly drunk, had said some dirty things to Tiddy and tried to kiss her right in front of Goddard's store. Unknown to Ches, Clell, the sixteen-year old Greeber brother, was there on the porch. Clell rose from his chair like he'd been shot out of it and almost had the boy whittled to ribbons with a Barlow knife before he could be dragged off. So…Buck was nervous.

On that same Sunday afternoon of the day of their meeting, Tiddy had come to the house after him and while he cowered in his attic room he had heard Old Henley order her off the place.

"My boy Buck hain't wantin' no doings with you outlanders," he'd crackled at her in an aged fury. "He's a good Christian boy and I ain't having him ruint by no little whorin' filly which runs wild in the woods not wearin' enough clothes to wad no shotgun. Git 'fore I lose my temper!" Trembling, while sweat dropped like lead from his arm pits, he'd heard her voice like soft violin music at nightfall, "I'll go, Mister Humphries, but I'll be back and I'll find him because I just mortal love him and cain't nobody make me stop."

He quit going to church and spent most of his time in the deep bottomlands. He changed his fishing and swimming spots on the river. Only at night did he venture to Firbank store to buy necessary supplies. But Tiddy wasn't fazed. Often he heard her whistle, like a partridge, and knew she was calling him. He had to fight with himself to keep from running to her. But always between doing what he so badly wanted to do and was too much of a coward to do was the horrendous image of Ard Greeber along with memory of Clell and the Barlow knife he wielded. Many times he had crept to the small gable window of his attic room and caught sight of her standing alone in the waving corn, so slim and beautiful in her open-neck white t-shirt and blue dungarees which she nearly always wore.

Suffering increasing torture because of his self-imposed isolation from her, he had lost all interest in his former pursuits. Now he went to the woods, but he only pretended to hunt or fish. In the deep bend of the river, he had found a new place to swim, a place well-hidden by the thick growth of willows along the banks. Here he had come to cool his burning body and to try and forget. But he couldn't forget. He didn't want to forget. Safe from her, she was still with him in spirit, and, in his imagination, she was in his arms in the flesh, pressed so closely against his naked body that he could feel the trickle of the blood in her veins.

How disgusted Luster would be with him, if he knew! Before his trouble with Tiddy began, he had gone once a week to see the big Cherokee hillman, although he was still ill at ease in the presence of one who was so in-drawn, uncommunicative and it flustered him mightily to have to talk to Miss Sudie, who, on every such visit, looked older, paler, and more out of place. An about-to-run expression was more and more noticeable in her greenish eyes, and her hair was beginning to streak with gray. He was downright sorry for her, even if no one had forced her to make the bed she lying in.

Suddenly, while lost in his thoughts, at a sound, strange and new, the boy sat up on the sand bar, listening, while goose pimples rose on his arms and legs. At first the noise was faraway in the thick forest and heavy undergrowth. After a short interval, he heard the popping of twigs, the clear partridge note alerting him to the presence of another nearby. As the willows parted, he took one startled look and scrambled to his feet.

Tiddy stood on the bank, slim, brown, and beautiful in her t-shirt and dungarees, her long silky hair blowing in a screen across her face. She held his clothes wadded under one arm.

He took one startled look and dived into the water. He stood on the sandy bottom and watched her through water-beaded lashes. The distance was short between them and he could see the sparkle of her blue eyes, the warm smile on her soft lips.

"Bucky boy!" she called cheerfully, "I knew I'd find you. But it taken a lot a-careful trailing. Why you been giving me the go-arounds?"

He leaned against the sand bar, hands buried in the sand. He had to sound his voice twice before the words came intelligently.

"What you doing a-way off down here, Tiddy?" he said in rising alarm, "Clell and your mammy'll skin you alive if they find out. H-how'd you find me?"

She laughed, "They'll never know anyways. Oh, I hid out in the cornfields and followed you. I almost lost you twice, but..."

His darting eyes stopped for a moment on a clump of hazelnut bushes. He had the vague feeling that somebody was hidden there watching them.

He gasped, "How long you been here?"

She dropped his clothes and clapped her hands childishly and replied, "About a half hour, I figger. You sure are a fine-built boy nekkid, Buck. I never would tire a-watching you."

The sun was like coals of fire against his face.

"It…it's not decent, Tiddy," he stammered, "y-you ain't been raised right for a girl. You…"

"Aw, flitter, Buck, I knowed about how you was built 'fore I seen you in the raw. Clothes don't make no Christian and they's nothin' wicked about a pretty body."

She tossed the hair out of her eyes, "Why don't you like me? I wanna be your sweetheart. We could have real fun hunting and fishing and swimming together. You sure grieve my heart like it has never been grieved on earth. I git so durn lonesome for you."

He had to put it straight to her. Now was his chance, now was the time. He cleared his throat hard to steady his voice.

"Listen, Tiddy, I ain't for you. I'm nigh eighteen years old and you ain't over fourteen. You're just a little kid not long outta hippings and don't have no more idea than a mule or a sick woodpecker what love really is. Your folks has let you run wild in the woods and…and even if they ain't took much good care of you, you're a child of God and are walking on dangerous ground and I ain't…"

"Don't try to preach me, Buck," she broke in, blue eyes glittering. "I know what you think and it ain't so. If I'm cravin' you, hit's because I'm just plumb crazy over you. I'm wantin' you for my man." Her voice had broken and she shook her head angrily.

"I ain't no common little bitch," she continued. "I'm wanting you for my boy forever, and like I told you, I ain't thinking it in no dirty way."

With sickness growing in his stomach, he said harshly, ""Well, I don't want you tagging after me no more. I don't love you a whoop. I…I got me a steady girl and we…we're gonna hitch up come fall."

He could see her biting her lips, eyes wide and glazed. She clenched her small fists hard at her sides.

She screamed at Buck, "You're lying black lies, Buck. I know all about you. I dare you to name me the girl!"

The boy swallowed hard. "It ain't no lie, Tiddy," he said doggedly. "Me…me and Birdie Kiler has been sweethearts a…a long old time. Me and her…"

He was sorry he said it the moment it left his lips, the words, the very thought scorched his throat. What if Birdie learned?

"Buck!" she cried a cry like piercing knife.

He couldn't back out now.

"It's so, Tiddy," he explained, "me and Birdie sinned together long ago. The old Squire wants me to marry her."

The girl stood very straight. Then her shoulders drooped.

She cried out, "You're lying as sinful as all the world, Buck! I heard about you and her, about how she waylaid and overcome you and how you hid out. You were nothing but a little boy, she ought to have been jailed or lynched! That was long ago and is long dead and forgotten. I heard tell all about you and her... you nothing but a little shaver hardly big enough to feed and dress yourself. She's a dirty, dirty slut, that's what...but she wouldn't marry you! She's got a b... bastard child but it ain't yours, You're just tellin' me so..." She stopped short, sobbed uncontrollably and grasped her hair in both hands for a moment.

Buck was puzzled, "Have you...do you know the baby, Tiddy?"

She wiped her eyes, "Yes, I've seen him several times."

"What does he look like?" he asked Tiddy.

"Aw, Buck, I dunno. Dink's right purty and cute, but he don't look nothing like you. He's sorter...oh, I just don't know!"

He turned his head to one side and admitted, "He could be mine, Tiddy. I been too big a coward to go over there to see. But I am going. I just ain't done Birdie right and I'll never really be forgive by my God till I see her and..."

"Buck," she yelled in childish anger, "you've made all that up just to git shed of me. I can tell by your wandering eyes! I can tell too that you'd like to sweetheart with me if you wasn't so queer and drawed off to yourself. We could meet here everyday

and nobody'd ever know it. Clell and Ard or none
of my brothers are studying you. They got enough
troubles, and…and Birdie Kiler's after men, not boys.
Why you think Ard and Luster's gonna go at each
other's throats when they meet today?"

"Luster don't give a hoot for Birdie," he said
uneasily, "Cain't I make you see it? She told Ard a
lie and he's gonna lose his life because of it."

"Oh, Buck!" she began crying and suddenly began
shedding her clothes, stripping herself of her jeans
and shirt, trying desperately to get down to her bare-
naked self.

He started to say something else, but without
warning she quickly concluded the job of shedding
her clothes. He watched, held motionless by a power
greater than himself, as she stood on the bank, a wisp
of a girl and the most beautiful creature he'd ever
seen as she raised her arms and dived into the river,
disappearing altogether and then not coming up. In
mounting terror, he waited, limbs paralyzed, eyes
bulging toward the swirling brown water where she
had gone in. He tried to peer below the surface to
where her naked body would be lying in the sand, cold
and lifeless. Already he could see the men dragging
the river with grappling hooks, the turtle-like Ard
waiting on the bank for him, arms outstretched.

He shivered suddenly in helplessness as the cold
crept up his body like some horrible slimy water creature climbing up to get at his throat. Then he tried
to leap high in the water as something soft like grass

brushed his thighs and swam between his legs. A golden head bobbed up and two cold, dripping arms clamped themselves firmly and fiercely around his waist, then his neck and a cold cheek pressed to his own hot one. He saw the golden fuzz on her neck and had to scotch himself to keep from brushing his open lips over it. He shook all over as if with buck ague, and, unguided by any will of his own, his long arms swept under the water and around her narrow waist and he felt the whole of her against him, curling and curving into him and as he closed his eyes against the day's brightness. He felt the soft lips, alive and apart, drawing childishly on his own but stripping him of his last strength, his last defense. Then the lips were brushing his cheeks like hot and soothing memories. And his own hand, as if guided by someone else, left her waist and cupped the girl's small firm buttocks hard.

She leaned back from him, the eyes with their pinkened whites, drooping and out of focus. Suddenly, the same eyes became wide and were water-fringed. Her eyelids flickered and drops burst against her cheeks. He tried to wriggle back from her, but she held him even tighter, burying her fingers in his straw-colored hair, her panting and her hot breath and words blowing into his ear like a consuming blaze.

"God Almighty, Buck, I love you something awful," Tiddy whimpered like a little puppy, "you're mine, mine! You'll never get shed of me now. And no one can ever take you away from me! Never!"

When he prized her arms away from his neck, and forced his hands between his stomach and her own to shove her back in the water, she lifted her spread legs and clamped them around his waist, her loosened arms coming back around him and pressing his face between her breasts, her fingers buried in his straw-colored hair. She began moving backward toward the sandbar, pulling him over with her.

His heart seemed as if it would burst through the spaces of his ribs. His lungs were so full of the wonderful odor of her, the half-wild wood's odor he could never forget, that it seemed too they would burst also in a great bang. She had captured him at last, and he was drawn between his love for her, his passion for her and the rising terror at the thought of her deadly brothers. He wished he could die right now, just fall asleep and never, never awaken.

Slowly he got control of his strangling breath. He had to get away before the worst happened. In another minute, he knew that the last of his restraint would fade from him and they would be on the sandbar. He would never forgive himself. He'd want to die, but not at the hands of that inhuman creature, the very thought of whom now drained all vestiges of passion from his mind.

He whirled about with her and again jerked her arms free. He fell to his knees, dropping her on the sandbar even as he wriggled free of her grasping thighs. In one long leap, he was standing on the sandbar. He glanced down at her for a moment, and saw the eyes, full of hurt surprise now, before he dove back into the water and swam frantically for the shore. He scrambled up the slick clay bank, hastily picked up his clothes from where she'd thrown them, and, not stopping to dress, tore out wildly toward the woods path, even as he heard her hit the water.

He reached the path and stooped down to put on his shoes. Behind him he heard the pat of bare feet and swung his head around to catch a glimpse of Tiddy rounding the bush-lined curves. She hadn't stopped to dress either and she was grasping her clothes in one hand.

"Bucky, wait!" she cried, "Please wait!"

Leaving the path, he broke through the prickly bushes and dodging a cane brake, cut out against the dense undergrowth. He was already winded from the recent excitement, the love-torture and any minute he felt that he might drop exhausted on the dark decaying leaves. But he ran on, twisting and tearing through the underbrush until he reached a small clearing. He fell face down on the moss under a clump of hazelnut bushes and sucked his breath in and out rapidly. He had eluded her. He had deserted her in this lonely bottom. If she tried to follow him, she would be lost. He felt sick and faint and full of shame. If only he knew she was safely on her way home, he'd feel some better.

He got to his feet and pulled on his pants and shirt. He turned to go, and there she stood, just behind the hazelnut clump and dressed in her own shirt and pants now, her hair still parted in wet strands on her forehead and cheeks. She looked so small, so free of any thought of wickedness.

He never moved as she strolled over to him, her cheeks darkened with blood as she hung her head like a teased little girl.

"You'll have to show me the way out," she said almost timidly.

She raised her clear eyes to him, "I hope you won't be hating me, Buck. Being next to your skin done something to me, but honest, I wasn't wantin' that... that. I never wanted to do such things. It's just...oh, I don't know!"

"I ain't hatin' you," he said hoarsely. "You know as well as me what'll happen if we're caught down here together."

She desperately pled with Buck, "I wasn't just spying on you, Buck, because I...because I knowed you'd be swimming. I wanted to tell you that a terrible trouble is brewing in Firbank. It may come to a head this evening. Ard is out to kill Luster because of Pappy. They's meeting this evening at the store. I heard Ard talking it over with Clell and Dodey Perkins. Knowing how much you think of Luster, I sneaked out to tell you. I...I thought you might want-a warn him."

A new fear tightened about him. His only friend was in grave danger.

"Luster can take care of hisself, but do they...your brothers all mean to gang him?"

"No, I heard Ard tell them plain and hard to stay away from Firbank, that he could handle that half-breed by hisself.. And, Buck...Ard...he can too," Tiddy said with conviction.

Her eyes widened as she continued, "You ain't got no idea how he can fight. Why, I've seen him whip Node, Dodey, Perk and Clell bloody all at one time. And once at a fish fry in Missouri he mixed with four niggers with razors and him unarmed. He broke one of them's back, another's neck and chewed out the third one's windpipe before the fourth one run like a striped-assed ape. And he was cut to ribbons and it taken over a hundred stitches to git his hide back in its normal place. But he was back to like common the next day."

"Luster Holder don't need no help," Buck said, trying to hide his growing alarm, "he didn't kill your pappy anyways, I'm sure of that."

"I'm ready to be going, Buck," she said in a whisper, "I'll leave you at the big road."

Buck broke a trail to the path. She linked her arm in his and they followed the path under the great hickories, beech and water oaks to reach an old logging road bordered on each side by dust-sheathed swale grass and flowering weeds. Where they left the woods, black-eyed susans dotted the grass. Here and there elderberries were beginning to ripen and the leaves on blackberry bushes were a dry, yellow-green. Lush growths of calamua grew close to the road, the root of which was good for colic and sweetens the breath. On the greenish slime of the sloughs were tuberous water lilies. Swamp milk weed encircled the soggy banks. A warm, sultry smell hung in the air. The bluish clay, baked and cracked, was hot to their feet. The heat waves danced devilishly before their eyes and brought sweat popping out on their foreheads.

At the intersection with the big road, Tiddy stopped and raised her face to him, "You...you was joking back there about...about Birdie Kiler, wasn't you, Buck?" she said uneasily, "You can't love her just because she led you off when you was just a little tapper not old enough to know what you was doing. Why, Buck, everybody...anyways, she ain't nothing but a...a whore."

He sucked in his breath sharply, "You mustn't use such ugly words, Tiddy. Your mouth's too purty to be smuttied up by them."

"I didn't mean to be nasty, Buck. I've heard bad things said around me since I was in hippings... me being the only girl and all. You don't really love Birdie, now do you?"

"I ain't saying, Tiddy," Buck explained, "Folks' talk always makes Birdie worse'n she is. I sinned against her once and I sorter got to kinda like her."

Her lips pouted, "Can't nobody rightly sin against a girl like Birdie. Don't you love me a teeny-weenie bit, Buck?"

She stood with her feet far apart, rocking back and forth. Water formed in Buck's mouth. He never ached so much for anyone in his life. He wanted to pick her up and take her home with him to love and worship her forever. With her, he wouldn't give a damn for anything else as long as he lived. But between them was a shadow of a terror.

He said as steadily as possible, "Please forget me, Tiddy. I won't never be worth nothing to you or nobody. You'll be finding you a nice feller someday, one that ain't sinned agin' his God."

She started to speak. Then she threw her arms around his neck, kissed him hard and fast on the mouth and ran up the dusty road like a frightened deer, leaving him there with the moisture of her abrupt kiss on his mouth. Absently, he ran his tongue along his burning lips and shook his head sadly.

For a long time, he stood where she left him, held by indecision. He longed to see Luster Holder, but what could he say to him? Luster resented advice from anyone. If only Squire Kiler would be on hand at the store, he would see to it that Luster wasn't ganged. But the boy didn't dare go to the Squire with the message. Without a doubt, he heard all about it and would be on hand. A great weight seemed to descend on his body. She had drained out his soul and carried it away with her. He had chased her off but she would be back. He could never escape her. He never wanted to escape her. But he could never surrender to her either, not as long as Ard and Clell were in the Nation country.

At the recollection of what Tiddy had left unsaid about Birdie's child, he came back to himself. What was it she had called him...Rink or Dink or something like that? Suddenly he remembered the vague reports which had come to him in round-about ways ever since that awful time four years ago. He had always closed his ears and passed it off as the old lie which the gossips would never let die. Up until now, he had been afraid to investigate.

He still wasn't satisfied. Taking a deep breath, he walked off in the direction of Firbank.

5

Sudie Lazenby sat on the side porch of the lean-to kitchen and watched the sun rise higher and higher above the hazy ridges to the east. Shadows danced on her peaked face as the summer breeze swept the hickory leaves near the back steps. In the woman's eyes, deeply shadowed, was an awareness. She sat very still in the cane-bottomed chair, her slim fingers primly clasped in her lap, and felt a chill like wiggly worms crawl continuously along her backbone. She kept edging her pointed tongue along her thin, pale lips, and occasionally raised a hand to pick a thread of graying black hair from an eyelid.

At a sound, she jerked her head around like a startled mare, catching her breath like a wheeze and cupping her hands hard on her sharp knees. She shot a quick glance through the open run between the two front rooms but didn't see anyone. She heard the plodding steps plainly now and they struck the hard-packed clay of the front yard and reached the cushioning crabgrass at the west end. She stood straight and stiff, then relaxed as Wurner Crouse waddled into view around the corner of the kitchen.

Wurner stopped just below her, a short stocky built man with heavy shoulders and powerful legs which bulged and knotted underneath his blue jumper and pants. His little agate eyes in a blank red face were blunt and turtlish and as they slanted up at her, the salmon pink lips, protruding like a blue gum Negro's, twisted into a spreading grin to reveal low-ground, horse-like teeth.

Sudie, still living with the increasing fear within her, sat back down. Wurner was a harmless creature, she knew, but she didn't want him around now. As he spraddled out on the ground and fingered the sling shot which swung on a cord from his bull neck, she choked back a sigh. Wurner Crouse was little more than an idiot, but next to Urfie Pearl Buckner, he was the best news carrier in the Nation. He seemed to have a sixth sense, for when anything happened in that vast expanse of pine covered hills, Wurner was either on hand to see or hear about it or he learned of it, and then waddled from house to house to let folks know. When he wasn't busy dispensing the news, he spent his time hunting squirrels with a slingshot in the bottomlands or grappling for fish in the sloughs and the river.

With a pang of miserable regret she remembered how he had spread the word of Dossie Bell Holder's death on that stormy night four years ago when she had turned her back on her God and lost her soul... the soul she must spend the rest of her days in recovering. She hoped Wurner would tell whatever he had learned and then leave, but once he was comfortably settled in one place he was hard to budge. But the idiot worshipped Luster and had come, she was sure to find out if he'd left for Firbank. She must urge him to be on his way, for on this one day she just had to be alone. This was the time, the time of the second turning point in her life. At the age of thirty-eight, she had again reached the crossroads and she was determined to leave the road grown over with brambles and brush and again take the path of righteousness and be made whole and at one with her Savior so that she might again know the joy which passes all other understanding.

"What is it, Wurner?" she said in a thin voice.

Wurner's own voice rumbled from deep in his barrel chest, "They's gatherin' there now...up there now. Firbank, hit's full, bustin' full. They hain't came yet, as the little boy says."

She pressed a lean thin hand to her heart, "Is that...that awful creature out there yet?"

"They hain't came yet? Folks sends me now... Mister Freel Goddard, he tells me to come find if Luster went?" Wurner answered.

"He's gone, Wurner," she whispered.

Wurner's mouth opened in a grin, amber oozing from the stained corners. He sucked it back in with a hissing sound, then his pig eyes hardened, glinting small and piercing from folds of flesh.

"Ard, he…that Ard, him, he pokes me, funs me, once kicked hard. My tap…hit missed eatin' his brains. But now…he…Ard…he'll meet his maker come sundown now."

He smacked his open hand hard against the ground and exclaimed, "What do you'uns think of that?"

"Oh, the wickedness of this awful place," Sudie moaned to herself, "Oh, to be delivered, Sweet Jesus, from the toils and iniquities which blacken and destroy my heart and soul!"

"God, He's good," Wurner said solemnly, "I go back now out there to Firbank. Gonna sing and preach and sang and save. Hit's bad needed right now."

Sudie saw him stand bare feet, with their blunt and blackened nails, splayed out on the clay, his big legs wide apart. She was glad the preaching idea had come to his head. She had heard how Wurner liked to gather children around him at the Firbank store and roar like a mad bull of the sins of this world, halting occasionally to sing an old hymn in his garbled way. Even the children listened to him in bemused silence, for they, like their parents before them, were afraid to make him mad. When the idiot's temper flared, he'd jerk the slingshot from around his neck, load it

with a railroad tap from his jeans pocket and shoot
in any direction or at anything he took a notion to
shoot. Otherwise he never bothered anyone and he
had a deep love for children.

As he reached the edge of the cabin, Wurner
turned back abruptly, blank face set, "Guts hurt and
growl. My stomach says eat now quick before…"

He paused and looked somewhere over his shoulder in the distance.

Sudie glanced around her uneasily. She wondered
just what was taking place. It was like that frightful night and day which seemed a thousand years
distant now. She wished Wurner would go on. She
wanted to be alone. There was so much to think on,
so much to do.

"Wait, Wurner," she said. She disappeared into the
kitchen and was back almost immediately with a paper
sack, "Here's some fried peach pies you can munch
on while you're on your way back to Firbank."

Greedily, the idiot took the sack from her. He
rammed a stubby hand into it and plopped one of the
flat pies into his mouth, and without another word,
waddled from sight.

Sudie sat back down. She reached into her blouse
and pulled out a crumpled envelope and held it
motionless in one hand for over a minute before she
smoothed it out and removed the contents. For how
many times since yesterday she'd never know, she
read the sprawling script, written with a hard lead
pencil on school tablet paper:

*Sudie, my own lawful wedded wife in the holy sight
of Jesus Lord—*

*I seat myself and take my pen in hand once more and
compose my rising spirits, my loved one, to let you know
that I'm leaving today and driving through to reclaim you
to my breast. It is glorious to know the forgiving power
of the Lord. Long ago I forgave you as you've forgiven
me. And now after months of prayer to Jesus Lord, He
has forgiven us both, for He doeth all things well and He
knows we belong back together.*

*I am following your directions so that no slip up can pos-
sibly come. It seems so long, and it's been so cruel, cruel.*

*It's such a long, hard drive across the Arkansas swamps
and the Tennessee hills and my car is old and the tires bad,
so I can't just say when I'll arrive. But it'll be some time
on the 25th. Just be ready. I'll hide the car where you said
and wait at the chosen spot.*

Until we're reunited in God.
Your Winnie

For a long minute after rereading it, Sudie held
the yellowed page in front of her, a warm flush suf-
fusing her sallow cheeks. God was good.

As she sat staring off toward the distant blue ridges, she again relived the dreadful saga of the past four
years and with the same terrifying grief she'd first
known, even though deliverance was close at hand. In
her imagination, the glazed blue of the heavens above
her turned threateningly dark, the lightning flashed,
the thunder rolled, and she was back once more in

the pastorage on the ridge east of Sobby Church and the horror was beginning. It was August 25th and that tall, silent man was there alone with her, telling of finding his woman dead in his cabin, telling it in a stolid way, like she was a prize mare or sow that had died on him and he wanted someone to take the burden of her burial off his shoulders. She could see the penetrating black eyes in the high-cheeked face which was bronzed by the sun and the wind, the jet black hair in cut-across bangs on his high forehead. With the powerful shoulders, the narrow waist, the lean legs, he was a wild animal out of the woods, and she was frightfully alarmed.

"I was drawn to him like a child to fire," she thought, "but he wouldn't of done it if I hadn't kept watching him so hungrily. He held to my eyes and drew them out like he was using them strong fingers of his." She was always thinking about her predicament.

She remained in her thoughts, "I couldn't no more help going with him than I could taking a drink of water when I'm dying of thirst. Something just seemed to come out of his body and go into me. I told him I'd come to his cabin for the sitting up and like a child I did, although I knew I was in danger and daring my God. He left me quivering like I had a fever.

She remembered the cabin, deserted by all except the dead Dossie Bell and those wailing cats. Elmer Runnels had driven her over in his wagon and she'd found Luster and her husband and that awful Squire Kiler already there. She'd had to sit helplessly and see the Squire drag Winnie away to the bottoms in that flood to search for a frightened boy that the vulgar talking Heber Kiler said had assaulted his daughter, a girl who, since the age of thirteen, had given herself to any boy or man who propositioned her. They had gone and left her alone with that savage man, and they'd sat opposite each other wordless in the dead room before he went out to change his wet clothes.

It was then she knew something damning was going to happen to her, but still she couldn't move a muscle. Even when he opened the door and stood there naked, she had been unable to drag her eyes from him. As she looked at the gleaming brown of his limbs, she knew now that whatever happened, she no longer cared.

When he said, "Come out to the kitchen a minute, Miss Lazenby," she had risen slowly as if hypnotized and followed him in there. She had stood like a statue as he undressed her, easing her gently to the quilt pallet on the floor. And as the rain pounded the tin roof and the cats wailed and the hound dogs howled she had forgotten her God and drifted off into a glorious world she'd never known. After it was over, he'd gone about his business as if nothing out of the ordinary had taken place, just as if he'd known all along he could have her or any other woman he wanted, and that he didn't give a damn.

And until near daybreak she had lain there wide awake and alone, her mind on the woman who lay dead in the next room, the woman she'd betrayed. She thought of Winnie whom she betrayed. She had committed adultery. In one short interval, she'd forgotten her husband and her God. She was irretrievably lost.

As the sun dropped faint rose petal rays on the wood floorboards of the kitchen, she had got up, dressed and gone to sit in a rocking chair in front of the blackened fireplace in that room of death. In something like a cataleptic state she had sat there while others arrived. She hadn't offered to help while Granny Blackburn, Urfie Pearl Buckner and Clemmie Bean bathed, dressed and lay out the corpse. The old women, happy-like in their morbid duties, had acted as if she was not present. Like three happy witches they went about their work, and later while they were in the kitchen cooking up a big meal for the curious, she realized they knew all and were discussing her fall, piecing together the pieces as if they were at a quilting and preparing to loose the scandal in every hollow, on every hill, in every crack and crevice of the Nation country.

When the Squire returned from the futile chase of that little boy, with her bedraggled husband in tow, she had blurted out the truth while Heber Kiler hooted at her like she was no better than he and his kind. She'd never knew how she'd managed to get home, dress and attend the burying at Sobby. Still in a daze, she half heard Winnie confess his sinful lust for Dossie Bell, how he had slipped out to Luster's cabin when the big Cherokee wasn't at home and tried to get her to leave the Nation with him, of how he'd accused her of having sexual relations with Buck Humphries, only to have her whisper, "Buck, he's my son" and fall dead with her heart misery. And through it all, while folks whispered and nudged and waited in an impatient sweat for the worst to happen, that solemn faced brown man had sat on a front seat, seemingly oblivious to it all.

Winnie hadn't shown up at the grave, and she knew he had fled the Nation. As dusk dark fell through the shaggy cedars, Luster turned to her and said, "Come on to my cabin. You can stay there." And as the wagon rolled deeper into the pine hills, into a country, strange, wild and forbidding, she had vanished from the world of Christian people. She withdrew, seemingly forever from the life she'd known, and like Dossie Bell before her, lived a life of sin without benefit of God's sanction, a damning life with a man in whose veins ran the savage blood of the Cherokee. And at every opportunity she had prayed to her God to forgive and rescue her from this lonely cabin. At first, the prayer didn't take hold, but as time went on and she never had a child, she knew that God was protecting her from further ties to the hell into which she'd cast herself.

Then, after four long years of torture, one day early this summer as she raised her streaming eyes and poured out her words from the decaying remnants of her lost soul, He had answered. She plainly heard the Mighty Voice as it rolled over hill and hollow and down through the mud-daubed chimney of the cabin.

"Find Winnie, your husband," it said, "you must reunite and pray out your iniquities together."

Spurred on by the Almighty's holy command, she had written the first letter to Winnie Lazenby's sister in eastern Arkansas. She had slipped from the house like a prisoner and crept five miles through the woods to the intersection of the Forked Deer and Firbank Roads, and hiding herself behind a clump of scrub oak, waited for the mail carrier's car. After that she went to meet him once a week and returned home tired and threadbare but heartened at following the command from Heaven.

Two weeks passed before an answer came. Winnie himself wrote that he was working as a hired hand on a farm. He had long thought of writing to her, but he had heard through a traveling salesman that she was imbedded in sin with Luster Holder. He had given her up as irredeemably lost. Then, with her golden message, his heart had overflowed with sorrow and joy that she'd repented her own black sin and forgave him his own. He had suffered a death of his own inside himself but had served his penance. God had answered his prayers too and what

a coincidence! The Heavenly Father had appeared
before him, the Great I Am of the Universe, with a
flowing white beard and flowing white robes, and in
a voice that shook the very waters of the rivers, had
commanded him to get in touch with the woman he'd
sworn to love and protect until death did them part,
that only by being reunited and by praying together
could they escape everlasting hell fire.

Together they could return to life as God's ser-
vants and bury the flesh and resurrect the spirit. He
would begin preaching again, this time not tying
himself to one place, but going to many, many out of
the way places where the Devil had anchored himself. Already he had saved enough to buy a second-
hand car. With his loud-speaker, he would spread the
word of God from the yards of courthouses all over
the South. He was busy at work on a plan for her
deliverance. Yes, he would rescue her from that terrible man and together they would again be washed
whiter than snow.

It had been hard to hide her happiness. She tried
to keep it from showing in her face as she sat opposite Luster Holder at mealtimes. He seemed to notice
nothing. As always, he said nothing which wasn't
absolutely necessary. And in his presence, she felt
convinced that he wouldn't care whether she stayed
on or left forever. But when she was alone, the old
fear returned. She must use every care in preparing
her escape. Luster had selected her as his woman to
take Dossie Bell's place, to cook his meals and fill

the vacancy in his bed and she had come without a protest. She must get far away or he would track her down and bring her back...or maybe, in cold animal wrath, slit her throat, and leave her in the woods where she'd never be found.

After her Lord and Savior had spoken to her, she tried to figure a way to keep her body from the giant hillman, although within the last year he had been less and less demanding of her. For the first time in her stay with him she had complained of being sick with a misery in her side. Luster had sent for Granny Gates, the old Negro midwife, who had many strange remedies. The old Negro woman gave her a horrible tasting concoction and said voodoo words over her. And when she still complained of nausea, Luster mixed her a strong toddy of charred corn whisky, that vile stuff she'd never tasted. It did nothing for her imagined misery, but it lulled her into a dreamy state of contentment. Fight against it she did, and, like one in a trance, she had once more forgotten Winnie. Only she did remember how they had buried all ideas of sex and during the last ten years together hadn't lived as a normal man and wife, although they were wedded in the Spirit of God. She had added more sin, which called for more prayers, more remorse, more striving for forgiveness.

Often she tried to explain it to herself. At fifteen, she was converted at Old Adcock Church over on the Cache River in Arkansas. She'd heard sweet, tingling chimes ringing in her ears and it was like she was lifted up and given a quick glance into the New Jerusalem. Twenty years passed without her again hearing the beautiful sound or experiencing the same glorious sensation. Then Luster had taken her on that rainy night and the chimes rang again clear and glorious and she was given another look at that celestial home beyond the skies.

It was hard to describe. As his hard arms crushed her against him, the chimes began low, tinkling, then louder, in ever increasing crescendo as she began climbing the golden stairs toward the pearly gates. She climbed slowly, soothingly at first, then more rapidly, more painfully, until she raised her voice to scream hosannas to Jesus Lord as the Heavenly Choir came forward singing preparatory to conducting her to the Heavenly Throne of God. And at that moment, a shriek of unsuppressed joy rose from her throat before it then died in a tortuous jerk of her whole body as the pearly gates were slammed shut in her face.

It happened that way every time he took her, and she realized that it was Satan's way of tempting her to continue her life of sin, forever to lead her up to the gates of Heaven, give her one hungry glance and then suddenly cast her in to the frightful darkness of hell where she could feel the heat of the eternal fires. That had been the story for four long years...lifted to the heights before bring cast into the depths.

And after each damning experience, she began trying to figure a way to keep from falling again.

She would purify her mind with prayer, add oint-
ment to her diseased soul and feel that she could
manage to hold off until the day of rescue. Then
when he pulled her over to him, the craving came
alive again, starting in her stomach like a small ball
which began spinning and spinning and swelling
larger and larger, until it seemed she'd die unless it
burst and gave her relief.

That was why she knew she had to get away
before the craving finally mastered her, overcame
the weakening power of her prayers, and made her
give up completely and forced her to replace her
kind and tender God with the ruthless and hard
Luster Holder. Only with Winnie was there hope of
deliverance here on earth and a chance of winning
Paradise hereafter.

Then, just when she thought that her God had
again forgotten her, the letter from Winnie had
arrived on yesterday and she again knew and realized that her deliverance was close at hand.

Still, last night she had fallen again, but for the
last time. She had lain awake and prayed silently
while that savage man slept softly beside her. It was
near daybreak before she felt the prayer catch and
take hold. The Lord's voice, so far away and deep
she could barely hear it, whispered, "Salvation is
close at hand."

Next day she walked the five miles and the mail
carrier handed her the letter of deliverance. And just
as if God Almighty were clearing away the last of

the big obstacles, something happened to intervene on her behalf.

It was at nine o'clock that Luster said, "I'm going out to Firbank later in the evenin' to get some flour, Sudie. I figger to not get back till maybe late. Be shore and see to Dimity. She's due to calf and'll need somebody on hand to granny her."

She averted his steady eyes and tried not to think of what was going to take place out at the store. Luster had never mentioned his troubles with the Greebers but Wurner had kept her posted. There was going to be a horrible fight. The death of Tank Greeber had set it all off, and the Nation was once more embroiled in the kind of dread trouble for which it existed.

She no longer cared, for she had long since ceased to take any interest in anything but her own salvation. There would be no peace in these rugged hills until more murders and more burying's took place. If Luster met his end, it would only be the fulfillment of the destiny set out for him before his birth. If he had been going to Birdie Kiler, that didn't matter to her either. She would never know the outcome of the fight, for by the time one or the other of the feudists was dead, she would be far, far away.

She watched the tall, muscular figure cross the rocky steep pasture and disappear in the pines near the springhouse on the way to that awful liquor still. She was alone with God once more. She had sat on the side porch to collect herself and to think on all that was to be done. The arrival of the idiot had interrupted her.

She heard the clock strike two. After Wurner had left, she went to the family room and stood in the center of the room motionless for several threading minutes, trying to keep her eyes from the old oak bed, the scene of her innumerable sins. She found her worn and battered suitcase and packed up the few clothes that belonged to her. She dressed in the black taffeta silk dress which she had worn on her wedding day fifteen years ago. The blue ribbon which she pinned tight up against around her thin waist was faded and frazzled.

The scarred faced mantle clock struck the half-hour, its ancient chimes hoarsely discordant after over a hundred years of time-marking. She carried the suitcase to the dog-run and stood there beside it for a while, her greenish eyes searching the locust thicket beyond the lane. She walked down the steps and hid the suitcase behind a lilac bush at the side of the house. Turning cautiously, she started to retrace her steps to the cabin when her eyes caught a movement in the underbrush directly across the lane. Her heart plugged her throat, choking her and for a minute she thought she might faint. She glued her anxious eyes to the spot and when no further movement came, she entered the cabin and brought a chair to the run.

It couldn't have been Luster. He just wasn't the type to spy on anyone. Possibly it was Cooter and

Carnes, the gray mules, or even the cow Pattie Pide. At the thought of the cow, she remembered Dimity, that she was due to calf. She couldn't see to her now.

She sat down to wait, the minutes crawled around her, holding back the hours. It must have been mid-afternoon when she thought she heard the faint rumble of the car laboring up the old wagon road in the valley back of the cabin. Even as she jerked erect, the noise abruptly ceased. She held herself taut, every nerve straining like tight catgut. She saw the bushes move out beyond the road bank. She wet her lips, swallowed and tried to sound her voice. A hoarse croak startled her and she took a backward step in the run. Then with catlike caution, she moved to the edge of the steps. The bushes parted and a dark head appeared momentarily before it ducked back down.

She breathed deeply, expanding her lungs to the hurting point, held it for a painful moment, then shot the air from her lungs in a desperate suspiration, the hoarsely garbled "Winnie!" riding over her tongue and into the humid air.

A long, stilty arm shot up and motioned to her. Feverishly Sudie picked up the suitcase and, like someone resurrected from the dead, ran staggeringly toward the clump of bushes. Salvation was at hand.

6

AT THE MAILBOXES, where the Forked Deer and Firbank roads intersected, Buck stopped and swept his eyes in all directions. Across a cornfield he could see the brick chimneys of the Kiler home peeping up through a fringe of leaves. He waited for only a minute, then setting his jaw muscles hard, he crossed the road and vaulted a vine-tangled rail fence. He followed a corn row, the browning tassels high above his head.

The high sun beat down torridly. It must be long past noon but maybe Heber Kiler was at home. Buck's wavering resolution to see him might be a crazy one. He didn't know anything else he could do to help Luster. The Squire was a powerful man, feared physically as well as politically, a brutal, vulgar type, but a mighty good fellow to have scotching for you in a time of trouble, and he was the only man who'd ever seemed to win the respect of Luster Holder, the only man the big hillman ever seemed to have any time for. Surely the Squire had heard the threatening news. He wasn't the kind to miss a good fight, and even at the age of sixty-five could still hold his own in a bear-hug contest with men half his age and was hell on wheels with most any weapon.

Buck felt little and awfully alone as he emerged from the corn and entered the cool shade of a long grove of oaks and hickories which led to an old two-storied frame house, where white paint had peeled off to leave a brown, forbidding exterior. He hadn't met the Squire face to face since the Birdie trouble four years ago. At church he had been able to avoid him, for the Squire never came inside to the service. With the passage of time, he was sure that thought of him never passed through Heber Kiler's mind. Still he dreaded a talk with the hard-bitten old man.

Maybe Buck had chosen the right time to come after all, for the Squire and Birdie had already left for Firbank, he was sure. A short distance from the long verandah, he stopped just behind a tree and peeked out cautiously. Except for the clucking of hens in the backyard and the distant lowing of a cow, there wasn't a sound. At first glance, the verandah seemed deserted. Then he saw a slight movement on the floor. At first, he couldn't make out what it was, as he left his hiding place and crept closer, careful to keep behind the rough-barked trunks of the aged trees.

He could see the whole of the porch now, and as his eyes swept it, he sucked in his breath with a noisy hiss. Seated on the floor near the steps was a naked child, a little boy. He could just see the straw-colored top of the curly head as he bent over a half-watermelon which was between his outspread thighs. The child was gouging at the red meat with his fingers and carrying the big hunks to his dripping mouth.

For a moment, Buck breathed a sigh of relief. He felt he'd been right after all...Birdie had left the kid at home by himself. The queerest feeling Buck had ever experienced ran over him, up from his short boots and spreading through his whole lithe body until he seemed transformed into something new, clean. His eyes remained glued on the child.

A twig popped under his foot and the little boy jerked up his head, listening, a piece of melon halfway to his mouth. Buck dodged his head back quickly and kept very still. He heard the screen door bang shut and a man say, "Bye, Dinks," and the kid grunt. He saw the man striding across the yard toward the lane road to the highway and recognized Freel Goddard, owner of the general store at Firbank. He didn't want to think about the stories which were so old now that they'd ceased to be rich fodder for the gossips' wagging tongues.

He watched until he heard a car start. He turned back slowly and gave a big start. Standing not five paces from him was the boy, a skinny little fellow whose sky-blue eyes were round with curiosity. He

still chewed a piece of melon and a trickling blood-
like stream of juice ran from the corners of his red
lips and dripped off his chin onto his chest, where
a collection of flies had gathered. Buck ran his eyes
over the olive-complexioned face, held in awe at the
beauty and perfection in the whole of the small figure. And his heart seemed to swell double its size
and threaten to burst through his ribs.

"He's mine," he thought, a pang of spontaneous
joy stabbing through him, "he's me all over, he's me
and he's the wonderfulest looking little scutter I ever
seen living and breathing. He come right outta me
and is blood of my blood."

The boy was studying him soberly, his smooth
forehead drawn into faint lines. He slapped at the
flies on his chest and rubbed his hands against his
round stomach before he clasped them behind his
back, his head thrown so far back that the hair fell
shaggy to his shoulders.

Then the clear piping voice came, which sent an
odd shiver over Buck, a shiver he hadn't known since
he professed religion at the Nazarene Church. The
voice said, "Who is you?"

Buck's throat was dry and he had to try his
voice twice before the dull sound came, "I'm Buck
Humphries."

The round eyes bulged, "Tiddy's Buck?"

"Ti-Tiddy?" Buck stammered.

The boy grinned, "She's telled me lots about you.
Why you never come see me before?"

Buck shuffled his feet and sheepishly replied, "I sorter been busy, what's your name?"

"Dink and I's four years old," the boy proudly informed him.

Buck wet his lips, "Who's your pappy?"

"I ain't got no pappy, just Birdie," Dink informed Buck.

As Buck stepped nearer, the little boy leaped suddenly toward him and snuggled deep in his arms, as if by instinct he also knew the truth which was glorious, sacred to both of them.

In Buck's mind, he played out the whole story of Dink's birth. Birdie had been midwifed by Murdie Blackburn herself in the crib at the Kiler barn. Buck had gathered that it wasn't his child at that time, that the child had favored someone else, a dark swarthy boy child and not fair and blue-eyed like Buck hisself.

Still not at all sure, he'd returned to Old Henley and learned that the Squire was no longer looking for him. Millie Kiler, Birdie's momma, had been found dead of a heart misery, and shortly afterwards Wurner had run across the bloated bodies of Luke Tolby, Birdie's uncle, and Bode Holly, rumored to have been the victim of Birdie's wrath and razor. These exciting things took the pressure off Buck. The Firbank settlement was in a furor, and there'd more burying to do under the shaggy cedars at Sobby graveyard before life resumed its usual course.

As the whole of the week of terror died away, he had heard that Birdie, with her mother gone, was wilder than ever before and that the Old Squire was not only reconciled to her way of living but was urging her on and profiting from her activities. He'd spread word that "even if the bastard turns out to belong to that 'ere Humphries boy, I hain't wanting the son of a bitch pollutin' my house. He'd be solid in the way and skeered as a mite-eat chicken."

Buck had tried to forget all about her. He was horrified when Wurner brought a message that she wanted to see him. He never went. He recalled her last words to him on that silver-sprinkled night, after he'd cried to her, "I can't see you no more, Birdie. I can't."

He was still recalling all that happened when a scent in the air brought Buck back to the here and now.

The smell of the watermelon on the boy filled Buck's nostrils. Buck pulled a blue bandana handkerchief from his pants pocket and rubbed off the boy's face, chest and belly. Dink leaned back his head and set his big eyes on Buck's. He grinned happily, showing two rows of teeth like the small even grains on an ear of immature corn.

"Tiddy said you'd come to play with me," the boy declared before asking, "you gonna stay with me all day, Buck?"

Buck thought momentarily of how mature the boy seemed for his age, how he could talk as he did and how he was aware of so much.

Finally Buck answered, "Maybe, where's your Momma?"

The child said nothing in reply but stared pleadingly at Buck when Buck turned slightly from him to look around.

"Stay Buck!" the child cried out suddenly and clung to Buck tightly.

Buck bent down to meet the excited boy's frantic hug.

Suddenly Buck became aware that they were being watched and Buck stood quickly, the child still clinging to him. Birdie was watching from the front porch. She wore a tight-fitting pink voile dress and high heeled shoes. Her busy black hair was tied back from her ears with a ribbon. Her eyes were the big, defiant brown ones he remembered and her lips, heavily painted, were larger, more puffed. She had filled out more now and at twenty-two was more voluptuous than she'd been at eighteen, stacked up, as the Squire often boasted, like a brick privy. As she stood there, hipped, her round breasts strutted under her dress, she had the look of something beautifully wild, graceful like a panther and just as dangerous. A memory brought the same dull ache to Buck's mind.

Her loud mocking laugh seemed to bounce off the tree trunks and ricochet into his throbbing ears.

"A touching scene," she said in a careless tone which once had corrupted his dreams.

"The pappy and his bastard son!" she harangued him, "The little peckerwood taken to you like a duck to water. You've taken a long time to gettin' around to seein' him, if you ask me. You'll have one hellacious time gettin' shed of him!"

She laughed a vile laugh.

Gently Buck pulled the boy's arms from around his neck and eased him astraddle his hip, the small hands digging into his back and stomach as Dink held on.

Buck licked his trembling lips. In her presence he was himself like a shamed little boy. He looked earnestly at the scoffing Birdie and asked, "Is he... is he really mine, Birdie?"

"Who the hell else's do you think he is?" she asked before spilling into a long talk about the boy, "He's your blood and bone, only knocked down about four feet. Can't you see he's the spittin' image? And he's as queer already as you was...sets playin' by hisself and a-starin' off into the durned sky like he was seein' angels or boogers or hisself as one of God-A-Mighty's own little sunbeams except he's full of devil as a stuffed goose."

She took a breath and continued, "And then turnin' like a skeered rabbit ever' time one of my friends comes to see me. You're the first man he ever got nigh, Buck, shore as sin, and you're just a boy at that and still don't look no older than you did when we was in school at Refuge. Dink…he seen you was his kind right short off."

"He's the purtiest little shaver I ever seen, Birdie," Buck announced proudly.

Birdie shrugged, "He's a right gracious little fart now, ain't he? He orght to be."

Then the girl sighed, "Buck, you're the purtiest piece of man meat I ever coupled with and if you hadn't been so religion sprung and skeered your Savior was gonna throw you right into the fars of Hell in a damn witch's swing, it'd be something!"

She shook her head, "Things mighta been different, 'y doggies."

Then looking at him with hope, her eyes stretched wide and she asked, "Say now, Buck, you ain't finally come to your senses, have you? You ain't actually come out here to see me, have you?"

Buck's face muscles twitched and he said quickly, "No, no, Birdie, I didn't come for that. I…"

She interrupted him, "I thought if you was, I'm ready. But I knowed you wouldn't dare. You was skeered as a treed coon before and you shore God wouldn't be around here if Old Pap was at home."

"He's the one I come to see, Birdie."

"Me?" the little boy looked up and asked.

Birdie's face reddened and she burst out, "You come to see that little bastard? You ain't expectin' me to believe that damn lie, are you?"

Buck shook his head, "It ain't no lie, Birdie. They's gonna be bad trouble up at the store this evening, and Luster may get hurt."

At the mention of Luster's name, Birdie's naturally dark face grew darker. Buck plainly saw a quiver ripple beneath her skin-tight dress.

She was very hoarse when she spoke.

"Wurner, he come by and told us and Old Pap's already went to the store," Birdie said uneasily, before continuing, "I'm a-going later. I got me some plans which has got to be carried out. I've heared me a piece of news which has set me a-far. For years the feeling's been backing up inside me till my teeth's a-floating. But I gotta wait till this here fracas at the store's over. Then I'll know just how to take hold. Wurner...he come back and told me."

Buck thought about Wurner Crouse. Buck knew most folks conceded that Wurner was an idiot. Folks said he had turtle eggs for brains.

As they stood there, Birdie set her hands on her hips and squirmed her shoulders before speaking, "Luster's just got to kill that varmint son-of-a-bitch, Buck. He's been pesterin' me for over six months now, a-scrabblin' up on the house to ketch me when Old Pap's not here. I keep the doors and winders barred most of the time and the double-barreled shotgun loaded and waitin' but sinst Old Pap got the drop on him and drove him off, he hides nigh the house waitin' to ketch me outside and pounce on me. My razor's always fresh-honed and round my neck, but

I'm afeared his scaly hide'll turn the blade. Before
God, Buck, I'd ruther be raped by a rhinoceros!"

Birdie hung her head and shook it before continuing to pour out her soul, "I git tired of this here
kind of life, slutting with every durned man Old Pap
digs up for me that's got an extry dollar or anything
to swap, and his taking most of it and laying 'round
drunk and boasting like he was a gentleman instead
a low-borned hog. But it's the only durned thing I
can do or care to do. Old Pap would've let Ard take
me long ago, but he's been holding out till he's sure
of that forty acres of Tolby bottomland. That's the
only reason he threatened him with the gun here
that day. Old Pap don't give a whoop in hell what
happens to me!"

The boy squeezed Buck's waist with his small
thighs and reached up one hand to pat his cheek,
"Let's play, Buck." The little boy, even at this early
age, knew Birdie would stand around yapping until
the sun went down.

"I figger I oughta be going, Birdie," Buck said.

"Pappy, he don't have no more idea than a rotten stump where I'm at. He may be needin' me for
something," Buck said as Birdie strolled over to the
verandah edge and leaned against one of the square
columns.

"Put the tapper down a minute, Buck, and come in
the house. I ain't forgot what a time we had us over at
the schoolhouse that night four years ago. I've had a
itchin' in me at the rememberin'. You was skeered in

your mind but they wasn't nothin' wrong with you physical and the proof of it's right there a-ridin' your hip. Before I take out to the fracas, I'd admire to git acquainted with you again. It won't cost you nuthin' and I figger it'll do you a lotta good. You certainly deserve it the way the other turned out...you scouring 'round that 'ere rainy bottom with Old Pap and that durned sissified preacher a-huntin' you to make you marry me...Old Winnie Lazenby, that was lustin' for Dossie Bell for over ten years hard-runnin.'"

The boy spurred his heels gently into Buck's leg, "Don't leave, Buck!"

Buck gripped the boy more tightly against him. In some way he felt protected with the boy in his arms. His heart drummed hard under his thin shirt as he thought of Tiddy. She was so innocent, so pure, so untouched.

"I...I can't, Birdie. It just ain't Christian and...and it'd be awful before the...the kid," Buck explained.

Her laugh was jarring.

"Before him! Hell far, the little piss ant don't have no more ideas than a rabbit what we'll be doing. Come on, Buck, I'm beginning to sizzle deep inside me and I'm sure it'll put new life in you to git your crankcase going again."

The boy watched quietly but began to cry just as quietly.

Buck looked at her and answered, "I just can't, Birdie. I ain't been forgive by my God for that other time. I can't bring more sin on both of us."

"Sin, my hind foot! God…He don't know nobody in Firbank's alive. It's Satan that watches over this here settlement. You're more interested in that bastard child of yor'n than you are me, and it gives me a prime idea. How'd you like to have him?"

"You mean…" Buck stammered.

She continued, "I mean I'll give him to you and you can take him home and keep him till Kingdom Come, 'y golly, if you're mindin' to. But first I'll bargain. Come on in the house for a while and then you can have him. I figure you'll be getting' bad cheated but it's your funeral, not mine."

Buck's stomach shriveled, "I couldn't do it, Birdie. I'd never be able to look him in the eye without rememberin' and feeling dirty, 'cause even if he's just a mite of a scutter, he'd know. Anyways, Pappy wouldn't let me keep him and…"

She broke in disgustedly, "You still gonna let that old moth-ate toot say what you'll do or don't? Why he's deaf and don't know it and orghta had his deceased old carcass planted at Sobby twenty years ago. Do you or don't you want your natural borned child? He's crazy as a bull frog over you already!"

She laughed raucously, "This here's the first damn time I ever offered a man a free ride and had him turn me down…And me throwing in a bastard to boot!"

Suddenly warm, wet lips kissed Buck's cheeks with a loud kiss, "Take me with you, Buck, please, please! Please take me!"

Buck shook his head, "I'm dying for him, but I can't make no such a sinful bargain."

He looked beyond her and apologized, "I...I'm sorry, Birdie, but I...I got me a girl and she's all I'm wantin'."

Birdie slapped her hand flat against her hips and had a roaring laugh, "What you gonna do, call in the neighbors to satisfy her or pray before you breed her? 'y God, you're worsen'r than that young Bibler Old Pap's got hid out in the shack down in the woods lot. Brother Dipple is as skeered as a plucked goose of me. But shoot, I'd just soon as lay up with Pistol Greeber and get just as much satisfaction. That preacher is skeered to death of seeing me but grows pale as can be at the thought of not getting' me. I'm here to tell you..."

She stopped short and seemed listening. Then she jumped off the porch and walked slowly toward Buck, swinging her buttocks tauntingly. She stopped so near that he could smell the candy-like odor of cheap perfume. It nauseated him. Dink burrowed his face into Buck's neck. Buck could feel the little fellow's hot breath as he drew it in and out jerkily, the wiggly body squirming in his arms.

Buck looked at Birdie and he saw that her large eyes were damp.

"I was just joking, Buck. I just thought it would be a favor to you, you not havin' none sinst I set you a-far and left you to smolder. I can wait for what I'm burnin' for," she said, her husky voice in her throat.

She continued, "I'm just bad jealous to actually see the kinda fellow I could'a had if I hadn't throwed myself away early and got down in the mud with the hogs. Mammy tried to raise me right, but they was too much of Old Pap in me. You're the only decent boy I ever had and I taken you like the bitch I was and never let you know I was the one that felt I'd dirtied you…a real clean boy…so that you'd always hate me and my kind. You'll make some girl a fine man if you ever git rid of them voodoo ideas your old Pappy brained into your ears and settled on your brain. Of all the men I've knowed, you was the only one plumb floatin' with real life. Skeered as you was, you rigged me in one beautiful try."

She caught her breath, "I wasn't really made for none of you. I'm needin' a strong man which can skeer all other men offen me and whomper hell out of me if I git outta line. I've had him back in my mind since I knowed what men was made for and if I hadn't got me a crazy notion about one of the sorriest bastards ever mis-birthed under God's sun, I'd a-went to him long ago. I let him slip outta my hands and the opportunity bust right in my face. After that, I didn't care what I done. Mammy went to meet her maker and left me with Old Pap. He seen how he could use me and I let him hire me out like I was a prize brood sow instead of a human. But I'm through now. I'm still young and I ain't begin to wear out. I'm a-goin' to him come hell or high water."

Her voice caught in a sob.

"Goddam, if I wouldn't let him cut my throat from ear to ear just to hold me in his arms and agin' my bouncing breasts just one time," Birdie confessed.

Buck didn't look at her but asked, "Who, Birdie?"

She looked hard at Buck, "You'll learn soon enough! It ain't for me to say right now, but Wurner... he brung me the word, and this makes it the day of my great decision."

She reached out a hand and grasped Buck by the arm. The boy Dink clove closer to him and she gave him a sharp smack on the buttocks.

"Don't be afraid, Dink," she said sneeringly, "I ain't gonna hurt your Pappy none, you little bastard. If I don't see hide nor hair of you again, it'll be one day too soon for both of us. You listen to me, Dink. You be good to Buck or I'll come over there and beat the paste outta you, because durn your pissified soul, I...I'm a-lovin' both of you and don't never wanna mess you up with my low-down presence."

"You...you mean I can still have him if I'm a-mind to?" Buck eagerly asked her.

She shook her head and smiled, "Sure as hell! I really admire you for being able to turn down what other men kill over."

"I'll be good to him, Birdie. Pappy's bedridden most of the time and he can't help himself now. This here's my own son and he can't make me give him up. I'll love him, Birdie and see he don't want for nothin.'"

The kid was trying to leap up and down in Buck's arms as he cried in a sing-song voice, "I'm going with Buck, I'm going with Buck!"

Birdie slapped his buttocks again, lightly.

"He's yo'rn to do with as you see fit and you'll spoil him till he stinks," she began, "I'm gonna miss the little piss ant a lot cause I just solid weaned him from his titty and I'll have to soundly admit I did git a lot of dreamy pleasure out of havin' him pull at my jugs and drain me when I was so overfull with milk I couldn't carry it comfortable. It was hell tryin' to break him. I painted my tits with quinine and soot and rubbed them with a mash of lard and jim-son blooms but it didn't faze the little bastard. He drug at them like they was covered in honey," she explained fully.

The boy blushed and hid his face.

Birdie laughed raucously, "I tapered him off on cow's milk. But I'm warnin' you…he likes it fresh and warm out of the cow. So keep your cow where he can't get to her handy or you'll be coming up short. He's bad as ere calf and Old Pap's whacked his little ass to a crisp the way he slips out to the pasture and nurses our old Jersey, Yellow Pride."

"We got a good cow, Birdie. She's just come in fresh. He'll have plenty of milk," he assured her.

Looking curious, Buck inquired, "Who'd you name him after, Birdie?"

She gave the jarring laugh that always made Buck want to run for cover and attempted to explain it to him, "That's the funny thing, Buck. I never rightly named him, I guess, and just called him 'Thingumbob' for a long time. Then as he growed bigger, he got so ever'time I bared my teats to feed him, he'd rear back and crow like a young rooster. I got to calling him Dink after a pet Rhode Island I used to have when I was a little spit."

She laughed again, "I'll be doggone. I figger the name comes right at him. He's as handsome-like as a spring mornin' just as sure as God made little apples."

Buck was surprised at the pride in her voice and on her face. Birdie shifted her hips.

Buck asked, "Can I take him now, Birdie?"

She exclaimed, "Jesus, yes, Buck! I been puttin' off bringin' him to you for I ain't got no more use for a child than a pig has for a side saddle. Keep him till Gabriel toots his mighty horn as far as I'm concerned. He's soundly in my way now that I've decided on a road of action which don't nobody but me know about yet. And…Dink…he's skeered of Old Pap and he'd like to get shed of him too."

Buck felt the boy nuzzle his hand into his chest. An icy chill ran up Buck's spine. Instinctively, he pressed his hand more firmly against the child's small, warm back.

"Go with him, Dink," Birdie said more softly, "He's your lawful borned pappy and has a right to you, 'cause you're two of a kind and orghta make it just fine. And he deserves you too 'cause gittin' you

nigh ruin't his soul and maybe he'll forget his imagined sin with you around him," she stated flatly. She
continued, "It'll be wonderful having you pissing on
someone else for a change."

She looked at Buck, "For if he sleeps with you
then you'll feel like you've been swimming in a warm
slough. I try to make him sleep on the floor, but he
gets skeered at night and crawls in by me unbeknow-
ing. Be extry keerful tonight, because ordinarily
he's the peeingest little snot this side of hell, but his
bladder is loaded with watermelon and I shore ain't
answerin' none for you and your sheets."

"I'll see to him, Birdie," he assured her, "is there
anything special he eats?"

She scoffed, "Any durn thing that's left lying
around loose, Buck. But mainly he likes crowder
peas, navy beans, cornpone, and fried sow belly. And
he really goes for catfish and hush puppies. But no
matter what you feed him on, Buck, you can't keep
no solid meat on him. I'll be durned if he don't run
it off as fast as it's ground. I tell him he's gonna grow
up lookin' like he swapped tails with a killdeer and
got cheated in the bargain."

She looked down at Dink, "Now, you mind Buck,
Puddin' Pie, or I'll truly come over and bust your little
ass till you cain't completely set down for a month."

Little Dink nodded but did so red in the face.

She raised her eyes to Buck and said uneasily,
"Are you going up the store?"

"I'm wantin' to bad, Birdie, but I'm hatin' to see it."

"I shore-God ain't gonna miss it, Buck. That varmint's spread word he'll be there at four sharp and I figger Luster'll show up too come that time. He won't take no dare."

Buck admitted, "I couldn't help him none, Birdie."

Birdie was excited and went on a spree and excitedly told Buck, "'y God, I can! I'm gonna be amongst them present and have my razor ready for any Greeber that tries to help that varmint out. Old Pap...he had his old forty-five Colt ready too. Freel Goddard was just here and he says folks has been pouring into Firbank sinst daybreak. Hell's a-brewing, Buck! Why didn't them durned Greebers stay out there in Missouri where they belonged at instead of coming out here to be killed! It was Luster no way which changed ends with Old Tank in that barrel of sour mash. I don't rightly know who done it but it sho-God ain't his way of doing no murder."

She continued, "I figger the other Greebers'll stay at home sinst Tiddy says Ard's ordered them to..."

"Tiddy!" Dink said, eyes opened wide.

"Tiddy?" Birdie's brown eyes bored into him a moment, her full mouth twisted into a knowing smile, "So that's the woman your pants are burnin' for? They say she...why Buck, she ain't no more'n twelve years old and..."

"She's thirteen coming fourteen, Birdie," Buck corrected her.

As usual Birdie had plenty to say, "Anyways, oh, Jesus God, forgit what I'm saying! I just keep rememberin' me things," she said, "Even if she wasn't but seven, she was made just for you Buck, and gals breed early in this here climate. I know Tiddy well. She come running through the grove one day in the early morning and saw Dink. First thing I know I looked outen a winder and they was playin' games like two on a featherbed. She come up to the house, with him a-ridin' on her back, and set them pretty eyes that look like they was meltin' and runnin' together all the time on me and says as bold and confident as you please, 'Miss Birdie, can I take Dink down to Sugar Creek swimming with me?' And I says, 'Yes, kid, if you can stand him.' I was expectin' a caller and glad to get shed of him till I was through entertaining. Well, she taken him swimming and he taken to her like a fly to sugar. That little split-tail come over often after that and she practically taken what raisin' I'd given Dink over. She bathed and dressed him and taken him home with her and been the biggest help on earth to me with him. And sometimes her brother, who's darker and swarthy like them other Greebers but a right favorable little snot, come with her. They'd bring along with a coal-black pick ninny who answers to the name Tadpole and the four of them spent most of the day in the creek, much to my unthrottled joy and Dink'd go on home with 'em and I figger they slept in the same bed...dogs, pick ninny and all. That Tiddy puts me in the mind of a young mare colt the way she runs, graceful as all get out and so purty she just makes you ache deep down in you a-wishin' you was built up in her."

As she had said it, Birdie had a devious look and grinned wickedly. It made Buck uncomfortable.

Dink had turned from Buck and was hanging on his mother's every word. He grinned and giggled and spat out, "Tiddy, my sweetheart."

Birdie kept on, "I'm just sayin' Buck, if you're wantin' her, take her and if your old man says anything, tell him to go clean straight to where he's headin' anyways. I figger she's as pure-minded as any female girl I ever seen and not no more Old Tank's daughter than I am. I figger she's a bastard and…"

"We's both bastards, Buck," Little Dink proudly announced.

"We're all bastards, Puddin," Birdie put in.

"Well, Buck, I gotta crawl into another dress and rush up to that darned store," she told him.

Buck shuffled and looked down at the ground, "I ain't sure I'll go yet, Birdie."

With that, he and Dink turned to go.

7

IT WAS COMMON PRACTICE for folks to come to town, to come to Firbank on Saturday because that was the one day they felt they could take off to go to town to the store and to learn the news. Seldom did they go to the bank because most folks around didn't have enough money to worry with having accounts. Folks went to Firbank because it was something to do. They didn't particularly go because they were up to trouble. They usually wanted something. Sometimes they just wanted to see something other than the backside of a draught horse or a mule. Sometimes they only wanted to stand around the livery stable or the blacksmith's shop or the corner of the one main street and listen and watch others just like them.

Luster Holder didn't want much. He'd left Sudie at home to go to Firbank because he needed something.

No more, no less. He didn't come to town to prove anything or because he had an ax to grind. Luster Holder just preferred to be left alone. But he also wasn't one to back down to a challenge. No matter, he hated crowds. He hated curious people. All he wanted was to get a sack of flour and get back home. Old Dimity would soon need his attention. She'd had a terrible time with her last calf.

He'd avoided the big road, which led straight down the red clay hill and ran on a level up to the store. He took a wide circle, clear around the school grounds, and climbed a board fence into Freel Goddard's vegetable garden. Half bent over, he walked through a patch of late tomatoes and stopped behind a trellis of morning glories to watch two men taking drinks at the rear of the store. After they left, he pushed back a wire gate and crossed to the store. No one was in the rear of the building. A constant hum of noise beat against Luster's ears. He'd uncorked a bottle and took a big swig. On the front porch, men were arguing loudly.

He had walked to a stack of flour and selected a forty-eight pound bag of Tennessee Rose, holding it out in front of him for a moment.

"A body could walk off with the whole damn store," he'd thought. The more he thought about it, the more he thought, "They's nobody got less sense than people."

His only thought had been to get away from all of it. If Sudie had told him sooner, they would never have run short of flour. But a meal wasn't a meal without hot biscuits. The Squire said folks would think he was afraid if he didn't accept Ard Greeber's dare. He didn't care a damn. He just wasn't going to lower himself by going at the beck and call of anyone, let alone a freak like Ard Greeber. And he never liked to fight in front of the curious. If that spider-legged ape would only leap out on him somewhere in the woods, he wouldn't mind it. When there was a fracas between two men, they should be the only ones concerned and not have to settle their differences with a mob looking on...a mob it didn't concern in the least.

He had lifted the sack to his shoulder and started to leave when a new voice at the front stopped him. It was the bull-like voice of Wurner. Someone was pestering the idiot, who without a doubt was taking advantage of the large assemblage to surround himself with youngsters to preach his own peculiar brand of the Gospel.

A roar had gone up. Then he heard a bellow. Laying the flour aside, he strode rapidly to the front. He peered over the heads on the porch just in time to see Ard Greeber advancing on the prone body of the idiot, scaly hands extended toward his throat.

His grandfather had always said, "Don't pick on no idiot nor hit no cripple." That was his belief too.

He had glided through the mass of folks on the porch and rapidly descended the steps. As Ard advanced on the poor idiot Wurner, his massive shoulders drooped toward his balloon-like belly, the spidery legs pressed flat against it as he propelled himself forward, churning the dust in a sort of weird canter as he neared the store.

Silence bore in almost unbearably as Ard scrabbled to the center of the wide-open space, the bristly stubble on his fiery purple scalp like dead grass in a sun-scorched field. He drew his narrow forehead into a mass of tangled wrinkles and swept his simmering eyes, red and beetly, over the wavering crowd. He shook his shoulders like a bear and rose high on his spindly legs like a bullfrog, then the legs disappeared under the belly once more and he set out for the porch in a jerky lope.

A sustained gasp was sucked in noisily by hundreds of throats as people rolled frantically back. These folks had been gathering since daybreak to witness a spectacle and they were certainly getting a spectacle.

Ard made a wide circle and stopped again just beyond the spot at the south end of the porch, where Wurner, still preaching, had raised his voice to a hysterical howl in an effort to hold the attention of his young listeners, who had begun to scatter, a few of them scrambling under the porch to join the white-faced Pistol and the gray-faced Tadpole.

"God He says now...says stay now," Wurner bellowed. "The Devil's came fastly. For is...beast form is...as Father says...the Devil must be cast out! He cain't be 'lowed to stay amongst his chil'ern."

Wurner kept up his preaching. Ard Greeber lowered his beady eyes to Wurner for a second, then
scrabbled slowly toward the prone figure. He squatted
back on his haunches and, still very slowly, reached
out his hands, the long, meaty fingers curled.

Folks watched, horrified, as he fitted the finger
clear around Wurner's bull neck. They saw the cord-
ed knots on the shoulders and arms as Ard bunched
his muscles preparatory to turning loose the whole
power of his iron body. They saw the pressure begin,
and at the same instant they saw a flash of brown
and heard Ard's gasp of surprise as he was flung violently backwards. He bounced on his semi-circular
hump and came back to his normal standing position in one movement to look up at Luster Holder
who stood above him.

Ard had the look of smoldering hatred in his eyes.
He hated Luster Holder for more reasons that his
hot head could count. He fixed those hating eyes on
the form of the big Cherokee and was determined to
kill him at last. Luster stood there staring at him, a
half-dead look in his eyes, the look of a stone-cold
killer who only kills when provoked but once he's
killed forgets it like a man forgets yesterday's frost.

Scrambling forward like the half-human spider he
was, Ard sprang upon the hillman and dug his claw-
like fingers into him. Luster let out an animal-like
growl. Ard's fingernails dug into Luster's skin and
flesh. He was truly like a wild animal from deep in
the forest. As he clung to Luster, the big half-Indian

used his own huge hands to grasp Ard Greeber and tear him off. With one huge and strongly-gripped effort he flung the hunched-back creature of a man onto the hard-packed clay ground sending clouds of dust boiling into the air. Ard again landed on his hump of a back and was just starting to climb to his feet when Luster pounced onto him and began striking him with heavy solid blows from his massive fists. The blows landed one by one with frightful rapidity. Luster said nothing as he beat Ard upon the head and neck.

Finally Ard managed to roll Luster until he broke free and got to his feet. In a split second, both the creature of a man and the big Cherokee were standing and facing one another. Luster moved in again. The half-breed's tall body swayed now as he stood with legs far apart. He resumed his attack with his fists and he poured murderous blows to Ard's temples. They had worked far out into the open space.

With this first lull in the suspense, if a lull it could be called, folks came back to life and surged slowly forward toward the combatants. Buck Humphries, with Dink astride his hip, was shoved with the spectators. White-faced, weak, he tried to hold back the mass, but like a piece of driftwood swept downstream by a raging flood, he was carried from the edge of the school grounds and across the dust-clogged road, until he was on the periphery of the human circle which now formed at a safe distance from Ard and

Luster...pressing in just so far, like wolves to await the kill.

Buck held tightly to the trembling little boy and tried to shield him from the insanely milling folks. Only one man, tall and gray, stood in front of him. He recognized Squire Heber Kiler, and for the first time in his life was glad to be near the powerful old man. Directly across the open space from him he saw Birdie, eyes wide and glazed, hair bushing out around her inflamed face, like some woman of the wilds.

There was no time for any further looking. A low rumbling in the mass rose to a hysterical roar as Ard suddenly lurched just in time to catch the toe of Luster's boot under his chin and be bowled back over.

As the big Cherokee rushed back in to stomp his assailant in the face, Ard leaped backwards six feet, then hunching together, sprang high, his little feet together. Ard jumped nearly to Luster and couldn't seem to check his forward progress. The feet caught him, as they had caught Wurner earlier, and turned him a complete flip. He struck on his back and rolled so rapidly that Ard, in his second leap, appeared to make his fatal mistake and give the fight to Luster Holder.

The big hillman regained his own feet and stooped back down in one movement. Before Ard could twist or leap away, Luster grasped him around the middle and lifted him high in the air, while Ard thrashed his long arms and twisted legs in an effort to free himself. Luster swung around and slammed the squirming body headfirst against the hard, packed clay.

"I figger that done hit," the Squire growled, shaking his head in decisive little shakes.

"Not yet, Squire. Look!" Freel Goddard cried.

Just as Ard's skull seemed to crack against the earth, he whirled over to one side just in time to avoid Luster's feet as the Cherokee jumped high to drive the head into the ground. A red gash showed on Luster's pants' leg where the butcher knife had sideswiped him.

As soon as the blood seeped from his leg and into his pants' leg and it was clear he'd been cut, Birdie saw it and screamed shrilly, "Luster! No!" She began to scream frantically for Luster out of fear.

Folks looked at her but she was unfazed. She was no longer afraid to show her affection for Luster Holder. Damn her old sorry pappy!

The brandishing of the butcher knife hadn't gone unnoticed.

"No weapons was to be allowed," Freel said loudly, "Up to now the fight's been fair and square."

"I figger so," the Squire said, "but I sorter admire seein' more action." His voice was edged with grave worry.

"He's done made a mistake drawin' that ere butcher knife, Squire," Freel declared.

The wily old Squire spat and shook his conniving head as he answered Freel, "I hain't so shore."

Luster was circling Ard, who was now holding the butcher knife. The hunchback rocked from one side to the other, lifting his small feet daintily. Then Ard jumped at Luster like a panther does its prey. He sprang forth from a half-crouched position but before he could land, Luster landed a solid blow to his chest while in mid-air forcing Ard to drop the big knife. He fell hard to the ground but like a cat sprang right back up and lunged again and landed square on Luster's chest wrapping his legs around Luster's waist and sinking his yellowed teeth into Luster's neck. As his teeth sank into the thin flesh covering his windpipe and jugular, Luster screamed in pain. He grabbed the hunchback by the hair on the back of his head and pulled hard while managing to wrap his free hand strongly around Ard's throat. As Ard continued to try and rip Luster's throat apart, Luster began to crush Ard's own throat with his strong bare hand. As he crushed, he felt the creature's jaws slacken and a gurgle came from his throat.

Luster then tossed the deformed Greeber into the air and he landed a few feet away. He intended to kick the ever-living life out of Ard but Ard recovered too quickly for him. Still Luster lunged and drove his fist square into Ard's mouth, his bony hard knuckles crashing into his teeth and breaking more than a few. The hunchback savagely shook his head and spit blood and broken teeth into the dust of the street. Luster started toward him and stopped. Ard stopped too but not before retrieving his knife.

For a moment they watched each other while the crowd choked back its breath. Then without any warning, Luster dove headlong at the scrabbling figure. There was a flurry of violent action. First one was visible in a cloud of dust, then the other, as the butcher knife flashed in the sunlight. Folks craned their necks forward to see. And it was at that given time that Buck felt Squire Kiler push back against him. With unbelieving eyes, he saw the old man jerk a .45 Colt from his shirt and begin cautiously raising it. At first, the boy thought he knew the reason, then he wasn't sure at all, for as he leaned over, he saw that the Squire had lowered his gun and was holding his fire. Although the fighters had slowed momentarily in their action and Ard Greeber's back was turned toward them, Buck was still confused about the Squire.

Buck squeezed Dink closer, cringing against the expected death about to occur.

Then all suddenly became quiet. There was no death, not yet. Ard Greeber stared at Luster Holder and his cold stare was returned. The road was deathly quiet as the two men continued to stare at one another. Both were bleeding and both were angry and spent. Although both were still standing, they were tired and their energies drained from them as if they'd been leeched by any old-time doctor of their lifeblood. As they stood there in the middle of Firbank in front of Freel Goddard, Squire Kiler,

Birdie, Buck, and the throngs of Nationites, all had grown still.

Suddenly, just as the street had grown quiet, Ard Greeber came thrashing and charging Luster like a mad bull, his face red and his teeth bared. His butcher knife gleamed in the sunlight. Its blade shone brightly and sharp. He had his head cocked slightly and as he reached Luster in a mad rage to plunge the knife deep inside the Indian, the quiet hillman stepped rapidly aside and hit Ard square in his thick neck. The blow landed solid. Ard let out a muffled groan and staggered wildly. Luster wasted no time. He rushed the deformed hunchback and landed another hard solid blow in his temple. Again, Ard let out a racket, this one more of an animal-like shriek than a groan. He continued in his staggered amble and tried to shake off Luster's blows.

Luster Holder was now in a blind rage and in the mood to kill his assailant. Despite his reputation, Luster was no cold-blooded killer. The man never killed for the sake of killing. He was either protecting himself or his property. But when someone crossed a line with Luster, they'd better be ready to make good on whatever threat they were making to the half-blood Cherokee at the moment. Ard pulling that knife had crossed the line.

Luster faced Ard and he saw quickly that he was in danger of losing his advantage. Ard was grappling for his butcher knife, which he had dropped again after Luster's last harsh blow. Luster moved in and grabbed one of Ard's long, unearthly arms, strong and sinewy, and turned it behind Ard's back twisting it violently in an effort to break it. With all his weight, he shoved Ard facedown onto the ground, sitting on him and forcing the arm until it snapped and he could hear bone cracking. Ard screamed in pain. With the arm freshly broken, Luster landed a huge fist into the back of Ard's bull neck. The blow stunned him. This was not a fair fight but pulling a knife on an unarmed man wasn't a fair fight either.

Just when Ard's body seemed to go limp, he fooled Luster, pushed himself up with his one remaining good arm and sent Luster sprawling into the dust. Still Luster saw an opportunity and took it. He grabbed the hunchback's butcher knife with one strong hand and as Ard attempted to spring on him, he slashed away at the hunchback. The first swipe sliced Ard's chest and a red gash of spurting blood slung on everyone close including on Luster. Ard screamed and fell to one side but still managed to get to his feet as did Luster. The Cherokee swung the knife again and caught Ard's arm and another massive gash appeared, this one bleeding more profusely than the first. Ard was bleeding badly now and he was growing pale. He staggered. Finally, sensing the end of this fight could be near, Luster rushed the staggering Ard Greeber and drove the gleaming butcher knife into his chest, killing him instantly. Ard Greeber would threaten Luster Holder, or anyone else for that matter, no more.

Luster stood and surveyed the damage he'd done. He looked upon the dead body of Ard Greeber and then looked around him. The crowd had moved back just a bit, widening the circle in which Luster was standing. He suspected the other Greeber boys were waiting in the woods to bushwhack him, and maybe they were. He stood there a long moment, studying the dead Ard Greeber and decided in his head that since Ard lived like an animal, he'd dispose of him just like he would a cow, a mule or hog he'd found dead in the pen.

True to his character, Luster did not even notice the silent crowd gawking at the dead creature of a man once known as Ard "Spider" Greeber. Many in the crowd simply stood there, slack-jawed, wide-eyed and some were horrified and others silently impressed, their faith in Luster Holder's coarse abilities reaffirmed by the bloody messy extermination of the eldest Greeber brother.

Slowly Luster picked up the deformed and dead body, shouldered it and walked across to the road to the edge of a deep gully and hurled it into the depths. The body crashed with a thud and a noise like that a man hears when a tree falls deep in the woods. Its heavy bulk crashed into the saw briars, bushes and dirt of the gulley deep below him. Those around him gasped. Even they didn't suspect such a coolness about the disposal of the body. As a rule, they'd just expected the body to be left where it fell. Even Luster had surprised them this time.

Finally Luster Holder, without so much as staring at a soul in the throng of lookers-on, turned back toward Goddard's Store. Bleeding and tired, he reached the porch of the store and leaned down and grabbed the big sack of flour and heaved it onto his shoulder. He balanced it and began his trek back home to his cabin. His path followed along an ancient lane that led into the deepest pine hills of the Nation. As he himself disappeared down the lane, the crowd began to disperse. There was news to knowrate.

Buck was confused and somewhat bewildered at what he'd witnessed but still relieved. After all, Luster was still among the living. Ard hadn't killed him and the Greeber brothers hadn't ganged up on him. He studied the quickly dispersing crowd. On this terrible fight, Birdie had been right and Tiddy gave her half-brother too much credit.

Still, Buck wondered at Squire Kiler's actions. Why had the old man pulled a gun? What were his intentions? Who was he gunning for? Was he gunning for someone at all? He was still thinking these things when he caught a glimpse of the filthy old Squire take out down the lane himself. Suddenly, he was worried about Luster. Something wasn't right. After all, he'd lowered that gun when Ard's back was turned to him, so he couldn't have been gunning for the hunchback. Buck caught Birdie by the arm.

"Birdie," he told her, "I need a favor."

She grinned wickedly, "I didn't think you's gonna ever ask."

He shook his head desperately and exclaimed, "I need you to watch Dink a bit. I got to go…"

"You ast' for him, and you keep him," she began to protest.

His face grew red and his temper too, "Shut up, Birdie, and listen. Luster's in danger, bad danger. He may get bushwhacked. I'm trying to he'p him. Git it?"

Suddenly her face went pale and she only nodded. She took Dink by the hand and the horrible thought occurred to her that her pappy was up to something and that the something would mean of the end of the man she truly loved. She watched Buck take off to the woods like a scared deer while Dink protested loudly his temporary return to Birdie's skirts.

Birdie Kiler was sure of one thing, just as was Buck, that damn black-hearted pappy of hers, Heber Kiler, was up to no good.

8

AFTER HE'D PUT his .45 Colt away quietly, Squire Heber Kiler had slowly receded back into the crowd. He wondered if anyone had seen him pull it, knowing they probably had. Buck Humphries had seen it. The old Squire's mind roamed and raced. He'd made deals with the Devil all his long life, including local devils and outlander devils like the Greebers too. He never went to church proper. He never came inside for the services but stayed under the trees with a few stragglers to chew tobacco, drink corn liquor and argue politics. He was an iron-built old man, a brutal, vulgar type. Some thought him a reliable ally, others saw him as the snake he was, low in the grass, waiting to strike.

The old Squire never missed a good fight, just as he hadn't missed today's fight either. It was rumored around Firbank and the Nation as a whole that his grandfather was a Negro, but no one had ever had the nerve to investigate the story too closely. The Squire was known far and wide as a Negro-hater and had been instrumental in keeping Negroes from buying land in the district.

Squire Kiler was indeed a Godless man. He blasphemed the Holy Ghost and was headed straight for the fires of Hell. His only actual reason for visiting the grounds of the Sobby Nazarene Church was to bring Brother Kester Dipple, who had the charge at Sobby since Brother Lazenby's sudden departure four years before. It brought shame, blood to Buck's cheeks to think of how Brother Dipple, against his will, was brought to Sobby to preach the Gospel. When Brother Lazenby left, a committee was appointed to secure a new minister. Elmer Runnells, Sam Tilford, and Ivey Hendricks scoured all of the western district of Tennessee and even went across the river into southern Missouri and northern Arkansas, but no preachers they saw would have the job. They had heard too much about the Nation country and Brother Lazenby's dismal experiences.

Then Squire Kiler, although he belonged to no church, appeared before the Sobby congregation one Sunday morning and took the rostrum. Everyone was quiet and curious as the crusty, irreverent Squire began to speak.

"If you'uns are still wantin' you somebody to spout Bible," he growled, "'y God, I'm just the man that can git you a first-rate spouter." The congregation simply stared at the old man.

And the very next Sunday, he showed up with a pale, hatchet-faced young man and introduced him as "Brother Kester Dipple, which'll fill this here pulpit with Gospel till hit spills over on the floor."

That was all. While folks sat wondering and supposing and the old Squire sat outside under a hickory tree, the new preacher sobbed out a nervous sermon, then sobbed out a prayer, agate eyes darting and bugging right and left, front and back as if he expected to be bushwhacked at any moment. After the benediction, the Squire came back in, took him by the arm, led him to his car, and drove off. Every Sunday morning and night the Squire showed up with him and, afterwards, took him away. It was a long time until folks knew the truth, Squire Kiler was using another scheme to make money. He let the preacher stay in a cabin behind his house, a virtual prisoner. He furnished him food and forced him to split the collection plate with him, for Sobby had a large congregation and quite a little cash was taken in every Sunday, not to mention the hundred dollars a month salary taken up on subscription.

The story of how the Squire found Brother Dipple was a weird one. He had heard of the summer revival meeting held by an itinerate preacher from Arkansas in a brush arbor over at Lizard Lick in eastern Neeley County. He drove over on closing night and waited until the minister started to leave the church. He waylaid him, forced two big drinks down him, and took him back to Firbank. He laid the plan before the preacher that night. Sick and dizzy from heat and the corn liquor, the minister agreed to take the church at Sobby. According to Freel Goddard, the Squire threatened to chase him down and castrate him if he tried to run away. He smoothed it over by offering to let him sleep for free with Birdie, an offer which Brother Dipple in mortal terror refused. Now the minister waited, hoping and praying that something would happen to gain him his release from the iron Squire.

Everybody in the Nation still remembered how the Squire dealt with old Aunt Bertha Coonce. The poor old woman owed him for a cord of firewood and died before she could pay for it. Being a pauper, the good folks at Sobby Church bought poor Aunt Bertha a tombstone so she'd have something better than a sandstone. The Squire levied on the dead woman's tombstone and took it up from the Sobby Graveyard and sold it for the debt.

The old Squire was a real pervert of a man as well. Aside from whoring out Birdie, his conversations were filled with debauchery. Only this morning, he'd been talking with Freel Goddard about Tiddy Greeber. Despite Birdie's own incest with Luke Tolby, her own blood uncle, the Squire enjoyed speculating about young Tiddy.

Freel had speculated about Tiddy's wildness and the Squire grinned a wicked smile as Freel declared,

"If that 'ere Clell and Tiddy was just down there in the dirt messin' with each other, that'd tell the story on the Greebers."

The Squire's old eyes shone brightly and sinister-like as he replied, "'y God, that Tiddy's gonna make some feller's backbone twitch 'fore many more crops is gathered."

"Well, Squire, I got a broad mind," the storekeeper responded, "even if I am a deacon in the church, but no gal of mine wouldn't tear around in the woods dressed like no boy, even if she ain't yet full-flowered."

"Hain't nothin' wrong with them god-apples of her'n, Freel, but I'm ready to agree, they hain't none of that fambly besides the mammy, Blanche, which is 'ere human."

The pure wickedness and lowdown sorry nature of Heber Kiler was hard for decent folks in the Nation to understand. They'd tolerated him for years, feared him, loathed him and tried to steer clear of him when they could. He went after what he wanted, no matter what he had to do to get it. Whether it be land, whisky, money or some other thing he aimed to have, he stayed after it until he got it. Now, he had his sights set on Blanche Greeber, the most beautiful woman in all the Nation and he'd kill to get her. He didn't aim to have any competition for her affections and he didn't really care if he had her affections as long as he had her. Yes, his was a wicked soul.

Someday, Heber Kiler's sins would find him out.

9

As Luster plodded along the lane toward his cabin, his body was tired. He was a strong man but even the 48-pound bag of flour seemed heavy on his shoulder. Still he was sure it wasn't the weight of the flour that burdened him today. His body was tired from the fight with Ard and his mind was tired from life in the hills with Sudie. She didn't love him no more than he loved her. They were a burden to each other. And the grudges held by folks like Greebers, even for imaginary slights, were a burden.

But that was life in the Nation. It was a complex place. There were good people and bad people. People who swore by Luster and people who simply swore about him. It was a place where gossip spread faster than a woods fire in the driest August. He thought about that damn Squire Kiler and his loose daughter, who the Squire had turned out himself. As low-rated as Luster knew some folks thought he was, he couldn't hold a light to that damn old devil of a man.

He'd seen Birdie in the crowd a bit ago in Firbank. He was sure she was wearing her razor around her neck. And she was quick with it. Talk still circulated how Birdie had killed Luke Tolby and Bode Holley four years ago. His ears still rang from a conversation he overheard at Firbank a little while back in front of the store. Two old Nationite women were gossiping about Birdie and her skill at wielding a straight-razor. The conversation, as he recollected it, went something like this:

> "I know she carries that razor around on a strang around her vile young neck and's ready to use it at a moment's notice."
>
> "Like she done on Luke and Bode, Doney?"
>
> "Piecola, I never believed that, mean as Birdie is. Wurner Crouse musta dreamed he seen her slipping out to her own uncle's and it musta been somebody else he seen in the bottoms that morning."
>
> "You may be right, only that idiot's mind is like 'ere camera you ever taken yore picture with. Hit don't make no mistake. But, to look at hit another way, no murder was ever soundly hung on no Nationite unless he done hit outen' the open."

"That's the cold-curdled truth, Piecola, even
if yore sayin' hit. In the Nation, some folks are
killed and others just found dead. But Birdie
hain't out here for no good."

"The prideless hussy! Tho' does she have
the nerve to pollute Christian folks with her
bed-rode presence?"

"Yeh, they's senseless men who'd tussle to
the death over her bedspring-warped carkiss!"

"How she kept her shape is more'n my motley brain can figger. She's still as young and
purty and fresh-bubbling as she was four year
ago, and her just coining money for herself
and that sorry old pappy of her'n in the un-
Christian way the Good Lord God won't let
them keep hit."

He could only imagine the kind of talk these old
tongue-waggers speculated in about him and Birdie
and him and everybody else. Luster was thankful that
he never really concerned himself with such talk.

He continued his walk. He didn't care to get home
to Sudie any faster than he had to but still he was
tired. He decided to take a shortcut across the old
Hearst farm. That old farm was overgrown and had
more unworkable land than tillable ground. No one
had much used it in thirty years. When the old man,
Lucius Hearst, died, his widow lived on a few more
years. When she died and took her place up on the hill
in their family graveyard under the cedars, hickories,

and black oaks, their daughter moved away. She was a gal with ambition and she got out. She moved to Memphis, which seemed a world away from these folks. And she hardly ever returned. She married a well-off man and didn't need the cropland rent or the timber. So the old place just sat still, growing up, kindly deserted and forlorn. The old house was still standing but not by much. The old cotton ground had gullied badly and there were deep gullies and washes that no amount of dirt could fill.

As he took out across the Hearst place, he neared the old cotton ground that had been washing for decades. He stopped momentarily to shift the weight of the flour sack weighing heavily on his tired shoulder. Just as he started back to walking, he heard a noise, not much of one, but still a noise. He stopped. Just as he stopped came the sound of a footstep in the woods to his right. It suddenly stopped just as he stopped. He looked to his right and started to step forward again, when he knew danger was lurking. He tried to make some noise to draw out the peril from the woods surrounding him and it worked. Again, he stopped in his now noisy tracks, but his pursuer didn't think to stop.

Luster threw the sack of flour onto the ground in front of him like it was a sack of hog feed. He turned abruptly just as the sack of flour crashed to the ground, wary and watching. He stood still a moment and then heard a soft call from beyond his line of sight.

"Luster, hit's me, Buck Humphries…are you okay?"

Luster shook his wary head. "Why on God's green earth is that 'ere Buck Humphries following me?" he thought to himself.

Finally, he spoke, "Yeh, what you doing out here, Buck?"

Suddenly Buck appeared out of the woods onto the lane and ran up to Luster pale-faced, short of breath and panic-like inquired of Luster, "Are you okay? I got worried and thought I'd better follow you in case you needed help…"

Luster shook his head, "I'm alright, Buck. What you doin' out here?"

"I wanted to warn you, Luster, 'cause they's laying for you," the boy explained.

"Well," Luster Holder informed him, "I'm much obliged but I'm onto their bushwhackin' ways. I won't let 'em catch me."

Buck looked at his only friend bewildered and explained, "I just don't want you caught unawares, Luster."

The big Cherokee smiled at him, and that almost made Buck nervous for Luster Holder hardly ever smiled, and let him know plainly, "I don't neither."

Luster looked at him flatly and said even flatter, "Ole Tank's boys may git me yet, Buck. But I don't aim for 'em to. And ain't no other damn son of a bitch gonna git me neither."

Buck tried to shake off his confusion and make sense of it all. He confessed, "I saw the old man, that Squire, make a move during the fight at the store, but I wud'nt sure what was going on then. He pulled his old .45 Colt and then stuck it back in his shirt"

"Hit's okay, Buck. Don't fret about hit," he stated, "I know what I got to do now if they's ever to be any peace. But I'll wait for hit to come to me first. Anyways, I got to git back home. Thangs may work out for ever'body now, Buck. Now, git goin.'"

Folks might be surprised at how much thinking actually went on in the quiet, mysterious mind of Luster Holder. As he walked his mind drifted to some of those folks. He was thankful for young Buck Humphries. As for Birdie Kiler, she'd been sizzling for Luster for a long time but he didn't give a tinker's damn for her and never would. His mind was on another woman and it wasn't Sudie Lazenby. He'd not killed Tank Greeber and despite Tank's hatred for him, he never personally took Tank serious-like. He didn't even understand why Tank seemed so durn intent on running him out of business and out of the Nation, except for pure greed. And that greed put Tank Greeber in cahoots with men like Heber Kiler and may have put him in his own damn sour mash.

As he shifted the bag of flour on his shoulder and continued his walk toward home, he decided one thing was for sure. He wouldn't be missing the setting up for old Ard. He'd sure be paying his respects. No sir, he wouldn't miss that for the world or a hundred romps in the barn loft with a hundred Birdie Kilers!

With Luster, once something was done, it was over. Luster put it away, out of his mind. It would be so with Ard Greeber's death too. It was all past history now and should be buried with Ard up there under the cedars at Sobby, once they pulled him out of that deep gully. But folks of the Nation wouldn't any more let the memory of it die than they'd let the trouble of four years ago fade away and lie in peace. For years and years their tongues would stir it like they were sticks and hoping with each stir that they'd dredge up another mess that had otherwise been settled deep down inside the stewpot that was the Nation.

He walked and he thought it over. He played it back in his mind, events that had just now occurred almost as if they had occurred years before. After he'd pitched Ard headfirst into the gully, and Buck Humphries had run up to him, pale as a sheet just lifted from the boiling kettle, he'd warned him to watch Squire Kiler and it was then Luster learned that Buck had seen the Squire make some move against him or had overheard some threat from his grizzly lips, although the Old Squire was very careful to keep his designs to himself. Birdie had warned him too, that night at the schoolhouse.

He took the flour and had barely reached his cabin when he sensed that something else was wrong. Parker and Hobart met him, prancing and yelping in distress. Old Pattie Pide, waiting by the lot gate to be milked, was lowing mournfully. He rushed to the barn. Dimity, the heifer which had been born the night of Dossie Bell's death, had birthed a bull calf with no one to granny her. She'd done it rather neatly and was contented licking its damp hide as she raised her velvety eyes to her master as if to say proudly, "Look what I brung you." He had been wanting a good bull for some time. This one was full of fine blood, for it had been pappied by Lem Runnel's registered Jersey. He decided to call it "Firebrand."

He walked immediately afterwards to the cabin and searched it and didn't see a sign of Sudie. No preparation had been made for supper. It was the second time in his life that a woman had let him down. Poor Dossie Bell had failed him because she was dead. He was puzzling over Sudie when Wurner waddled up and finally made him understand that he'd hid in the bushes shortly after noon and seen her drive off with Brother Lazenby. The idiot had been to see her a short time before and, in his animal alertness, had figured that something was wrong with her, that something big was about to happen.

Wurner told Luster how he came to see it all. He had waddled up to Luster and explained, "Miss Sudie give me fried pies. She seem in a hurry to git me gone…God, He tole me 'you wait here in bushes. Watch.' He come then, my eyes seen him. She went and pulled big box in hand. Then now was car and sputter-sputter and dust in nose. I seen them up there. They was gone fastly."

So that was it. Sudie had decided to go back to her weak-kneed preacher. What Luster didn't know at the moment was that others had seen the spectacle play out. In the Nation, there were eyes always on the wrong things. He could just hear the tongues a-waggin' in and around Firbank and the countryside now. And it was.

When the news sank in, he took a double drink from the jug behind the cookstove and sat down. As the liquor took hold, a feeling of infinite relief came over him. He was shed of her at last.

Luster stood and worked another bottle out of the back pocket of his pants. This drink brought the relief back to him. He hadn't eaten since morning and hoped that there would be plenty to eat up at the Greeber house, once Ard was laid out.

Nothing was in his way now. Surely she must have been expecting him for a long time, even if she was most afraid of what Ard would do. Ard couldn't well do anything now. After four long years it would be good to have someone who looked and acted like a woman to come with him to his cabin. They had never said a word to each other, but he had read it in her eyes over four weeks ago now. He could read a woman's eyes just like he could a dog's. Her sky-blue ones had told him she was ready.

He got up from his chair, went outside and started toward the lane to the old house on the hill.

10

U RFIE PEARL BUCKNER and Clemmie Bean sat on
the road bank of the school grounds waiting for
the crowd to thin out. Dust swirled around, as cars,
trucks, wagons and horseman jumped every mud-
clogged road leading from Firbank. The sun was a
crimson disk just above the hazy western hills.

"I hope to roast out my miseries with the devil, if
it wasn't the durndest fracas which ever taken place
before human eye," Urfie Pearl said. "It's sich a pity
Granny Blackburn missed out on it. She sure…"

At a hoarse cackle behind her, she whirled quickly
to look up into the withered face of the older woman,
who stood just behind her leaned over on a knotty
hickory stick.

"I never missed a smidgen of it, Urf," Granny
Blackburn said with grim satisfaction. "I got tard

waitin' out at your place and come humpin' it for the store. I couldn't set thar held betwixt a sweat and a stroke tryin' to figger out who'd end up breathless. Hit was a sight to nurse in the heart for the rest of my endurin' days."

The thin old Murdie Blackburn's black cotton dress hung shapelessly from her stooped shoulders. Her bone-thin nose hooked sharply toward a hairy, upturned chin and her palsied head vibrated in ceaseless and rhythmic negation. She stretched her turtlish neck and spat a stream of amber on the road below. It splattered on the hard-packed clay ground. The flaps of her black poke bonnet jiggered up and down as she worked her toothless gums together and her breath wheezed audibly.

"It was now, Granny," Urfie Pearl said. "It's something a body can describe to their grandchildren fifty years hence. Him finishin' Ard off with the varmint's own knife and throwin' the body in the gully like it was a cow dead of bloat, then walkin' off like nothing had took place, sure beats nothin' that ever happened in God's own wicked world."

Clemmie nodded, "Yeah, just like he was leavin' church, if he ever went. This here's sure a blow them Greebers'll never take without no comeback." Clemmie looked at her companions and shook her head. She kept fiddling with a snuffbox in the lap of her black woolen skirt, reaching up occasionally to pull at the top of her gray bonnet.

Granny sat down beside them. "Where do you keep yourself at durin' wakin' hours, Clemmie? Hit's well knowed around Firbank that the brothers was mortal afeerd of Ard and wished strong to see him graved…whether hit was by Luster Holder or somebody else. They say he was cock of the walk at his house and ordered them big men around like they was snot-nosed tappers just outta clouts. They say he's whompered hell outta them many a time and even had his own pappy buffaloed so he was keerful how he crossed him. And more…him being the oldest, they knowed he'd settle his pappy's estate and willed hisself all the land and money on hand. You never seen a one of 'em out here to he'p him, did you?"

"I hear tell Ard ordered them to stay away," Urfie Pearl said.

"They would'a did it anyways," Granny countered.

"Still and all," Clemmie said, "with their pappy just fresh murdered too, they'll be out for real revengence now or they'll be a laughing stock and have to leave the Nation."

"You're spouting truth now, Clemmie," Urfie Pearl said. "They cain't afford not to at least try to git Luster." She pulled out her under lip and driveled a fresh dip of Rooster Snuff between it and her gums.

"Who's denyin' it?" Granny snapped angrily. She swabbed snuff into her gums and tapped her stick against the ground in rapid taps. "Elmer Runnels says he'll haul us back home in his wagon soon as they git Ard's body drawed up outta that durned gully."

She turned toward the spot where over twenty-five men lined the gully edge. Cautiously holding to bushes, several were sliding down the sharp forty-foot drop-off with ropes to tie around the remains of Ard Greeber, preparatory to pulling him out. Squire Kiler, tall and gray, was shouting orders. A team of gray mules, tended by a Negro, was backed up to the depression.

Clemmie tucked wisps of cottony white hair under her gray bonnet. "Ain't you goin' to the settin' up, Granny?" she asked anxiously.

"Now that ere's a damn fool question. I hain't a-goin to skip it." She rubbed her dark-spotted hands together. "I shore want-a he'p lay out that critter and see just how the Good Lord God ever concocked sich a human mess. They say he weighed fifteen pound at birth and hit nigh killed his mammy when the doctor and four women grabbled him out. I 'low we'uns just better have Elmer drop us off at Greebers and save time. They'll be plenty of vittles, I know, 'cause I heerd some'un a-saying that folks has been trompin' over that way with them ever since the news of old Ard's death was knowrated."

"You know, when old Tank died, them darkies took his body up to Jackson," Clemmie said, "That was when the Meedon levee was in an awful bad shape."

"I 'low I r'member that," Granny said, ""cause they had theirselves a passel of trouble gittin' thar and back. Anyways if they had trouble, hit's no matter for 'em...haulin' the old bastard over thar to git him preserved modern."

"Hit's a sin and a shame, Granny, and a personal insult to all of us...cheatin' us outta a doin' what's been our bound duty in the Nation for over sixty years now."

Granny cackled, "I figger the worms'll git to him jest as soon, Urf, as if he'd been laid up in camphor."

"As for me," Clemmie said, "I want to be put to rest like the Good Lord God intended and not have no man fiddlin' with my carkiss and drainin' all Nature's blood outen it. But I'm ready to help all a body can."

Clemmie leaned closer to her two companions, "Did you'uns hear Birdie Kiler scream to Luster? She's sure come out in the open over him, and him already with a married excuse of a woman on his hands!"

"They's no doubt she's gonna make a strong play for him if she overtakes him in the woods," Granny said. "Ard being dead, she hain't afeerd to traipse anywhere now, and maybe she's got to believin' them rumors about Sudie Lazenby not being out thar. As for me, I don't put no stock in it. She's jest ashamed to show herself, and I'm shore she hides when anybody goes around. I've been ha'f a mind to go out thar and see fer myself ever since the stories got to being strong knowrated enduring the last year, but hit's a hard drive and my laigs wouldn't hold out for no walkin' in them God-awful hills. And, too, I've always liked Luster and wouldn't want him to think I was pryin' into his business."

"You wouldn't learn nothin' noways, Granny," Urfie Pearl informed her plainly.

"I figger not. Sudie'd shore run like a guinea hen if she seen me. Anyways, if she'd left Luster, he'd a-already got him up another woman. I don't put no stock a-tall in them stories that he done away with her. His enemies started that, even goin' so far as to tell the High Shuriff. But you ain't saw him snoopin' around out thar," Granny instructed Urfie Pearl with a definite resolve to settle the matter.

"If she's left, they's a mighty lustful lookin' woman open for Luster now," Urfie Pearl speculated.

Clemmie broke in, "Who could you be meanin', Urf?"

"Why, Blanche Greeber, of course," Urfie Pearl quickly answered.

The women went quiet for a moment, staring out at the scene playing out before them. Then Urfie Pearl spoke up again, "Well, I knowed this…the old Squire shore don't look none too happy over the outcome of this here fight. That bottomland's went vanishing."

"You don't mean you think the Squire wanted him to kill Luster, him a close friend and all?" Clemmie asked in astonishment.

Urfie Pearl drilled the smaller woman with buggy eyes, "I ain't meanin' nothing, Clemmie. How'd you git the idear that Luster's a friend of anybody's? I've soundly saw me enough to know it's gonna take every mite of power Heber Kiler has to save the livin' Birdie's been bringin' in to him. Shorely you seen Buck Humphries up here with that bastard child of his'n and Birdie's. I jest imagine she's give it to Buck so she'll be free to git away from the Squire."

Clemmie looked about her uneasily, "You durn well know Old Henley Humphries won't let him keep that young'un. He…"

Urfie Pearl looked at the Negro working the mules and chided Clemmie, "Hursh, Clemmie! They's fixin' to snake him out."

"Hit's high time," Granny snorted, "I coulda already had him on the coolin' board by now!"

The men on the edge of the gully were moving back now.

"Git up dere! You Nell! You 'Cilla! Hah!" the Negro called to the two sturdy mules. They hunched their backs and started straining forward, but nothing happened. The Negro started laying on his rawhide whip, raising it high and swishing it through the air so hard that it wrapped clear around the mules' bellies and had to be jerked loose.

"Dig in, mules," he yelled to them, "Git on now! Git on! Is you glued to this here earth?"

A barefooted sharecropper, stooped and wizened, slouched over to the Negro and tapped him on the shoulder, "Was I you, Hoss, I'd sorter back up and git a runnin' start. That'll tear him loose from them bushes right short off."

The Negro lowered the whip and set his big brown eyes on the intruder. "You isn't me," he said, turning away and again raising the whip.

The barefooted man spit and edged in closer, "Well, now, nigger, I just figger I've snaked enough logs to know how to..."

The whip cracked in the air and the mules strained forward again as the sharecropper began shouting, "Hup! Hup!" in an effort to stop the Negro.

"Hup Hell!" Squire Kiler roared, coming over from the ditch. He whirled the sharecropper about and drove a big boot into his seat. "Git on and quit holdin' up the team with yore ig'rant advice, you rabbit chasin', tater eatin' son of a bitch!"

There was a sound of crashing bushes and a bumping body.

"Here comes Ard," Clemmie whispered mysteriously. The three old women, arm in arm, stood now, huddled together. They saw a sight, the like of which they'd never witnessed in all their years in the Nation. As the dusty, bloody body of Ard Greeber shot over the edge of the gully, something alive and screaming leaped out of the bushes and flung itself on the breast of the hunched-backed corpse, wrapping its tiny legs as best it could about the barrel-chest and kissing the smeared and blackened face... eyes, nose, mouth...with loud resounding smacks. A dark little body followed it, arms slung around the other, and likewise screaming.

Squire Kiler reached down and peeled off first the Negro boy and then the white, like they were sticking plasters. They fought, scratched, screamed and cursed at him.

"It's his little brother, Pistol, and his nigger play-mate, Tadpole," Urfie Pearl said curiously, "They just mortally worshipped Ard. They say he never come in from Firbank, Melburg or anywhere's excepting he brought them candy and crackers and thing-um-bobs little peckerwoods like them like."

"I wonder where they were during the fight?" Clemmie said.

Urfie Pearl's eyes remained on the spot where the men were now gathered around the battered and slashed remains of Ard Greeber. Freel Goddard, with Pistol under one arm and Tadpole under the other, was walking rapidly toward the store, the boys still kicking, cursing and screaming.

"I ain't got no more idear than a wet dishrag, Clemmie, but I suppose the little fellers stayed hid at the store, them being too small to git through the mob to watch. I hear tell, several children was bad trampled, and Leslie Pandrey's youngest boy got a leg broke in two places."

"Here comes Elmer, " Granny said, "His wagon's about ready to go. I reckon the Squire and Freel'll haul the corpse over. I'm hangin' betwixt a fever and a bowel action to see that varmint without no clothes on, but how the hell we gonna git clothes back on him oncet he's undressed is more'n my motley soul can now tell. He hain't got no more God-borned shape than a two-headed calf."

"Let's go git in the wagon, Granny," Urfie Pearl said as she moved forward to meet Elmer Runnels, "This here's gonna be a night to remember. Are you ready, Elmer?"

Runnels spoke jerkily, "Yeah, I'm past ready. Freel just told me them Greebers are on their way out here after the remains. I ain't hankerin' to be 'round when they show up."

Granny Blackburn set her dull eyes on the west. The sun was sinking behind a thick purple bank. "They's another storm a-brewin'" she said, "I look for a God-awful whirly-gust back yonder."

11

THE CUSTOM OF SITTING UP with the dead had a long and rich history in the Nation. There were folks who looked forward to a good "setting up." They got plumb disappointed when they missed one or the family decided to be so private that they buried their dead soon as they'd breathed their last. The old women of the Nation, like Granny Blackburn, Urfie Pearl Buckner, and Clemmie Bean, among so many others, were experts at the art of sitting up and knew the customs and manners of the art. Sometimes folks came who'd you be surprised to see there. There were folks who you wondered why in the name of the Good Lord they had bothered to show up but they did.

The folks would come out of the woods, away from their stills, away from their crops, their chores and gossip, just to gawk and gander at the spectacle in front of them and gather new gossip. A funeral was a social event, a spectacle, a reason to break from the burden of toil and an everyday world that was harsh. It was also like a settling up of accounts...accounts of this life...accounts full of grudges, moral debts, feuds and other human tragedies. Folks came out to put away Dossie Bell Holder, some out of curiosity, some out of mourning and some for the entertainment of it. They'd come out to see Tank Greeber put away too. Now they'd come out to put Ard Greeber away and, no doubt, they'd come out in big numbers.

Unlike Dossie Bell or anybody else the ladies of the Nation had ever laid out, Ard Greeber would be a different sort to lay out. His body didn't lend itself to an easy laying out. When they pushed his chest and upper body down, his feet and legs kicked up.

As they stood on the porch of the Greeber house, Squire Kiler commented on the chore to another gentleman, "Push his feet and laigs down, hit was the head then. That damb hump made him jest like a rockin' cheer. I thought oncet of askin' why they didn't saw out a hole fer the hump to fit down in... the varmint wouldn't showed no difference...but, instid, I suggested they try him on his side, sorter kitty-cornered in the box. That ere Clell, which wears his hair long as a gal's, looked at me like a bull at a bastard calf and says, 'Hell naw, Ard's gonna be buried so he can look up at his God.' Hit was the first damb time I ever heard hit hinted that they even knowed they is sich a thing as a God."

"I reckon he wouldn't a-rode no easier on his side, Squire," Frodie Ingle said.

"Maybe not, Frodie. Anyways, while two of them held down his head, the others bore down on his feet and laigs, and, the fifth, he tied him down with a plow line at both ends. Forcing him down in thar like that'll practical bust out the sides of the coffin and I figgerhit'll be all whomper-jawed before burying time. I offered to he'p, but that ere Clell waved me back. He jest solid wouldn't let no soul tech him. Hit's a prime wonder he'd let Granny, Urfie Pearl, and Clemmie lay him out, but you jest cain't natural stop them three. And, 'y doggies, they's the best hands with corpses ever borned on this here Earth."

"You churned out a mouthful of truth then, Squire. Have you saw his mammy?" Frodie asked.

The Squire didn't answer right away. There was the sound of his chair scraping the wall. Then he leaned over and spit. "Gimme that ere jar of drinkin' liquor again, Freel. I'm wantin' to warsh out the taste of that stale cud." The jar made a dull flash as it was raised and lowered.

"That ere's fine. Hain't nobody makes whisky like Luster Holder," the Squire declared.

"Have you saw Ard's mammy, Squire?"

"No, goddammit, I hain't, Frodie. And she hain't his mammy noways. You…you don't think a purty woman like her could of birthed a homely creature like him. Anyways, she hain't much more'n no thirty year ole, and I figger her grief won't be no hard one to throttle. As for me I wouldn't think no more of havin' him dead than I would a garden mole," the crooked old Squire declared.

"About that 'ere Blanche," Frodie persisted, "How'd you like to have a settin' of her eggs, Squire?"

"'y God," the Squire growled, "I durned well got what hit takes to hatch 'em."

Varney Lemons cleared his throat long and hard, "Uh-uh, Squire," he said, low, cautious, "layin' all jokes aside, but that 'ere Blanche sho' would make some man a good woman."

"You jest hain't spreadin' no bull manure now, Varney. She sho' as hell would. But I'm thinkin' you'd better not," Frodie broke in.

The Squire gnawed and chewed at his lips a minute. He scratched his head and cast a scornful but inquiring look around him. He watched the people standing around and rubbed his foul old mouth with his hand.

"Well," the Squire finally spoke up, "ole Blanche is sho' one fine lookin' gal…but they's drawbacks even to a purty woman. Now you take them boys of Tank's. Who in the Devil's name would wanna take them on as fambly? I sho' wouldn't. That damn Birdie of mine is bad enough."

Some folks cackled. Others looked away. Folks had plenty of mixed emotions about Heber Kiler. Some feared him, some liked him, some detested him and others just plain didn't give a damn for the son of a bitch. Some of the old tongue-waggers in the Nation wondered at times aloud at how the settin' up for Squire Kiler would go when the time came.

The conversation turned back to Tank Greeber, whose sour mash drowning made a widow woman out of Blanche Greeber.

Freel Goddard spoke up, "Well, Blanche and all of them Greebers is well shut of Tank anyways, no matter, and probably glad."

"Yeah, I 'low they are, but I shore wouldn't be in Luster's place," Varney declared.

Freel Goddard spat before predicting, "Me and you both, Freel. Luster's time is sho' about to run out."

"Squire, reckon he'll be over here for the settin' up?" Frodie asked curiously.

The old Squire hawked his throat and spat out, "He's sho'ly got more damb sense than that, hoss! Hell far, he killed the hunchback dead!"

"I disremember him ever missin' a settin' up, Squire. He shore believes in helpin' out in time of trouble. Hit may be, though, he wouldn't leave his woman a way off out there by herself," Frodie contemplated as he rubbed his grizzled chin.

Squire Kiler laughed, squinted his eyes and informed Frodie, "Hell, hoss, he hain't affeered to come, if that's what yo're hintin' at. But even at that, they hain't nobody gonna stick their head in a wild-cat's den when they don't haft to, especial when he's all tard out anyways. As for leavin' Sudie, he don't pay her half as much mind as he does Dossie Bell's cow, Old Pattie Pide."

A rock crashed against the side of the house, followed by a prolonged yowl, causing the assembled men to jerk their heads in the direction of the racket.

The high voice came clear, fierce, "I bus' yo doddam brains out, you meowin' ole sonna bitch!"

"You's hit him, Pist!"

Pistol and Tadpole were watching out to keep the cats off the corpse of the man who had been their best friend.

"'At orghta hole 'm for a while, Taddy. It's beginnin' to mizzle rain. Le's me'n you go to bed. Tid's still out som'ers."

12

———→✤←———

TIDDY WAITED in the purple shadows of the barn hallway. Across the horse lot she could see the lights at the house, hear the high voices of men and women and the screams of children. She was glad to be away from all of it, although she wished Pistol and Tadpole were with her. The presence of death had made her afraid for the first time in her life. The little fellows said they wished to stay near and keep anything from bothering Ard.

The Ard she knew was gone, and she wanted the night to be over so they could put the shell of him under the ground and let life go on like it had before that awful Indian so brutally murdered him. But more death must come, for now her brothers would never breathe another free breath until Luster Holder was stretched out cold before them.

Poor Mammy was going to have an awful time now that her great protector was gone. It was just simply terrible that she'd been robbed all of her life from knowing a real man to love and care for her. God Almighty just hadn't been much kind to her about men. That seemed the way of this awful, dreary life sometimes.

She, Clell, Pistol, and Tadpole were going to miss Ard awfully much too and were just bound to suffer. Clell just hadn't been acting like himself for the past month. He was frightfully torn up and it would take a long time to get back together. She worried about the future for the first time ever really.

If only she could see Buck...she did hope he would come. She couldn't understand at all why he continued to give her the run-around. No other boy ever had. Even when she went to the store or to church now, the eyes of men and boys seemed to bore vulgarly underneath her clothes and make her feel cold and naked. Since Clell romped on that sharecropper boy at the store, no one else had dared to do more than stare. But just knowing what they were thinking and what they wanted filled her with shame. It made her want Buck more too. And it made her wish she'd been born a boy. Then she and Buck could have had a time without boy-and-girl thoughts to disturb them. All she wished was to be his sweetheart and tear around with him doing the things he did just as she would with Pistol, Tadpole, and Dink. She'd like to go fishing and swimming with him and spend the night. Yes, if he'd let her she'd like to bathe and dress him and rub him to sleep just like she did with the little fellows.

A pure boy like Buck just couldn't care for a slut like Birdie Kiler. She would purely ruin him and he wouldn't be clean anymore. She had taken advantage of him once when he was a little shaver that didn't have any idea what was happening. It had taken four years for him to grow clean again. Birdie just wasn't satisfied unless she was doing evil with a man. She would even take Pistol and Tadpole if they were only old enough, because according to what a girl at school told her, she had tried to get Clell to come to her. Why, she shuddered, she would even take Dink himself, because she'd heard the story about how Birdie used to go to bed with her own uncle, Luke Tolby.

She was sure Dink belonged to Buck, a product of the time of his one fall. That's why she loved the little mess so much. When she slept with him cuddled in her arms, she always imagined it was Buck, and it made her feel good all over. Since Buck was Dink's pappy, she wondered if he wet the bed too. A body could stand anything when her heart was soft and full of the one she loved.

She jerked up her head and listened. Someone was crossing the horse lot. She drew further back against the crib door and peered out into the greenish-yellow moonlight.

There were two of them...a boy and a girl. They came straight toward her, and she pressed hard against the rough-hewn log wall. They passed so close she could have touched them, and she could smell the sour odor of sweat mixed with a musty perfume.

She caught their wary whispers.

"Let's go up in the loft," the boy said hoarsely.

"I'm afraid, Rink!"

"We cain't do nothin' here. Come on, Perline."

The girl climbed the ladder first, he right behind her.

Tiddy's breath tickled her throat. She knew them now: Rink Bailey, a tall gangling boy from over near Sweetlips, and Perline Medlock from Finger. She'd seen them often at the County Singing Convention in Melburg. Rink must have brought Perline to the sitting up for the free food.

All at once she was afraid too. But she couldn't move, straining her ears to listen. She thought of going to the top of the ladder, only it'd be too dark to see good. Her face burned.

She heard the dry rustle of straw, and particles of dust and trash began settling around her and choking her lungs. The noise above her seemed to deafen her now. She'd never had such a curious feeling in her whole life. She wished to run. Her legs were drained of all blood and strength and tingled numbly.

"O God!" the girl moaned.

Tiddy wondered if she should tear loose for the door of the barn and get help. She found her legs and reached the open door. The hoarse voice from above stopped her momentarily.

"Do you want me to stop, honey?"

"Oh, oh no, Sweet Jesus!"

Tiddy heard a low cry. It came from her own throat. She broke frantically for the house and ran headlong into someone who was cutting across the lot on the way there too.

She leapt back, screaming, as she beat at the dark form with both fists. Her wrists were caught by two hard hands and a voice cried in her face, "Tiddy! Tiddy! What's come into you?"

She dropped her arms and looked up at him unbelievingly before she sprang toward him and clasped her arms around his neck, holding to him fiercely, her whole body shaking with sobs.

"Buck, Buck, Buck, my Buck," she moaned over and over.

His arms girded her waist and pressed her so hard against him she could scarcely breathe. Her ribs were about to pop. She pulled down his head and kissed his eyes, nose, cheeks, mouth, feeling the trail of saliva which she left there.

She could barely see him now, for a black blanket of clouds had wiped out the moon. Thunder grumbled in the west and heat lightning flashed like car lights clicked on and off.

"Who scared you, Tiddy?" Buck said huskily. He was trembling as bad as she now.

"Oh, Buck," she bawled like a little child, "I...I can't never tell you!"

"It'll be all right because nobody'll ever know it from me."

"I...I can't say it out loud, Buck," she wailed. "Stoop down and I'll...I'll whisper it in your ear quiet-like. That won't really be saying it."

The words seemed to bubble and pour into his ear and hurt him like it was poison coming out of her mouth.

He unclasped her arms and held her hands in his own big warm hands. Suddenly she felt awfully safe and no longer afraid.

"Don't you wanna go back to the house?" Buck asked. "It's gonna rain hellaciously in a few minutes."

She pled with Buck, "No, no, Buck. There's death up there. Let's go somewhere else. Please."

Buck looked at her a long moment, stared past her toward the house filled with death and took her by the hand. He made no move and finally, being impatient, Tiddy began to run, tugging at Buck's hand and pulling him behind her in the dark wet night, the rain now falling heavy upon them. The two followed a split rail fence and ran together down the lane until they reached a small shed in which cotton seed was stored. Tiddy opened the door and jumped in with Buck close behind her. The interior of the shed was half full of seed.

She lay flat on her stomach and Buck plopped down beside her. The oily smell of the soft seed mixed with the steamy smell of their wet clothes. On the east was a wide opening, through which seed were shoveled from the wagons. The cover was propped back with poles, and the water ran off it in gushing spouts as it beat against the tin roof with a clanging, deafening roar.

It was so good to have him with her like this and she hoped they could stay a long time. With all the excitement and confusion at the house, she'd never be missed. There was no one who'd come searching for her now that Ard was dead. Her grown brothers had other things on their minds, and Clell was too sick at heart to think of anything else.

At a sudden idea, she threw one arm around Buck's slender back and leaned her face toward his cheek.

"Is your pappy out here, Buck?" she timidly inquired.

Buck shook his head and answered, "Yeah, he started early a-muleback."

Suddenly she lowered her eyes and asked, "How long you suppose he'll stay?"

"He'll stay as long as he's needed. Since he's got old and feeble he admires to be around the dead. Says he don't feel so lonesome in their presence," Buck explained to the shaken girl.

"Let's stay here all night, Buck," she pled earnestly.

He felt a shiver run over his wet body, "You can't mean what you're sayin', Tiddy."

She just had to know whether he cared for her. "It ain't what you're thinking, Buck. It ain't what they was…oh, Buck, I'm just sick and alone far down in me. A great big hurt keeps gathering inside my heart and makes it beat with misery. My stomach's weak and upset."

He looked at her seriously and instructed her, "I orght to take you to the house, Tiddy. You orght to pull off yore wet clothes and get into something dry. You may take a bad cold and come down with pneumony."

She smiled at Buck's concern and exclaimed, "I feel warm and cozy, Buck! You can't take me up there…I'd just simply die!"

He turned half toward her and rested his hand lightly on the small of her back, and she snuggled closer and closer to him, puppishly, holding his cheeks between her moist hands. She tasted the gathering saliva in her mouth.

"You know what, Buck," she said carefully, "I'll go out to your house and stay there with you tonight, if you'd not mind too much."

"Pappy wouldn't stand for it, Tiddy. He lives soundly by the Good Book. And he won't abide by us lying in a bed out-of-wedlock," Buck warned her.

She pouted and seemed almost childish for a moment. Buck knew her thoughts.

"Listen, Tiddy," he said very seriously, "we got to go up there, It just ain't right for no boy and girl to be lying here in this shed without no grown-ups near. If your brothers found us, they'd kill me and beat you bad. You go on to the house, and I'll follow you up there shortly. You're wet anyways and the rain can't soak you no worse'n it's already done."

"My brothers ain't studying me now, Buck. All they're thinkin' of is gitting even with Luster Holder," the girl confessed.

"Is Luster up there?" Buck whispered, concerned about his only true friend.

She laughed, "Buck! You shorely ain't crazy enough to think he'd show hisself at our house now? He'd be dead before he got inside the door."

Buck shook his worried head and scratched the side of his face, "You don't know Luster Holder, Tiddy..."

"That ain't nothin' to us anyhow, Buck. Please stay," she stopped him.

"It just ain't right, Tiddy," he said, complaining to her as always like she was a little girl and he was a settled man. "It ain't treating Ard with the respect that's due him."

She took on a serious look and declared, "Ard ain't with us anymore now, Buck, and what I do now cain't disturb his eternal rest. If he'd known you, he'd a-liked you and you'd a-liked him. He had an awful good heart and mind, even if his body was all stoved up."

Buck was silent and she wiggled closer to him. She turned him toward her and wrapped her arms hard about his waist. She brushed her lips against his nose, then found his mouth. A sweet tingling went through her and made her feel so good she wanted to cry when he swept her in close and drew on her mouth ever so gently.

Her lips sort of stuck to his, pulling them with her, as she moved her head back, squirming as far as she could into his soggy clothes. She liked that a lot. She kind of longed to bite his cheek, only not to hurt any at all. She did it gently. His laugh was high, unnatural. He spanked her bottom lightly.

Buck smiled but nodded his head. He looked toward the door of the shed, almost nervously, and told Tiddy, "We'd better get gone, Tiddy. Someone might find us in here. We don't need no trouble."

Her face reddened and she blurted out, "Oh, hell, Buck, what's hit matter? Some of the old gossips have been spreading tales that we been together. I really come down here to warn you that Clell's awful jealous of me. He's always sorter acted like he owned me and….and if he wasn't my brother, I'd sometimes think he was in love with me hisself."

The hair on Buck's neck seemed to rise, "Has he said anything about us?"

Tiddy's face flushed a deep red. "Aw, Buck, he'd hate any boy he thought I loved, but he ain't gonna find out I've ever been with you again. We can sweetheart right here or somewhere on your land and when I know he's nowhere about."

Buck's words trembled from his lips, "I can't afford to git in no more trouble, Tiddy. I was lucky to come out alive the last time." He cleared his throat and hardened his words. "I don't want you to come around me no more. Do you understand me?"

She paled beneath her tan, "You cain't chase me off like this, Buck!"

"Do you want me to be killed?" Buck asked her frustratedly.

She began crying, "Buck, I don't want nothing but to love you. When you kissed me the other day, you just naturally drained out my soul and made you and me belong to each other forever. After that, I knowed I'd follow you the rest of my life, no matter if I get laid low in my cold and lonely grave."

Her tears continued to flow and she kept on, "If… if Clell tries to harm you, I'll git me a gun and shoot him even if he is my favorite brother! Do…do you really mean you don't want to never see me a'gin?"

"I mean…" His voice broke, "Please go on home, Tiddy."

She pushed at one of his legs with her foot.

"I tell you what, Buck," she said, as an old idea came back fresh and new. "I am gitting kinda chilly with the wet duds, Buck. Let's pull off neekid and I'll let you rub my back and then I'll rub yours, just like I often times do with Pistol, Tadpole, and Dink. It's the most fun ever!"

Indeed Tiddy was chilled. They were the most heavenly chills on Earth and they spread out over her as Buck began to stroke her like she was a lost little kitten. She put her mouth to his ear and blew into it. He jerked upward, and when he goosed her lightly in the ribs, she jumped, giggling and shoved him away from her. As he half turned, she shoved him on over on his back and sprang over on him, sitting up astride his lean belly before she leaned over and rubbed her nose hard against his own.

As she started to rise back up, he pulled her down to him and held her motionless while she wiggled to free herself. His mouth was new, strange, unlike any kiss she'd ever known. It was like he was trying to draw all of her mouth into his and maybe just turn her wrong side out and draw all of her deep inside him until only her feet stuck out. The whistling of his nose was like he was smothering and fighting to get air to his perishing lungs. His heart jumped so fast it seemed to be trying to drown out the fast pitty-pat of her own breast. Then his hands, so big and hard and yet so easy, clasped her a way down low and pulled her higher until her small firm breasts were mashed out against his chest right under his chin.

All of a sudden it just seemed that something unknown and threatening had entered the shed and was hovering over them. A stream of instantaneous fear shot through her brain and flashed to her whole body.

She unclasped her arms and gave a mighty push-up against his chest with her open hands and jumped from him, rolling over and over in the cotton seed before she came to her feet near the door, dizzying and teetering from the roll.

The fear was still in her when she heard him cry in a choke, "Jesus-Lord, forgive me, Tiddy, for what I was a mind to do!"

She sucked her breath noisily in and out, and it was chilled by the cooling air. She tried to say words, and something in her parched mouth stuffed them right back down her gullet. She stood for a moment, shivering and undecided. Then she snatched up her clothes and leaped from the shed.

She bounded through the sheet of rain, and it met her and raced on by, more and more of it aiming to take its place. She stopped at the horse lot gate and pulled on her dripping shirt and pants. She held very still and listened. From the front porch she could hear the endless talk, still loud like you'd expect to hear on the porch at Goddard's Store. The conversation from the death room was more muffled, and that seemed odd. A body could scream and Ard wouldn't hear it. Through the kitchen window she could see light, but not the loaded table. She knew if she tried to eat a bite, her stomach would throw it solidly back in her face.

She opened the lot gate and entered the house by the open side window of her own room. She stripped and crept slowly toward a far corner. She ran her hand along the bed until she touched soft warm flesh. She jerked back and waited, shaking uncontrollably, before she sat on the side of the mattress and lay down on the narrow ledge, worming herself to a good body hold before she twisted over and eased Pistol or Tadpole, she couldn't tell which, more toward the center. One arm encircled the small naked boy, and he awoke and started violently upward, jamming a sharp elbow stiffly into her before she said in a hiss, "It's me...Tiddy." Her hand stroked his head and she knew it was Pistol.

He wormed close to her and clamped his arms around her neck.

"I thought you'd never git here, Tid," he whimpered, "I dot so doddam tard I hadda leave Ard's torpse. Will he fo'give me, huh, Tid?"

"Sure he'll forgive you, Wiggletail," she sympathetically explained before asking, "Did Tadpole stay with him?"

"Nuhhuh. He over on t'uther side!" He took her hand. "Feel."

Her fingers touched the Negro boy's wiry hair. He muttered mellowly in his sleep.

"Why you tremblin' so, Tid?" Pistol said.

"I guess I'm just upset some, Pistol."

"I's affeered but I hain't with you 'round me." He relaxed against her like a soft, warm weight, and she began rubbing his skinny back. He raised his head and smiled.

13

LUSTER HOLDER CLIMBED the last ridge and came out of the woods into a lane, which ran from the fields to the back of the Greeber home. Although the house was shut off from view by a clump of persimmon trees, light from the kitchen seeped dully through the dripping foliage. The rain was holding up. It had turned to a fine mist which burst against the face and blinded the eyes.

From the distance, the sound of folks, many folks, came to his ears. From the forest he could hear the hoarse cough of motors, the chinking of traces, as more cars and wagons arrived. He took a sack of tobacco from his pocket and rolled a cigarette, shielding it from the mist by bending slightly over. He was in no hurry to reach the Greebers. The main part of the sitting up would come later, after the crowd thinned out. Mindless of the wet grass, he sat down on the lane bank to wait.

It had been a hard, hard day and he was awfully tired. His limbs were stiffening and soring from the fight at the store. His throat was slightly swollen where Ard had sunk his teeth, and it was hard to swallow comfortably. He hadn't handled that fight in a proud way. If only it were to do over, he would shoot the creature right between the eyes with his .32-20 or slit his throat fast with his frog-sticker, in spite of Ard's stated notion not to use any weapon. The hunchback must have aimed not to use anything but his teeth, but when he saw he was losing his life, he forgot everything, pulled his knife and Luster didn't hold it against him.

He hated messy killings and this one had sure been one. He liked to end them quick and clean. He hoped he'd never again spend another such time as he had from sunrise to sunset. He thought of how Sudie had looked at him as he prepared to leave the cabin for the store. She'd had the expression of a close relative getting a last view of a loved one before the coffin's lowered into the grave. In her greenish eyes was hope mixed with fear and until he returned in the afternoon, he'd been sure she was praying that the Greebers freed her from him forever. Even now he could see her on her knees begging her Maker for deliverance from bondage to a murderer. Unbeknownst to her, he had seen her, tear-streaked face raised to Heaven, crying for succor from the God she felt she had betrayed.

Nobody on Earth had forced her to live with him. If she'd only known he didn't care near as much about her as he did Pattie Pide and Dimity, maybe she would have gone off long ago. If those cows had been human and could have kept his cabin and his bed, he would have taken them instead of her any old day, for she was the poorest excuse for a female he'd ever seen, even if she did go hog-wild over him in the dark, where she could feel but not see. But it just tired the hell out of a man lying with a woman that felt she was being raped every time he took her. She was just a bag of bones anyway and that didn't make it so pleasurable either.

Brother Lazenby had run out on her after Dossie Bell's funeral, and Luster had felt sorry for her and taken her to his cabin, just like he'd done Dossie Bell before her. She wasn't pretty and she was scared to death, but he figured she might change after he'd mated with her on the kitchen floor the stormy night of the sitting-up. She didn't. She acted like she'd sold her soul to the Devil himself.

Luster couldn't understand it. Although Dossie Bell had been a good, Christian woman, she was faithful to him and never seemed to mind that he never married her. She never acted like she was sinning against her God, for she damn well knew He'd forgive her.

Luster worked a pint bottle from the inside of his khaki hunting coat and took a long drink. He rolled another cigarette and continued to wait on the bank of the lane. The clouds had rolled back and the egg-shaped moon reappeared, casting a vague grayish-yellow light over the countryside.

The thoughts spun wearily in his mind, "Hit jest pesticates the livin' hell outta man having a skairt woman 'round him, and I wished she'd went long ago. When I crawled in bed and pulled her to me, she shaken so I could barely hold her. Then she nigh smothered me and bleated like a dying calf and screamed, 'O Lord Jesus, into your arms, I come!' Hit would askeered the daylights outta somebody like Buck Humphries, because hit jest sounded like she went clean outta her head. I never seen a woman loved hit like she done unless hit's Birdie Kiler. But Birdie…she don't moan and groan after hit's over like the Devil was adraggin' her t'wards the fiery furnace."

The way he saw it, God made her the same way he did so she could be a good, sound mate for some man…that's what he had in mind when He made any woman. He didn't give a holy damn what she did just so she served her earthly purpose and offered up her prayers to Him. It must just gripe his Heavenly Guts to know He slipped up so in letting folks like Sudie and Winnie be born on the land he created for human beings.

He had known for some time that Sudie was trying to get back in touch with her husband. Wurner had seen her slipping out to the mail carrier and reported it to him. He had warned the idiot to keep shut-mouth on it. Wurner worshipped him and let the news go no farther. Although he had no sound idea to whom she was writing, Luster had guessed it easily. He had read it in her watering green eyes, which showed more sparkle after each message. He was positive she was planning an escape and that Brother Lazenby was coming back after her.

From the barn hallway, he had seen her hugging a letter to her shaggy breasts and was sure it brought the happy news. After that, he stayed away from the cabin as much as possible to give the minister every chance to reclaim his long-strayed wife. They were two of a kind and should live out their lives together and not spoil two families. Like Squire Kiler once said, "Winnie Lazenby was nothing but a woman in men's breeches."

It was downright amusing that the preacher had run off, following the confession of his love for the dead Dossie Bell, for if there ever on earth was a man Dossie Bell wouldn't have given her love to, it was Winnie Lazenby. All he meant to her was a go-between for her God. Even Sudie had spent four miserable years milling over whether to give up the joy of the flesh for a return to the man she'd been tied to in holy wedlock.

After his forty-two years of life, Luster figured that all the trouble in the world between folks was not because they didn't understand each other, but because they misunderstood each other the wrong way. Sudie thought he was holding her there at his cabin, when actually he would have been glad to see her get herself as far away as was possible for a body to go. Brother Lazenby thought he would kill him for what he tried to do with Dossie Bell when actually he didn't think anymore about him than he would a dead lizard on a sand hill.

Folks around the Nation thought that Squire Kiler had planned to marry off Birdie to Ard Greeber, and maybe he had at first. But he had certainly changed those plans even before Ard's death. Just what he had in mind now, Luster wasn't sure. The Squire pretended to be Luster's friend and didn't know that Luster had the Squire figured out as a son of a bitch thirty years ago, even since when he, Luster, was just a scutter himself. Funny enough, most Nationites also seemed to think Luster and the Squire were friends too. They didn't know Luster's secret insight either.

Wurner had seen the Squire riding out to Greeber's every day for the past three weeks but Luster didn't understand what was going on any more than had the idiot. The Greebers thought Luster had drowned their old pappy in that now infamous barrel of sour mash to get revenge for their beating up Crip and stealing a load of liquor. In the first place, the old man himself didn't have a thing to do with the hijacking. In the second, it wasn't Tank he was aiming to get. Somebody who wanted him out the way bad had done the killing, and Luster just about had that party figured out. Take Buck...he was Dossie Bell's own bastard son. He surely worshipped the big Cherokee but was scared because he thought Luster didn't have any time for him, when actually he thought more of him than he did any scutter on earth.

And then there was Birdie Kiler. Ard Greeber and the Firbank bone carriers had low-rated it that he had been going to the Kiler home to see her but he never had, although she'd been running after him since she was fourteen years old. He would have taken her long ago if she hadn't been so loud and wide open, for he reasoned that he would have been doing her and her family a favor to cool her off, but he knew too that he'd light a fire he'd have to keep trying to put out, because she would have followed him around like a chick does its mother.

He took another drink. The red whisky was mellow, over a year charred. Over at the Greebers the crowd was growing larger, as more folks slushed up out of the wet night. It was the most pleasure Nationites had had since his woman died, although many a one had come to this very house not a month back to guard over the remains of Tank and to get a good square meal.

Ard Greeber had wanted Luster out of the way bad...not because of the murder of his pappy Tank, but because he thought Luster was the reason why Birdie Kiler had refused to be his wife. Even after Ard offered the Squire forty rich acres of that Tolby bottom land, he believed Luster'd gone to Birdie when she sent for him. He hadn't. Birdie had shot off her mouth about it and Ard had heard it and put two and two together.

Nearly four years ago now, and even while Birdie was heavy with Buck's child, she had waylaid Luster on the Meedon Levee Road. He paid her no mind and left her cursing lung-loud against the cypress trees. But she never gave up. Think of the she-devil and she'll appear. Luster looked back down the road and in the near distance, there was Birdie Kiler, buxom and big as life. As he drew near, her face lit up. Apparently, she had cut through the woods after he left Firbank and headed him off as he was crossing the road by the Refuge Schoolhouse. She ran up to him, big breasts flopping under her thin silky dress, and gushed out the words.

"Luster, I rushed out here first. God, I thought he was gonna take you away from me forever. I..."

He cut her off. "I hain't got no time to fiddle with you now, Bird, and I hain't never gonna have none. I'm tard out and sore and'd admire to git to the settin' up soon as I can."

"You hain't goin' up to the Greebers?" she said like she was hearing things out of the night.

He didn't answer her. Instead he said, "You better git on home 'fore your old pappy misses you."

"Old Pap's drunker'n a bitch by now, Luster, and don't have no more idear than a fresh skinned possum where I'm at. I got to have you...right now...for the fires of Hell are cracklin' inside me!"

He'd watched her in silence as she stood swaying on her big legs, her breasts now bubbling and quivering over the top of her low-cut dress like separate live things. Her eyes were round and dark and the moon, just peeping through the pines, glittered off the oily blue-black of her bushy hair.

"Oh, good Lord God, Luster," she panted wildly, "don't jest stand there. Take me! Hurt me! I'm jest mortal-frizzled sprung waiting fer you. Ever since I first knowed you when I was just a little split in bleached-domestic drawers, I've had a plaguing itch deep in me that only you can scratch."

"Git on home, Birdie," he said. "I'm so damn wore out I jest don't wanta be pestered by you."

"You won't be tard long, Luster," she begged. "I'll put new life in you, and shor'ly Ard didn't destroy what I'm a'cravin' most."

He watched her for a long time, moodily. Then as he turned to go, she leaped on him, panther-like, and wrapped herself around him like a fog. He'd thought, "I shore hope Dossie Bell's not watchin' me from a way off up there in the silver sky."

He tried to shove her away, but she clove to him. He shook her loose and, fitting one hand in the neck of her voile dress, ripped it off of her in one sweep. It was all she was wearing, except for the ribbon in her hair. Luster stared at the naked girl for a moment and she smiled. She was getting what she wanted. She pressed herself close to the big Cherokee. She'd longed for this moment and she planned to make the most of it. She wanted to take Dossie Bell's place in his bed, for good.

Luster threw Birdie's crumpled dress on the wet bank of the lane and pushed her onto it. She didn't complain. He crawled between her legs and took her. She was wild and loud. He gave little thought to what anyone might see. He was determined to quench Birdie Kiler's fire and shut her up. He was tired of her pursuit of him, tired of her constant and exhausting nagging for him. She was nothing like Dossie Bell, but then to him, no one was, not Sudie Lazenby and not Birdie Kiler either. And now it seemed she'd won. She'd gotten what she was after. If he was honest with himself, the hillman had lusted after her at moments too. But he knew she was dangerous, and he knew even he ought to stay away from her.

As soon as he stood up and the act was finished, Luster Holder was over Birdie Kiler. Even now he didn't want to think about it. After it was over, he thought glumly, "I jest nat'ral felt wors'n than after that scrap with Ard Greeber. Hit's all night to like hit, but when a body jest nat'ral goes mad, hit's somethin' else. A feller figgers to enjoy his pleasure without havin' to fight no wildcat. No wonder a kid boy like Buck Humphries was skeered to death of her."

She begged him to take her for his steady woman. "Git shut of that goddurned preacher's wife and I'll be a faithful woman tonight. I'll never touch no other man but you, Luster. I swear to my dear, sweet Jesus." He thought to himself, "no need to tell her no news about Sudie leavin.'" And when he pulled on his clothes and said nothing, she changed her tune. "If you won't do that, Luster, meet me here a'gin... every night. They pay me, Luster, but I'll pay you. I'll give you every durned red cent of my earnings," she pleaded.

When he still said nothing, she became frantic. "For Christes's sake, Luster, save me from Old Pap, like you've done saved me from that human mud turkle!"

As he turned from her and resumed on his way, she cried a final word, "Watch out for Old Pap, Luster. You cain't trust him no more'n you can a cottonmouth snake. I'm soundly shore he was wantin' Ard to kill you, and now I'm shore he's figgerin' dirt which he thinks you might not take to too hearty."

As she talked on, he waited to take a drink.

"I cain't say for certain what his idears are, Luster, but I'm a'thinkin' hit has to do with another woman which I'm shore you don't even know. But his main plan, I suspicion, is to still git that forty acres of Greeber land by tryin' to talk one of them remaining Greebers into marrying me. He's still pos'tive you got yore eyes set fer me," she explained desperately.

He looked at her a moment, then left her lying there naked alone on the rain-soaked bank of the road. Right then, he knew he'd never crave another woman if the experience had to be as sordid as that one. Some fellows must not mind, for she did a land office business up there in that rotting old Kiler home. She made the Old Squire a good comfortable living and followed the kind of life she most desired.

But he pitied the man who'd ever be fool enough to take her for wife or woman. She'd wreck him physically and there'd be no peace for him day or night. Like dogs, men and boys would catch the scent on the wind and be drawn to her. He'd have to stay close with a shotgun handy to drive them off like blackbirds from a wheat field. That's the way it was now. Why should a body think it'd ever be any different? When Birdie got satisfied, the jaybirds would be crying, "Who'd a-thought it?"

"I set her a-far," Luster thought, "worse'n she's ever been set, but somebody else can put hit out. If I wanna rassle myself to death I'll do hit with a man. She shore ain't the kind of woman I'm a-wantin'. I've had one in the back of my mind for over a year now. I jest been bidin' my time because of Sudie. Now, the way's open at last, and God, man nor the Devil hain't gonna stop me. But I shore God got to watch that old Squire."

He stopped in his tracks and raised the bottle. It cast red shadows on his big brown hand as the moon broke through. He drained it and tossed the empty aside. It fell in the bushes with a dry chink. After rolling another cigarette he sat back down. A few folks were beginning to leave the Greeber house. The now still night became alive with sputtering motors, squeaking wheels, tramping animals, which drowned out the choruses of frogs, crickets and katydids in the bushes and along the pond banks. Sleepy from liquor or grub or too much talk and excitement, they were pulling out for the drive home. It would soon be time to go up there.

In fact, it was time to go. He always liked to be on hand when a dead corpse belonging to somebody he knew needed to be watched over and kept in peace until the soul had a chance to safely take its flight in peace, even if such didn't pleasure him like they did Granny Blackburn, Urfie Pearl and Clemmie. Those old women scented out a death like soaring and circling buzzards above the pine woods, but they were mighty good hands with those who had crossed the Great Golden River for the last long journey.

After this drink got to circulating in his veins, he'd go on up there. They might think hard of him if he didn't come. He'd helped put their old pappy away and it was his bounden duty to do the same for the son. The Greeber boys might be aiming to do away with him some time, but they wouldn't try it until the funeral and the period of grief was past. He gave little thought of their hatred. The way he saw it, a man didn't have but one life to live and if he was afraid of losing it, he didn't have any business here on earth anyway. He should go where he wants to and when the spirit tells him to go. Folks said God meant for a body to take care of himself and live out his time. To Luster, a man's time was right now and what happened afterwards wasn't any of his damn worry, God had figured long ago just the minute his time would run out, and He kept it soundly to Himself and no manner of praying would make him tell it.

It was funny, and not much funny either, how folks thought he went out to Firbank this afternoon just to tangle with Ard Greeber. There again was the misunderstanding which made of life a hellaciously tangled path. He'd actually gone to the store for a sack of flour. Sure, he didn't give a damn for the Greebers. They'd all made their threats to put him out of the moonshining business and run him out of the Nation. They well knew they could never do either one. That, given the chance, they would bushwhack him, he well knew. So far, they hadn't hurt him in the liquor trade. They made rot-gut that only lowdown whites and coloreds bought.

No, he hadn't meant to meet Ard Greeber. Although he didn't think any more of killing Ard than he would have an alligator turtle or a terrapin, he didn't wish to lower himself by fighting a cripple, even if that cripple was bull-strong and vicious as a mad dog. But when a man jumped you, that called for action. You either had to act or be destroyed. You could have fought a man fair and square, but Ard hadn't been a man. Fighting with Ard was like fighting an idiot. A body shouldn't pick on abnormal people anymore than he should pick on Wurner. He's an idiot and well-known as one. God just hadn't done right by them in their birthing as if he's punishing their folks for some terrible sin they'd committed before the cripple or the idiot was even conceived. A body should, at least, look something like the folks he lived around and not as Ard had looked.

Wurner looked passably well, while Ard Greeber looked like something that ought to have stayed buried under a log. But when a man jumped you, you had to act or be wiped out. And, once the fight started, killing Ard was as easy as shooting a water moccasin or a mad dog and you'd never give it a second thought afterwards. Luster could kill a man like Ard and still get a good night's sleep. He figured most any man could, it seemed natural enough. It was just something that had to be done. He'd like the other Greebers out of the way alright but he didn't mean to go out of his way to get them. Killing the Greeber clan off, the menfolk that is, could be done all in Luster's own good time and not on their dares. Even though they were too near his part of the Nation country and disturbed the peace with their sorry presence, as long as they stayed out of his country proper, he'd pay them no mind. It'd be good to get shed of them all at one time, but that might be too much to hope for.

Ard hadn't been afraid. He'd meant to meet Luster where everyone could see him and had ordered his brothers to stay at home. He was positive he could do the job alone. Of all the Greebers, he was the most fearless, the sharpest, the meanest. Luster thought about that. He thought about Ard's fearlessness. Anyway, after he'd thrown Ard's body into the gully, Luster set out through the woods for home.

He recalled it all as he continued to walk and continued to replay the events and the facts in his mind. He'd taken his time walking and had reached the woods' path which led to the Firbank Road when he sensed the presence of something hidden nearby. He's stopped quickly and, not turning, as he slanted his eyes toward the bushes, and through the small opening between the leaves plainly made out a motionless bulk. He couldn't see the form very well, but he knew it must be Ard. The hidden hunchback gave off a queer animal odor. And indeed it had been him.

He'd been ready to wheel and fire at the slightest sign or sound out of the ordinary. Nothing happened, so he walked on, for he knew Ard wouldn't try a shot at him. He wanted only to be sure Luster had accepted his challenge. He was unafraid, but he meant to meet his enemy where everyone could see him.

Wurner had kept him posted on Ard, and Luster had him figured out right down to the ground. Of all the Greebers, Ard had been the least slinking. He never killed unless he could get his hands on a man. A horribly ugly creature, not human, not animal, but betwixt and between, Ard had little cared for life unless it gave him what normal folks had. He'd wanted Birdie, and was ready to crush anyone she craved, whether or not that anyone craved her. But Birdie had spurned him and when she turned down any male thing on two legs, then whatever it was, it just wasn't made to breed with humankind and should have been glad for somebody to put it out of its misery, although Luster hadn't asked for the job.

The way Luster now saw it, he did Ard a big favor in removing him from this world. Ard just didn't fit in with normal people. He had sent him where he could be all straightened out and made whole, and he must be happy for the first time in his memory. It was all past history and should be buried with Ard up there under the cedars of Sobby. But folks of the Nation wouldn't ever let it go, he just knew that. Well, some things never change. So on Luster walked, his mind recording today's events in Nation history and his own.

As Luster walked, his bearing became easier. As the liquor took hold, a feeling of infinite relief came over him. He was shed of Birdie and Sudie both, at last. Too as he walked, it was all making more sense to him now. Those events had put him on the trail to the truth. Now he was on his way to the sitting up for the man he'd killed. He was lost in his thoughts still when he suddenly dove face-down to the ground as three sharp cracks came from the bushes opposite him. He had been wary and on guard like a rabbit listening for a bobcat stalking him and had just about allowed himself to be at ease. Then as he heard his assailant, or assailants, tear through the underbrush, crashing and thrashing wildly, he was alert again. Now Luster had his own gun in his hand, spurts of red vomiting from the barrel. He was shooting in the general direction of the guilty and hoped for a hit. He heard a snapping of twigs, a wild scrambling and someone fled wildly in the darkness. Luster got off shots somewhere around head high of his assailant. He knew by their wild thrashing about in the woods that he'd not actually hit them.

His worn mind and body had made him careless, even if he had taken the back route. He'd never thought that the Greebers would try to get him so soon. Here at the path-side he'd been well hidden. Someone must have trailed him here or from the distance and the fire of his cigarettes. Possibly Wurner had let it be known he was on his way to the sitting up. He hadn't bothered to tell the idiot to keep it quiet, for it was sure no secret. He'd told Wurner about the shortcut he was taking too, and he didn't ask his poor simple friend to keep that a secret either.

He thought as he resumed his walk toward the Greeber house. Maybe it wasn't a Greeber after all. They'd be apt to work together at any ambushing. He was tired but now awake and ready for anything that came his way. He hadn't eaten since morning and hoped there was something left up at the Greebers. Nothing was in his way now.

All these thoughts and remembrances were still rolling through his mind as he neared his destination.

14

WHILE THE RAIN BEAT the roof and slashed at the windows, Granny Blackburn stood over the hot wood range in the kitchen watching simmering pots and skillets of food. The odor of frying ham, roasted meat, barbecue and coffee was fused with the oily stench of coal oil and settled over the steaming hot room. Occasionally, the aged woman stood to take a fast look in the oven, the dewlaps on her reddened throat quivering. Dressed in a loose-fitting black cotton dress, she was humped, her chest caved in, but her bright black eyes were alive to all about her as they darted here and there over the room.

"You better stand over there by the hall door, Norey," she said. "I don't want a soul in here till we're good and ready to turn hit loose, no matter how thar guts rumble and groan." She stretched her turtlish neck and spit into the wood box at the side of the stove. The flaps of her black poke bonnet jiggered up and down as she worked her toothless gums together, and her breath wheezed audibly.

A blotchy-faced woman, whose big breasts swung free from her body, pressed closer to the door. "I won't let nobody by, Mammy."

Granny nodded, "I'm shore glad they's a solid wall betwixt this here and the family room. Hit he'ps out a lot, but somebody orght to calm them durn young'uns down. They's makin' enough noise to wake the dead."

She sighed and continued, "Just so the little bastards stays outta here, because the front porch and every other room is bustin' full. Hit'll take the rest of the night to clean up the mud and slush." She showed her pink gums in a wicked grin, "I figger the weather's done slowed down the bush-work and drove the courters back to their cars."

"I'll be glad when it slacks so they can all git back out in the yard where they belong at," Norey said. "It's got my nerves bouncing all over me."

Urfie Pearl Buckner, the rail-thin old woman in gray-checked gingham, directed the arrangement of the food as two other women helped get the long oak table ready for the hungry. A coal-oil lamp sat at each end of the table, and the blue-flowered oilcloth cover was scarcely visible underneath the assortment of platters and bowls.

Granny fanned with her apron. Her palsied head vibrated rapidly. "I be goddurned if I ever seen as many vittles even at a all-day singing," she said drawing her lips far in over her toothless gums. "I 'low they's enough to feed half the county."

"It's the most grub I've saw since Dossie Bell Holder passed away," Urfie Pearl said. "I just cain't git it straight, Granny, the Greebers being strangers and all." She pulled out her underlip and driveled a fresh dip of a Rooster Snuff between it and her gums, a habit she had of doing throughout the day.

"I look at it this a-way, Miss Urfie Pearl," a harelipped old woman said firmly, "not many folks had saw Ard Greeber up to today. And during the fight, there wasn't much chance to git more than a teasing glance at him. They've come out to git a close up squint now, and they sorter felt like they orght to bring a dish of something out of respect and to give them an excuse to git in on it. Not many folks ain't ever saw a sight like him even in no side show at the circus over to Melburg."

Urfie Pearl rubbed a hand across her watery blue eyes, "That's about it, Miss Tessie. But I'm shore glad we hain't got to wait on a corpse like ever'body had to when them niggers took so long with old Tank's remains?"

"They takened that detour, Miss Urfie," Tessie said, "and that'd throwed 'em late."

Granny slid her lips slowly in and out, "If they'd brung him on here and let us lay him out proper wouldn't everybody had been held betwixt a chill and a stroke just wonderin' whar he was."

"It's the cold-curdled truth, Granny," Urfie Pearl nodded. "I've said it before, but hit's a sin and a shame and a personal insult to all us…cheatin' us outta a doin' what's been our bounded duty for over sixty odd year now."

The women mulled that thought over again. They didn't care much for progress and modern ways, especially those of new-fangled undertakers.

"Anyways, back to the here and now, any way you look at it," Urfie Pearl said, "we'uns'll haft to stay here till up in the day tomorrow."

Granny laughed rattlingly, "I's glad they never taken sich pains with Ard, 'cause he's all laid out proper. I jest cain't figger, though, whar in the devil they got that durned red box at?"

"Why, I 'low they brung it around by the detour, Granny," Urfie Pearl said.

"If they did, they flew through the durn sky in that old truck of their'n."

"Well, they coulda went to Colterville for it. That ain't but fifteen mile."

"Quit worrin' your brain about it, Urf. No matter whar they got hit at, Ard's ridin' in hit and'll be thar a long, long time."

"I 'magine so," Urfie Pearl lifted a cover from a large bowl on the table, "Have you'uns tried any of Purdie Colt's persimmon puddin'? It melts right in your mouth."

Granny snorted, "I've tasted so many durn things, my stomach's ropin'. Who's settin' in with the corpse now?"

"They's a room full, and folks keeps pouring in and out to git a look at him," Urfie Pearl said, "I seen Trudy Hacker last time I glanced in."

Granny snorted, "She orghtn't to look at him, Urf, her all swoll out...shaped like a bolster case in a strong north wind. She may git skeered and mark the child and birth a monster herself." Granny took a fresh dip. She talked over it in a mumble, "I hope to stoke the fars of Hell with a sauce pan if that ere hunchback warn't the hardest corpse to git in clothes I ever see'd in all my eighty-five odd years. Hit was his Sunday blue serge which that ere Clell boy laid out and I be durned if he didn't might nigh haft to bring in a pair of mules to draw hit on him. He jest looked like he'd been poured in hit, and hit was already bustin' at the seams. We done the best job we could fer the shape he was in, but I'm mortal skeered he'll spoil 'fore the buryin' the way Luster bunged him up."

Urfie Pearl smiled understandingly, "I reckon he'll keep till he's planted, Granny. We give him a good going over with camphor to start with, and Clemmie, she keeps dampening his hands and face by the hour. But I'm affeered somebody'll haft to git Freel to open the store and fetch another bottle."

Granny cackled, "Hit wouldn't be no bad idear to let him age overnight in a barrel of hit like his old pappy done in that 'ere sour mash. They wasn't no sense in embalmin' him no ways. What was you fixin' to say, Mod?"

A little woman with a large goiter chuckled, "I'll be durned if it ain't a sight the way that little snort hangs to that coffin and that little darky hangs to him."

Granny slapped her withered hands together, "I be goddurned if hit warn't hard to know who we was preparin' for burial. Oncet I even found myself undressin' and warshin' the nigger. Pickin' Tadpole offen' Pistol and Pistol offen' the corpse beat anything I ever see'd since I laid out Banford Mercer's idiot gal, Mirander, and had to slap at bedbugs and lice even to know that part of her I was workin' on at any one time. Them little piss ants bellerin' and cussin' to high heavens that we was hurtin' Ard and that Ard was their'n to see to...'y God, hit shore whupped me!"

Tessie Burress chuckled, "It was kinder cute when Pistol sunk his teeth into Clemmie's ankle and she squalled like a choked Dominicker hen."

"Shoot, it taken all my stren'th to unclamp the little scutter from her, and him no more'n coming seven," Urfie Pearl said, shaking her head. "Then to hear him say, 'I'll tick yo ass outta my house, doddam old bitty! You let Ard's torpse 'lone.' Made me wanta kill him or hug him or something. He is a right pert little peanut and just kinder melts my heart down to the point of nothin'. The poor little feller ain't been raised in no very Christian way, I'm thinking. But was I you, Granny, I'd put some of my shank salve for white-swelling on Clemmie's ankle. She may come down with lockjaw."

Granny swabbed snuff around her gums with a blackgum toothbrush and spat back, "I'll doctor her as soon as I can git home and make me up another batch. I jest hain't got no time for young'uns. I 'low hit'd save the settlement a lot of trouble later to go on and bury them two little turdheads with Ard. And that 'ere Tiddy too. Whar'd she wander off to?"

"I seen her goin' t'wards the barn earlier in the evenin'," Tessie put in.

"Well, I'm sayin' hit and I hain't stutterin'. She's gonna git a might young and tender tit caught in a mighty old and rusty fence if she hain't awful keerful," Granny Blackburn prognosticated.

"Why, Granny, she's just a little snot-nose gal," Tessie said, "and ain't yet reached the full age of full female deevelopmint."

Granny scoffed, "I hain't stripped her to see whether she is or she hain't, but I 'low she's got ever'thing a full-growed gal has. They say she's horsin' bad for that 'ere Buck Humphries."

"I've heered it hinted," Tessie said, "but I plain wonder what Birdie's up to…givin' him that young'un of his'n."

"That hain't hard to know a-tall, Tess," Granny said. "He's gittin too big and's in her way, and they say the Squire hated him like sin and taken special delight in whomperin' hell outen the little bastard. Birdie don't keer a damn about him, but what a boy like Buck can do with him is more'n my motley mind can figger."

Maybe he's aimin' to marry hisself a woman, Granny," Mod said. "He's gittin' old enough."

Granny pondered and asked, "You wouldn't be meanin' Tiddy, I hope? All I'm sayin' is…Buck jest gotten outen that trouble with Birdie Kiler by the skin of his teeth. This time he's playin' with shore death."

"They's just too much happening to keep up with," Mod declared. "have any of ya'll saw Blanche Greeber?"

"I ain't saw a sight or a smell of her, Miss Mod," Tessie said. "Now, she's the one which's got half the males of Firbank snortin' and buckin' like prize stallions."

"She has now at that," Mod declared.

Granny sat a high-stacked platter of sizzling ham on the table. "Hit shorely couldn't be grief a-hold-in' her, wherever she is. Did any of you'uns see whar them stepsons of her'n went off to? The rain musta drove them in some'r's or 'nother."

Mod's eyes blinked rapidly. "I'm shore they musta went to the barn too. They didn't come in the house."

Norey Blackburn was shoved back as the hallway door bumped against her. Squire Kiler tromped in, gray eyes squinting toward the table.

"Hain't the grub ready yet, Granny?" he said gruffly. "'y God, I'm so hungry I could eat a bull and hits ballerin.'"

"Hit ain't nigh ready, Squire," Granny snarled. "Hit do look like you men folks'd quit pesticatin' the very devil outen us while we're walkin' our hind laigs off tryin' to clabber together a decent meal to fill yore whistlin' guts."

The Squire lowered his eyes and told the old gal, "Forgit hit, Granny. I can calm down my comin' appetite fer a while yet. I was jest wantin' to ask if..."

The outside screen squeaked and the door burst open, rebounding against the wall. Wurner saddled in.

"Lord God preserve us, what next?" Urfie Pearl cried. Granny Blackburn threw up her hands and turned back to the stove.

Wurner's denim shirt was plastered to his arms and chest, the hairs showing transparently through it. His pants were rolled high above his knees. Red clay squished between his thick toes. Water ran off his short black hair and down his greasy red cheeks like gobs of lard. A smoky steam began oozing from his body as heat seeped into him.

"He's comin' now," he rumbled from low in his belly as he waddled toward the stove, "I was out there now and seen him oncet. He was comin'. I left fastly."

Granny turned slowly to face him, "You're shorely hain't meanin'..."

"Hit's Mister Luster now, comin' to the settin' up." He slapped his hand flat against the corner of the cook table. Pans and dishes rattled together and a bottle fell to the floor and shattered into a thousand glistening pieces.

"What do you'uns think o' that?" Wurner asked solemnly.

A momentary quiet settled over the hot kitchen. From outside came the droning noise of the steady downpour.

The Squire stood very straight, big-knuckled hands gripped. His face went bloodless and his eyes bulged slightly as he seemed to see something which wasn't there.

"What's chewin' on you, Squire?" Granny demanded.

The old man veered his eyes from her. Then a leering frown drew his face down longer. "I was just thinkin', Granny," he hawked his throat, "while you'uns finish preparin' the vittles, I'll jest meander out to the barn and feed my stud."

"You'll get soaked to the hide," Granny predicted flatly.

The Squire scratched his head and feebly mumbled, "Cain't he'p hit. Blaze...he ain't ate since mornin.'"

He strode to the side door, opened it to the wet night, and was gone. Wurner started to follow, but catching sight of the food on the table, he grinned absently and seemed to forget.

"Goddurned old fool," Granny snorted, "with them filthy corduroys he already smells like a moltin' squirrel and when he gits wet he'll stink up things wors'na mangy ole dog. Hit's a mare and no stud he's thinkin' about anyways, and I figger she might answer to the name of a certain woman in this here very house."

"What could you be meaning now, Granny?" Mod Pullins said anxiously. "Who would give that old toot a tumble?"

"Oh, nothin' a-tall. Them that's blind should remain blind. But as fer who'd be entrusted in him, accordin' to reliable reports which shoulda come first-hand, he hain't never left no woman disappointed." She drew her lips far inward, "Of course," she added thoughtfully, "he could wanta sorter warn them boys about Luster being on his way, him tryin' to..." her voice rumbled off.

Urfie Pearl sidled over to the older woman, "Granny, did you see the print of a gun in his pants' pocket?"

"I can still see, Urf," she snapped. "I only wished I had me the Godly pow'r to know what he's actual up to. Hit's the first durn time I ever see'd the old bastard so nervous."

"The worst is yit to come," Urfie Pearl said hollowly, "if Luster's actual on his way out here."

Granny Blackburn cackled, "Norey, I may haft to send you home for a change of clothes. Hit looks like we'uns may be here for a solid week."

"I can't still see how he'd have the nerve to come, mammy?" Norey said incredulously.

"Me neither, Miss Norey," Tessie declared. "It does look like he could let the corpse rest in peace."

"I sorter wished he'd stayed put too," Urfie Pearl said, "they's enough excitement to hold Firbank for a while."

"That's what I shout, Miss Urfie," Mod said. "he ain't got no lordly right to try to barge in where there's grief at, him so god-awful cold and unfeeling-like."

"Hain't got no right, your hind foot!" Granny exploded, "Like me, Luster hain't never missed no settin' ups in his part of the country. He's a prime hand around the sick and the dead. You hadn't forgottin' he was right here when Old Tank lay a corpse and him supposed to of done the killing. Nothin' happened then and hit won't happen now."

"They wasn't shore that time, Granny," Tessie said, "but this time they really know."

There was a pause in the conversation.

"They shore won't be wantin' him, Granny," Tessie said. "He's just coming out here as a dare, and's asking loud for a coffin box."

Granny cackled, "That hain't got a goddurned thing to do with it, Tess. Hit'll surprise them boys so bad to see him, they'll tuck their tails and run. But he hain't lookin' for no trouble. Luster's always ready and willin' to give a hep'pin' hand to his neighbors in time of trouble. I figger he's got more actual right here than anybody outside from the family, him being direct responsible for the whole thing and havin' a pers'nel interest in the corpse hisself." She stopped and chucked, "I 'low when a man kills off another, the body rightful belongs to him if he wants hit, jest like 'ere squirrel he shot outen a hickory. Everybody concerned orghta give thanks to the Good Lord-God that He let Luster remove sich a varmint from the face of the Earth."

"Maybe like the Squire, he's got him another reason for coming, Granny," Urfie Pearl said.

"Urf, you might be figgerin' under full steam now," Granny grinned and winked.

"Wonder if Miss Sudie's coming with him?" Tessie said.

"I won't even lower myself by answerin' sich a damn fool question," Granny hooted.

Mod Pullins chimed up, "Well, anyways, Granny, like I was sayin' previous, I don't believe she's out there."

Granny spit in the woodbox. She wiped her mouth on the back of her purple-spotted hand and drilled Mod with her sharp black eyes. "Let's don't git started on that 'ere again. She may or may not be out thar. Wurner here could clear hit up, if he would, but he's sich a stark idiot. Anyways, I 'low Luster's tole him to keep shut-mouth on hit. I've pumped a hundred odd time without no result." She tottered toward him. "Wurner, lissern close to me. Is Miss Sudie still out to Luster's cabin?"

Wurner showed his yellow, horse-like teeth in a spreading grin. "Miss Sudie was preacher man's wife. Goes then and lives way back."

Granny's head shook in steady vibration, as she asked again, "Is she or ain't she out thar, you turtle-brained hog?"

"Miss Sudie. Green eyes like a cat at settin' up on Dossie Bell. Preacher man he leaves fastly," the poor idiot answered.

Granny flung up her withered arms and hobbled back to the stove. "Set down, Wurner," she said in disgust. "The idiot's talkin' about Dossie Bell's death. Time don't mean nothin' to him. The only way we'll ever know is to go out thar, and my carkiss wouldn't hold out fer no sich a trip. Anyhow, she might hide out if she's thar and see'd us coming, and as I've said I shore wouldn't want Luster to think I was pryin' into his business."

The other women stared at Wurner Crouse and the thought crossed their collected minds that Wurner might not be as idiotic as he was crafty. Just maybe he knew exactly what he was doing.

"All I got to say, Granny," Tessie said thoughtfully, "is that if he's did away with Miss Sudie, they's a dozen women right here at this house right tonight that'd fly to him like a child to its long-lost mommy if he'd just crook his finger in their direction."

Granny cackled, "Hit's Birdie Kiler that'll fly first and fastest. She wants to git out from under that durn old Squire's thumb so bad she has to wake up at night to spit it out."

"I'm here to tell you'uns one sound thing," Urfie Pearl said. "Luster could shore break her to harness and make her work double."

Granny wiped her brow and cackled loud, "Yore idears are hatchin' deep under the hide now, Urf. That half-breed'd shore cool off that brush far ragin' inside her."

Mod Pullins listened to all this speculation and grinned. Finally she spoke up, "Well, guess what I fount' out a bit ago?"

Granny stared hard at her and declared, "Hell's bells, Mod! Just tell us!"

Mod smirked, "Miss Sudie ain't out there no more."

Everyone looked at her incredulously but Granny, who scoffed, "Mod Pullins! What in the name of sin and Satan are you bleatin' about?"

Mod shook her head and began to explain, "No, Granny, old Wurner knows. Card seen 'em. I was gittin' the chillern' dressed for the fight. Card was out hitching the mules to the wagon to haul us over to Firbank when he seen this old Chevy touring car pass by in a cloud of dust. He come runnin' in like a whipped cur and says, 'Mod, I may hope never to reach no Promised Land if I didn't just see Sudie Lazenby pass with...with...' He couldn't go on and suddenly stood there froze solid like he'd seen a ghost. So I give him a finger-poke in his navel and hollered, 'Quit standin' there like a dazed hen and tell me who!' And he says, face pale as a lye-scoured floor, 'I'm afraid it was Brother Lazenby hisself, Mod.' And I says, 'Card Pullins, you been drinkin' or you're bad needin' your eyes treated with fresh lady-water. Don't you touch another drop till you take me and the chillern' and drop us safe at the store at Firbank!'"

Mod let out a long sigh, "But my poor man was spoutin' out true words after all."

"May my poor heart skip a beat!" Urfie Pearl gasped.

Furiously Granny rolled her althea toothbrush around her toothless gums, "Old Scratch has done come to the Nation. I knowed she was skeered to death of Luster, not never regaining her rightful self since he takened her that night his woman lay dead. If she's left, hit was because Luster was tard of her. He's free agin' so look out!"

Granny hobbled to the dining table and shoved Wurner back. He already had a whole roast hen in one big hand. She jerked it from him and pointed to the cook table. "Quit standin' thar grinnin' like a mule eatin' briars and git over thar and set down, Wurner. I'll give you something t' eat, but I be god-durned if I'm gonna have you snortin' into the main table like a durn boar hog."

The idiot smiled vacantly at her. He waddled on to the cook table and sat down, both elbows on the edge of it, huge hands upheld. "Aigs and 'lasses...aigs and 'lasses…aigs and 'lasses," he crowed in a kind of weird chant.

"What's he s…sayin', Granny?" Tessie said bewilderedly.

"He's wantin' a dish of scrambled eggs with sorghum molasses poured over hit, but I solid balk. Git a stewer and fill hit with chittlins', squirrel stew, and chestnut dressin' to start him off on, Urf, and dump in some stewed okry and tomaters, whippoorwill peas, turnip greens and cabbage. Throw a hunk of that sow belly in with hit and then crumble a mess of corndodgers on top of all of hit. Don't give him a smell of the barbecued 'possum, hog, goat, or sheep, or any of the roast chickens, beef or ham, nor none of the cakes or pies. Mix all the stuff up together… he won't know no difference…and bring a gallon of sorghum outta the pantry. He'll pour hit over his food so long as they's a drop left and hit'll save the best dishes for normal folks. Fetch a pitcher of buttermilk too and I'll sugar hit for him. Maybe we can fill him before the others is ready, but we'll haft to stand right over him and see he don't git outta hand. He shovels hit down faster'n you can pour hit out to him. 'y God, he could gobble down every durn thing on the table and still be gut-beggin'!"

"He orghta ate last, Granny," Urfie Pearl said.

Granny laughed, "That's what I shout, but you cain't hold him off oncet he starts…git your broom, Norey. I hear that durn cat comin' back. Every cat in the Nation'll be here before morning."

15

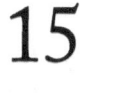

WITH ARD SUDDENLY DEAD, the Greeber men-folk would be looking for vengeance. The history of the Greeber clan was long and vicious and it spanned all the way back to Missouri. The Greebers had been there and they were just as questionable in their character there as they were in the Nation. No one doubted they were dangerous and no one doubted they'd probably gotten in trouble across the river in Missouri.

Tank Greeber's death had set his sons' blood to boiling. They were the kind of folks that craved revenge. They were just the kind who couldn't rest until someone else's blood was spilled in return for that of their kinsman. They all figured that Luster Holder had killed their pappy. Tank's manner of dying seemed just the kind of thing they'd suspect of

Luster. They were competitors after all. Both were in the business of moonshining. Luster and his bunch had been at it a long time. The Greebers fought for the same business as the big Cherokee. So finding Tank's body pickled in his own sour mash seemed like the deepest insult the violent hillman could dish out to them. Still, all of this really proved just one thing, the Greebers didn't know Luster Holder at all.

Then Ard was killed. The older brother was the one they looked up to after their pappy met the Lord and the Holy Spirit or the Devil himself in a vat of boiling spirits. No sooner than the mules pulled Ard out of that damn gulley, the remaining Greeber brothers began making plans to seek out their vengeance on Luster Holder. And once the decision was made, there was no turning back. They'd spill Luster's Indian blood or bust Hell wide open! Their pride demanded it.

Clell Greeber's muscles jerked and an elbow shot into his brother Sarl's ribs. The brother just older shoved him away with a curse. The boy leaned forward, hands holding his knees to steady him against the vibrations of the speeding car. The boys drove toward the house and their own destiny too. They'd made up their minds to take Luster Holder out for once and for all.

You really had to go back to Missouri and pick up the pieces to know the whole story of why things were now rounding off in this violent fashion. Folks said they had moved out to Tennessee because Tank

Greeber, through pure accident, finally learned of Luke Tolby's death and decided to come out here to this savage country in the hopes of getting the former Tolby holdings. That was the talk.

That wasn't completely true at all. Tank had run a general store at a small river landing in Missouri and bought cotton on the side. His trade had come from the sharecropper class whose open accounts he carried on a twenty percent basis until fall. Taking advantage of them, he added to his books many items not purchased and was able to keep them always broke and in his debt. The farmers of his territory had a deep distrust of banks and financial institutions. As for cotton, Clell later learned that on several occasions his pappy had not only bought it from the farmers, but it wasn't unusual for Tank to send men to rob his customers of their cotton money on their way home. That way, the Greebers got not only the cotton but kept their money too. Such proved Tank Greeber's level of greed.

This trickery of Tank's went on for several years and he grew pretty well-off from it. After a few years, folks got smart to Tank and he learned through his sons that the sharecroppers of the territory had indeed gotten wise to his treachery and were planning revenge. Tank had had a conversation with a jobber, a grocery salesman, and the subject of the Tolbys back in West Tennessee came up. After a good bit of talk, the jobber learned from Tank that the Greebers were related to the Tolbys. The jobber

knew of the Tolbys in Tennessee and informed Tank
that his distant cousin, Luke Tolby, the last of the
Tolby menfolk, had died. The jobber had learned,
during a visit to Goddard's Store at Firbank, that
Luke Tolby had been found dead in the hills of the
Nation. Tank also learned that Luke's death wasn't
from any natural causes.

Indeed, this jobber had learned a lot during his
trip to Goddard's and he passed it on Tank. The jobber talked long and loud of the history lesson he'd
received at Freel Goddard's store counter. He learned
how, back before the Civil War, a Cherokee Indian
had stolen the vast Tolby holdings from its rightful
owners. The man spoke of Birdie Kiler, Luke's niece,
but said she, like her uncle before her, would never
claim the land of their forefathers.

Upon hearing all of this, Tank was interested
in the possibilities that lay in the hills of the Tolby
Nation. He felt those possibilities were untapped and
ready to be seen about. So Tank drew his money out
of two banks in an adjoining town and got himself
ready to act. He set fire to his store in the dead of
night and, with his family, skipped out of Missouri
before anyone had time to act or catch him. The
Greebers fled Missouri in the same Buick car in
which Clell and his brothers were now speeding
toward the house. Old Tank Greeber had decided
that Tennessee was a safer place for the Greebers and
full of rich opportunity. At that time, neither Clell

nor his brothers, for that matter, really had any idea what was hidden back in Tank's twisted old mind.

It had broken Clell up badly to flee Missouri, and he never forgave his father for deserting the place where his mother was buried. And Mammy Blanche and brother Ard bitterly resented leaving too. After they had come to Firbank and his pappy bought the Luke Tolby place from Squire Kiler, he became more reconciled to the situation, because it seemed they might be settled for a long, peaceful time.

Not so. His pappy, ignoring that Birdie Kiler was the closest kin, let it be known that he intended by kinfolk's rights to have the thousand acres that John Holder, Luster's grandfather, had wrested from the Tolbys. Tank instilled in the minds of his sons that they must do away with the half-breed and claim the land. He began forming plans toward this end, and, as a beginner, put up a still down in the bottoms near the Forked Deer River to run whisky in competition with Luster Holder.

Ard had opposed the plan. There were hard words and Tank insultingly referred to his eldest son as a curse sent against him. Ard never forgave him for that remark. And when Clell sided with Ard, his brothers ganged him to beat some sense into his "simlin head." He never told Ard about it.

The boy was forced to help them at the still. Knowing nothing of distilling, they made little headway against Luster, who was himself a master of the art. Nearly a year passed and the half-breed continued to ignore the Greebers, just as he had ignored all other slanderers and competitors in the past. Then Code Greeber got the idea of hijacking a load of Luster's whisky to try to test it and find out just what made it sell in such large quantities over at the county seat, Melburg. Clell saw through the excuse right away. All his brothers wanted was to provoke the big Cherokee so he'd come out of the farthest reaches of the Nation and give them an opportunity to bushwhack him and they forced Clell to help them. They waylaid and overpowered Crip, Luster's Negro man, beat him with their fists and brought back Luster's charred corn liquor to their barn.

Clell had spent a night of terror, at any moment expecting the appearance of Luster Holder, and now he was certain that the half-breed hadn't come because he was working on a plan which called for one decisive stroke. Ard was furious, but since it was done, nothing could be done to undo the damage. And although Tank was not in the plot, he was the one who paid. The very next afternoon, while the brothers were in Melburg, their pappy was brutally murdered at the still.

Ard had sided with the brothers now, and so did Clell. They all swore a quick revenge. Then Luster's astounding appearance at Tank's sitting up had cast a doubt in their minds. Had he been the murderer, he wouldn't have dared come out to their home. Folks at Firbank said it wasn't his method of killing anyway. He might be a half-Cherokee, but he certainly wasn't treacherous. The whole thing was puzzling, especially to Clell and Ard. But who else could have done it? No one else in the whole Nation had anything against them. Clell had suggested that someone from Missouri, someone who'd been cheated at the store or robbed of his cotton money, might have slipped quietly over the river, got his revenge, and then slipped just as quietly back. His brothers scoffed at him, but he could see that it worried them.

Then they remembered the forty acres Ard wanted to swap to Squire Kiler for Birdie and the violent quarrel between him and his pappy because of it. In Clell's presence, and safely out of earshot of Ard, they hinted that it might have been the hunchback himself who did the foul deed. He hadn't gone to town with them on the day of the murder, and the unusual method of the killing could certainly have originated in his twisted brain.

Clell was horrified. He gave it the lie, and they threatened him if he ever let Ard know their suspicions. He wouldn't have told him for the world, because Ard hated them enough already. And he was afraid Ard might think he was not so sure himself, although he would have more quickly believed that the others had done-in their pappy. Until this day you just couldn't know who actually did it. But it wasn't Ard. He might not have cared much for Tank, but he sure wouldn't have killed his own blood-pappy.

Clell straightened up and looked around him. They were whizzing through Goose Cackle, the halfway mark on the road to Melburg. There were eight more miles to go. He shot a fast glance at his brothers. They still slouched moodily in their seats, hooded eyes distanced. All but Code. He hunched over the wheel and urged on the car with the same cold fury.

Clell had got his first good look at Luster Holder the night of the wake for their pappy Tank. Even now he could see the powerful but relaxed body, the distinctly carved features, with the glittering black eyes. Luster seemed so calm, so sure of himself, so out of the world of people. A soft tingling had gone over Clell's body. Shame filled him, for he couldn't bury a certain admiration for this man who may have murdered his father. He remembered that Mammy Blanche had come in the room to see the body, but had set her eyes on Luster instead and kept them there. He searched for hate in her eyes and could find neither hate nor grief. It was something else. He realized she must be relieved at the death of the husband she had never loved. With her mellow blue eyes it seemed as if she were trying to tell the big hillman she held nothing against him even if he were the murderer.

Later on that night he had seen her talking with Luster behind the hickory in the backyard, while someone else eavesdropped from the shadows around the corner of the house, one of his brothers he supposed, although he couldn't tell which one and couldn't even be sure it was indeed one of his brothers. He was sure Mammy Blanche was trying to learn enough to satisfy herself that Luster was innocent so she could tell Ard and not have Firbank gossip that Luster had been seeing Birdie Kiler and might take her for his woman as soon as he could rid himself of Sudie Lazenby. Clell was sure Luster wasn't the type to lower himself by going to Birdie. He longed to reason with Ard, but knew it would be futile. Even when Ard called him off to the barn early this morning and told him that the big Cherokee was coming out to meet him at the store, the boy was too stuffed up with worry and fear to plead with him to call it off.

Ard's last words still rang in his ears: "I'm doing this all by myself, Didapper, so don't come around there. I've done told the others." Then he added something which sent purple shivers over the boy. "If I don't come out alive, I want you to promise me you'll always look after Mammy Blanche and the little chaps. All of you git away from here and return to Missouri. Be sure."

"I promise, Ard," he'd said, fighting to keep from breaking down and showing tears.

The long arm had squeezed his shoulders. The laugh had rumbled deep in his throat. "Perk up, Didapper. I'll be here for Luster Holder's burying."

These men who surrounded him here in the car would force him to help them kill the Cherokee. If he refused, they'd shoot him down too. He had no hatred for one who had tended strictly to his own business. Ard had hurled the challenge and died in a fair, if savage, fight. Of course, given a good chance, it would pleasure him mightily to send Luster Holder on after Ard.

Ard's death had finally decided him, it and his promise to flee to Missouri if Ard died. Those thoughts and his own personal decision were still rumbling through his head when the quiet in the car was broken when Code spoke up and addressed his brothers.

"Alright, boys," Code Greeber began, "I been thinkin' about this and here's something else. The way I got it planned, we'll slip out to his cabin tonight and git him while he's weak from that fight. We'll use the Indian style on him...surround the cabin while he's asleep, set it afire, and blow him to hell when he comes out."

"I still think it'd be best to bushwhack him, Code," Seeby said. "That's what Ard orghta did instead of tryin' to meet him head-on. For one thing, we don't know the layout of his cabin or the country 'round it, and I just don't trust that..."

"Shut your damn trap, Seeby!" Code snapped. He spit against the wind and poured more gas to the swaying machine. "Bushwhackin' him out in the open has been tried before and them which tried it are sleeping at Sobby. That damn Cherokee sees through underbrush and can smell like a hound. In following my plan I done planned so keerful, we'll be bushwhackin' him anyways."

"I still think…" Seeby began.

Code snapped back, "Goddam what you think! I'm the boss of this here family now and you'll do it just like I got it worked out to do."

After that, no more was said.

The boy Clell agreed with Seeby but he well knew the uselessness of backing him up. He had ventured opinions before, and all opposed him. They still considered him a boy whose judgment was not worth consulting. All he prayed for was to see Ard safely put away in the churchyard so he could start his long journey to his home above. Then he himself would carry out his own plans, long delayed by the trouble between Ard and Luster.

When Luster Holder killed Ard this afternoon, it finished the boy too. He had loved Ard as much as he despised Code, Corbin, Seeby, and Sarl. He hated every drop of Greeber blood in his veins and damned to Hell his own pappy for putting it in them.

God, how good Ard had been to them! If folks had only known what he was really like they would have forgotten his horrible looks, for his insides were just as beautiful as his outsides were ugly. And when you were around him and loved him, he wasn't ugly at all.

While Ard lived, there'd been little fear in the Greeber household. He wasn't a bully. With those he cared for, he was kind and gentle as a woman. He liked the small things of nature which other folks didn't notice…like stones, vines, moss, wild flowers, insects, and birds. He brought to the house sick or wounded animals he found in his wood's wanderings and constructed screened boxes for them behind the house. He fed and doctored them until they were well, then gave them their freedom.

When he got back from this dismal trip, Clell must turn loose the screech owl, crow, and coon… Ard's last patients. And he must remember to pour out saucers of milk for the tom cat, Muddyspring, and the pussy, Noble Preen, with her six new kittens. Ard had raised them and petted them and they were going to miss him God-awfully too.

Ard had brought things like mussel shells, old bird's nests and feathers, moth cocoons, Indian arrowheads, and many, many things to delight the younger ones. He carved beautiful objects out of wood with his knife….animals and flowers and funny little people, whittling, sandpapering, shining and painting on them long after bedtime, while he, Tiddy, Pistol and Tadpole watched in wide-eyed fascination. He built martin and pigeon boxes, so wonderfully carved and printed in such dazzling colors that the birds broke into wild song at the very sight of them.

Even now Clell could see the pitifully misshapen body being swung aloft by the iron-muscled arms to give the finishing touches to a tree-house for the children, or he could see the massive hump seeming to weight him down as he stooped over Mammy Blanche to help her figure out a crocheting or knitting design, often taking the needle from her hands and starting the pattern himself, the powerful fingers moving with great speed and accuracy.

Ard had strange ways and he became stranger and stranger after he got crazed over Birdie Kiler. He began to bay the full moon, his loud, deep-toned howls resounding mournfully over the countryside and causing one to draw up in a knot under the covers. He seemed to be crying to God of his hard lot here on Earth and pleading with Him for help. Ard had lived a way off somewhere and he had the power to see things common folks couldn't, for the Lord had given him unusual powers to make up for the mess He had made in molding him.

Ard was the master of all these marvelous things. Yet, he had fallen under the dark spell of Birdie Kiler, and his unreasonable craving and imagined love for her had brought his downfall.

16

AFTER TIDDY RAN AWAY from the cottonseed shed, Buck lay on his back, for a long time while the chill of the advancing night seeped into his bones. It was unforgivable the way he had frightened her. All along he'd been a fool and thought she wanted him that way. With the soft weight of her warm body on top of his own naked one, with her small lips wet and drawing, his mind could no longer control his body. Even as his passion began rising and getting beyond his control, he had struggled futilely to scotch it. Not since the experience with Birdie Kiler had he felt so helpless and forgotten himself. Then just as he was on the verge of turning his physical self completely loose, she had sensed what was happening to him. Only then, his fears had to overcome his passions.

She had leaped from him and snatched up her clothes. She looked so small and child-like in the revealing flashes of lightening that shame had flooded over him, drowning the lust of the body and again restoring the peace of the mind. He had almost sinned again and God had prompted her to flee before its consummation. But even in his hurt, he was elated to know that all of her seeming recklessness was born naturally within her and didn't come from the Evil Wile One. She was a child of the woods and so pure and beautiful in the inside and out as an early spring violet pearled with dew. Like a fool, he had ruined himself with her, and she'd avoid him now as he'd tried to avoid her in the past. Too late he'd realized just what she was and what she meant. He would spend the rest of his life in regret and live on her memory alone. He never wanted to think of any other girl.

He had faith she'd never say a word to anybody about being alone with him. He just hoped for the sake of both of them that no one had seen them. He got up, dressed, replaced his .32 Smith & Wesson in his shirt and walked toward the house. The rain had about stopped, the night now dank and dripping, but the moon was again peeping through rifts in the dark clouds. It was going to clear off. As he stepped over the strands of wire at the horse lot, he stopped short. In the misty green light, he saw a couple creeping from the barn hallway. He wondered if it was the same boy and girl Tiddy had seen. He supposed not. Then from the direction of the barn, he heard men's voices.

To avoid the thickest part of the crowd, he entered the house by the back porch. He stopped there and waited. In the kitchen, he could hear the mumbled talk of folks eating, from the front verandah and yard, a continuous hum of conversation interspersed with sharp exclamations and jarring laughter. A woman's voice shrilled into the night as she rounded up her children to leave. Most of the crowd, their curiosity satisfied and their bellies tight with the feast, would be on their way to close or distant points to get a good night's sleep before the funeral up at Sobby tomorrow afternoon. Drowned motors coughed hoarsely, horses neighed and traces jingled.

He took a deep breath and entered. He eased up the hallway, hugging the wall and stopped just before he reached the white square of light from a room on his left. Hesitantly he veered his eyes about the large, high-ceilinged room, which had been stripped of all furniture to make room for the coffin and chairs of the watchers. Across from the fireplace on two carpenter's horses rested the mahogany painted pine casket and spreading out from it in a semi-circle were over twenty-five people, most of them seated, the old-line sitters-up, the majority of whom stay all night.

Buck tried to set his gaze over their heads and on the rain-stained pink wallpaper just above the heat-cracked mantel. Near the door he saw Elmer Runnels' long face longer now, silver-rimmed glasses shining in the light from the Coleman gas lamp on the mantel and Banford Mercer, who held his face in his open hands, and there were others he knew, most of them from the Firbank settlement. There was Doney Pandrey, Thible Plusser, Doretha Winkle, Jodey Peaks, Narcissa Tacker, Lady Bob Buthren, and others he didn't know, most of them from distant communities in the county.

At the head of the coffin sat his pappy, Henley Humphries, dressed in a dark suit, against which his drooping mustache and beard gleamed snow white and didn't show the normal tobacco stains. He leaned over on a hickory stick, watery eyes squinted toward the floor and the crown of his bald head, surrounded by a fringe of hair, was a dull honey brown. He chewed absent-mindedly on the hairs around his mouth. With his eyes badly cataracted, he'd had a hard time seeing well enough to see anyone. There was a scattering of women, old and young, and three of them held sleeping babies, while a fourth pillowed in her lap the head of a youngster of ten or twelve, who sat on the floor. He knew the latter two: Oney Phelps and Okker Lee, a big nine-year old boy who never got out of her sight, good, religious, afraid, and knowrated to be still un-weaned.

The men looked blankly at the walls or dozed in their chairs. Occasionally a woman would lean over and whisper to her neighbor, then straighten up and set her lips back in a stern line, letting her eyes stare vacantly. Buck knew now he was the subject of conversation. In one corner, a young girl was blubbering as she dabbed at her eyes with a man's handkerchief. An old woman beside her kept patting her eyes and saying, "Shhhh." Buck knew the girl, Trula Priddy, the organist at Sobby. She was noted for the crying fits she threw at all funerals, for she had a tender heart for all mankind.

He didn't see any of the Greebers. He prayed that Tiddy had gone to bed. He couldn't stand ever to face her again, although at the very thought of her his heart fell low in his chest. Because of his unquenchable love for her, he would never spend another moment of peace or happiness on this earth.

He wished to get this gruesome duty over with and hurry back to his home before his pappy rode in on the mule and found Dink. Even though the old fellow was nearly deaf, he might hear the boy crying, if Dink awoke before Buck returned. And, before he retired, his pappy nearly always stumped to his room and struck a match to see if his son was safely in bed. He'd surely discover Dink.

Buck desired daylight before Old Henley discovered Dink. Birdie had brought him back to him and Buck was determined to keep him. Still he dreaded the violent scene he knew would take place when Old Henley found out about Dink. His heart melted as he thought of the little fellow sleeping there at the old house alone. But Dink said he wouldn't be scared. He recalled how he had pulled him close and said softly, "Dink, I got to go over to the settin' up awhile."

"Settin' up?" the boy had asked puzzled.

"Yeah, over Ard's body," Buck answered, "Ever'body goes to show folks they're proper grieved and to keep nothin' from botherin' the corpse."

"The corpse?" the boy asked.

"Yeah, what's left of him down here sinst Jesus called his soul up there," Buck explained.

"Soul?" the confused boy asked.

He had seen he wasn't getting anywhere so he just said, "I got to go he'p out with the dead man and git him ready to bury. You wouldn't wanna be there."

"Oh!" he clung to him, "I'm skeered to death of dead mans, Buck. Bird…she tole me they had boogers in they heads. She wouldn't take me to see Old Tank when he was coffined."

Buck embraced the boy and undressed him and waited until he was sound asleep before he left.

Buck dreaded the ordeal of crossing the room and viewing the remains. It had to be done. If a body failed to do so, he was showing disrespect toward the departed and his family and there would be bad talk about it for long afterwards.

He had just steeled himself and was about to start forward when someone touched his shoulder. His nerves jerked painfully and he whirled around to face Clemmie Bean, a cottony-haired little woman in black, from whose sharp upturned chin, a brown trickle of spit dangled.

"Have you saw Ard?" she whispered mysteriously, and before he could answer she grasped his arm with

a bony hand and urged him forward, almost dragging him like a mother with her little boy.

His eyes bugged as they came to rest on the man
in the coffin…the most horrendous sight it had ever
been his misfortune to behold. The huge head rested deep in a pillow and the bristly hairs were turned
to a rusty red in the light from the lamp above him.
One eye was not well closed and, through the slit of
the lid, glinted evilly. Despite the fact that a strip of
domestic had been looped under the chin and tied in
a bow at the crown of the head, the tips of his tusks
showed dully yellow over the puffed lower lip. He was
the color of a grub found under a log in the river bottom. Ard was dressed in a blue serge suit with a blue
shirt and orange cravat, and his bull-wide shoulders
were wedged against the edges of the box, his chest
bulging far above the opening. With sickness grov-
eling up inside him, Buck saw the plow lines across
the chest and around the withered legs. The ropes
went clear around the coffin at head and foot and
must have been tied underneath, for the knots were
not visible. An odor of camphor struck his nostrils in
a nauseating way that almost knocked him down.

The old woman was watching him and he knew
he was expected to say something. He dampened his
lips and the sound came from a distance, like he was
a way off somewhere mumbling it to himself.

"Don't he look natural?" Buck feebly ventured.

"Yes," she whispered, like it was a deep-dyed
secret, "just like he was asleep. But it shore was one

more job to git him settled in that box for his last long ride."

Clemmie motioned him to one side to make room for a rail-thin woman who was pregnant almost to the necessity of delivery. A big toddler was astride her hip, a little girl of three held to her loose hand and a boy of four to her sleeve. Two boys and three girls, ranging in age from five to ten, pushed in closely behind her. She stopped, removed a black-gum toothbrush from her brown-rimmed mouth and, putting spread fingers to her lips, spit over the coffin and into the blackened fireplace. Brown specks settled waveringly on Ard's tallowy face. She stooped and lifted each of the smaller children in her arms and held it out over the coffin saying, "Hit's Ard, Sugar Tit. He's went to live with Jesus."

The seven-year old screamed, "Lemme down, Ma, lemme down! I gotta go to the bushes!"

She dropped him on his bottom and he ran bleating from the room.

The oldest boy looked up at his mother, solemn-faced, "Durn, Ma, he's uglier'n 'ere tree toad."

She struck a back-handed blow at him, but he dodged her. He stuck out his tongue and cried, "You missed me, you ole sway-backed heifer!"

"Wait'll I git you home, boy," she said, completely unruffled, "I'll pure scour out yore durned nasty mouth with lye soap."

Buck watched all of this nervously. The grim duty performed, he moved back quickly now. He wanted out of the room, but didn't know just how to leave respectfully. A body was supposed to hang around for a while to show that he properly felt the loss that the removal of a fellowman had brought to the settlement. Someone had vacated a chair in the corner near the verandah window.

He was lowering his body into it when something caught his ear...it was the sudden silence. All sound inside and outside the house and even in the kitchen had abruptly ceased, as if shut off at one sharp command. Everyone leaned forward, eyes toward the door. He heard someone suck in his breath like a last dying gasp!

Luster Holder entered as silently as a breeze. Tall, khaki-clad, he seemed unaware of the presence of anyone as he strode across the floor, took one sweeping glance at the corpse, then stepped back and began rolling a cigarette. As always, Buck had eyes for no one else. The big hillman looked out of place in the confines of any room. The dark, flashing eyes in the deeply bronzed face with its high cheek bones and thin firm mouth, the straight nose, the straight black hair in bangs, the powerful, drooping shoulders, and relaxed animal body...all belonged in the open air in the thick woods.

Luster spoke to no one and no one said a thing to him.

The silence was broken by the hollow sound of heavy boots in the hallway. Squire Heber Kiler entered, a tall, rangy man dressed in a yellow corduroy suit, which was slick and blackened from long use. The Squire was gray-eyed, iron-gray haired and his whole body slouched as he walked.

"I'd heered you'd arrove, Luster," he said in a resounding voice as he stopped near the big Cherokee. "I'll be dambed if I ever see'd so many curious people sinst yore own woman quit four years ago. Figger to set up fer the rest of the night?"

"I'low I will if I'm needed, Squire," Luster answered him.

The Squire hawked his throat and glanced uncertainly at Luster.

"I sorter figgered on hangin' around till daybreak. Birdie, she can take keer of things at the house. We'uns'll be needed all night 'cause most ever'body'll hump hit for home when they git their empty guts stuffed."

Buck leaned farther back in the corner. The old man mustn't see him even though he was sure the Squire would never mention the incident of the afternoon. The underhanded old fellow, a vicious man when roused, would wait until he caught him alone. Buck didn't mean for that to happen if he could possibly prevent it.

The Squire set his eyes on the corpse and drawled, "That ere's a right purty and costful box to be put in the ground to rot. The way I see hit, thar hain't no damb use on God's green earth spending a lot of money to put folks away in high-falutin' coffins. All hit does is make the worms hafta bide their time a little longer. And what in the glorious hell does time mean to a dead man or worm neither?"

When Luster made no comment, the Squire shot a doubtful look at him.

"Who-eee," the Squire growled, "They's enough camphor on him to preserve ever' corpse in the county. 'y God, if he was living, he'd be drowned in the durn fumes. But I figger they don't want him to git too ripe before he's planted or he'll sho-God stink up that church house worsen' ere polecat!"

The Squire looked around again, shifted his weight and asked Luster, "You hain't got none of that ere good chartered stuff on you, have you now, Luster? I need my strength if I'm gonna stay in here."

The big hillman handed him a full pint and the Squire drank half of it and handed it back.

Just as Brother Blankfield, a local Holiness preacher, started toward the door, the ghastly thing happened...something that was to be remembered as long as Firbank existed.

With a sharp, popping crack, Ard Greeber bounced straight up in his coffin and rocked back and forth for a moment before the deformed body sat straight up to face the room with a leering dead look.

The catch and hiss of breath was clearly audible, like a bucket of water dashed on live coals. Trula Priddy, the Sobby organist, gave one soul stirring and very dismal shriek and fainted in a heap on the floor. Brother Blankfield took one horrified look and fled up the hall. Buck saw the circling flock of blood-less faces, the open mouths, the stampeding bodies as folks broke madly for the door leading to the hall-way. Squire Kiler stood there, suddenly gawking at the awful scene himself. He was a superstitious man and Buck watched him carefully knowing that fact. The old Squire had some Negro blood in his veins and was given to their peculiar brand of superstition. The fact was that the rangy old Squire was just as jumpy, just as spooked as anyone else in that stuffy room. He was suddenly in as big a hurry as the rest of the Nation folk to get out of that room. As Buck watched aghast too, Squire Kiler was close behind the mass of hysterical mourners, pushing, shoving, and kicking, the Squire's voice was in a high bellow, "Git on, good Lawd! Git on! The varmint's done come to life! Goddam a room with jest one door!"

Buck stayed in the corner, stiff and straight against the wall. Soon the room was empty except Ard, Luster, the unconscious and trampled Trula, Buck and, to his great relief, his pappy. At least the old man wouldn't discover Dink, now, for the time being. Old Henley still leaned over on his cane, now happily chewing the hairs around the corners of his mouth. Buck was sure his pappy knew of the com-motion, but he was too deaf to hear it, to cataracted to see it and too stiffened with rheumatism in his aged limbs to move very far anyway.

Luster rolled a cigarette and lighted it just as Granny Blackburn hobbled in from the hall. Behind her bobbed the heads of several others. The old woman shot her reddish eyes around the room.

"y God, I thought the whole durned world was a-ending," she said as she rubbed her weathered chin, "Ard, he's practical up from the dead even if he don't know hit!"

"I figger we need some baling wire, Granny," Luster said calmly, "them ropes was rotten as hell." He was examining the broken ropes from the coffin.

"I'll jest go tell Norey to git some, Luster," she cackled. "We got to bind the varmint down till we can earth-weight him. Some of you women pick up the durn organist and take her out to the air." She hobbled away, stick pecking the floor in front of her. Clemmie, Urfie Pearl and a couple of other women lifted Trula Priddy to her feet and helped carry her into the hallway.

There was a commotion outside, heavy feet pounded the floor boards, people at the door were roughly shoved back, and the Greeber menfolk stalked into the room…Code, Corbin, Seeby and Sarl…tall, rawboned men with dark hooded eyes and snarling lips. The boy Clell trailed them.

17

BUCK FELT THE BLOOD rising in his veins. He could almost see it just as plainly as he saw those five frightful men grouped just inside the doorway. Even to look at them was to think trouble, bad trouble, death. All of them were over six feet tall, dark robust men on whose gaunt faces showed the black stubble of two days growth, all except Clell, the youngest, who was still a smoothed-faced boy and wiry as a snake. They were all dressed alike, in blue jumpers and dungarees and hard brogan shoes. Their complexion was not the weathered copper-brown of Luster Holder, but rather a swarthy, dirty brown, which with their beaked noses and thick meeting eyebrows gave to them the collective expression of sullenness, hate, and irritability. They stood slouched, saying nothing, but their black eyes smoldered in their sockets, dull, reptilian but watchful. Those eyes darted back and forth from the upright body in the coffin to the tall, relaxed figure of Luster Holder, who stood rolling a cigarette as if utterly oblivious to their presence.

He lighted the cigarette and funneled the smoke through his nose as he regarded the five men with his emotionless eyes.

"The harness broke," the big hillman said offhandedly, "Granny Blackburn, she's fetchin' some balin' wire. I figger that orgn't to hold him." Otherwise, he was completely unmoved, unchanged and obscenely bland.

Code, the oldest now that Ard was dead, veered his eyes to his brothers. None of them said a word. Clell kept tossing his horse mane hair out of his eyes.

Granny Blackburn hobbled back in shoving a path through the Greebers with several coils of rusty baling wire in one hand.

"Goddurned if hit didn't take all hands and the cook to rustle up this here wire, Luster," she said plainly, handing it to the big hillman. "I 'low hit'll hold him down secure till the Judgment."

As Luster unwound the wire, he stepped to the head of the coffin and placed one brown hand flat on Ard's chest. He pressed hard and the body flopped back down in place. The feet and legs strained against the remaining rope and Granny Blackburn started shoving them down to keep the rope from breaking.

Granny turned her vibrating head toward the men at the back of the room.

"Don't stand thar like a covey of Goddurned partridges sit by a birddog.," she growled, "Come on and give us a hand, he's yore kin, not our'n."

None of the Greebers moved.

Granny tottered and clung to the feet of the corpse to keep her balance. "Well, then," she snorted, "go to Hell and tell the Devil hits a passel of shoats I've sent him."

Buck noticed that as Luster worked, although he seemed wholly occupied with the job at hand, his dark eyes kept the group of men under close surveillance. Luster finished with the head, then wired the feet. He rubbed his hands together and said to Granny, "That ere'll right do hit, Granny."

"Shore hit will, Luster," she cackled, "I'll 'low it'll take the fars of Hell to melt 'em loose, but I be dog if he hain't been the contrariest corpse I ever see'd. I got to go back to the cook room, Luster. If yore a-needin' me, just bray out and I'll come a-humpin' hit, but I wish't to the good Lord God you'd tell me how to git Wurner outen thar. No starved boar hog ever done away with as much grub as that idiot's gobbled down tonight." With that, she hurried from the room.

Buck continued to sit far back in the north corner of the room. He grasped his knees to steady his hands and arms as well as his legs. He didn't look toward the Greebers. He prayed to God they hadn't noticed him. Even in his rising terror, he was certain they had eyes for Luster alone. He tried not to watch Luster. He just couldn't stand to see him cut into bacon strips or shot full of holes. He'd be helpless to give him the aid he needed, for if he moved they'd let him have it too. As best he could, he held his eyes on his pappy, who sat in the same motionless position in the chair far back in a corner near the wide window just behind Luster. He might be tied there with baling wire too!

The stillness was unbearable. If something didn't happen soon, he was afraid of what he might do. It would be purely awful to show yellow in front of Luster Holder. He fingered the .32 Smith and Wesson underneath his shirt and wished he'd left it at home. He felt more helpless with it on him, for if the Greebers knew he was armed, they'd finish him off quickly. He wished now he'd slipped it to Luster, but surely the big hillman hadn't ventured out here without his revolver. A knife and brass knucks wouldn't be enough this time. "O' God," he thought dismally, "Luster oughta had more sense than to of come, him being fearless is gonna cost him his life. God! He ain't gonna always protect him. Luster Holder's time is running out. If they start something, he's a goner."

And even as he thought, he shot a quick glance toward the Greebers just in time to see Code nod his head.

It was a signal. At the nod, a pistol flashed in Code's hand and two shots cracked at the same instant. The gas lamp went out in a shattering and tinkling of glass leaving every object in the house in the dark. Someone cursed loudly.

"Keep low and scatter," a hoarse voice ordered. "Remember what I tole you. Don't far till you're shore whar he's at. You know the rest."

"Did he plug you, Code?" a boy's voice said, high, alarmed.

"The half-breed bastard got me in the right hand, but I can far as good from the left. Scatter and quit talking. He's dead shot and sees in the dark like 'ere animal."

No sounds came from the spot where Luster was last standing. On his knees in the corner, his racing blood came to a frozen halt, Buck could imagine the big Cherokee crouched somewhere in that room, which was coal dark now that the moon had fallen behind the hills. Luster would be calm, alert, and wouldn't be the first to fire at anytime.

All that was heard was the slight shuffling of squatting men, their queer manner of breathing as they tried to control their lungs against the rising tension. It was truly awful to be hemmed in here with death.

Fire roared at his left and not four feet from him a red spurt blinded him. Someone moaned.

"You hit, Corbin?"

"G...Goddammit...I..." the voice died in a sucking gasp.

"He's gone! He's gone!" the boy Clell called out, "I tole you to wait, Code! I tole you we could bush-whack him easy!"

"Shut up, scutter!" a new voice growled. It must be Seebey. A pistol cracked twice in succession, and over to the left of the coffin came an answering shot.

"Side-swiped me," the Seebey voice said curtly.

"I think he's hid behind the coffin, Code."

"We might hit Ard."

"Goddamn Ard," Clell almost screamed, "He's deader'n Hell anyways!"

There were five fast spurts of flame in that direc-tion, the sound of splintering wood. Then two flashes of crimson, closely followed by a scream of real pain.

Silence for a moment.

"They done got Code, Clell!"

"Not quite, he hain't!"

The boy's voice was high and sobbing, "The son of a bitch'll git all of us, Seebey! Let's rush him with our knives! Come on, Sarl!"

"Wait, boy!"

There was a rush of feet, a stumble and a fall. "Goddam, I fell over Corbin." Sudden noise filled the room. There was a warm gurgling, a sound like someone strangling on water. Then silence again.

"I tole you not to do hit, Code!"

The silence broke again as feet shuffled and one mighty blast came from the middle of the room before silence again took over. No shot came in answer. Just then two Greebers slipped out into the hall and came back in with a double-barreled shotgun.

All was still quiet.

"I think we got him, Code."

"Durn if I don't too. I…"

A gun roared close, once, twice, followed by a violent thrashing of feet. All was still as death once more, and Buck knew that death at last was in complete control, only always kind to his best lieutenants, he may have possibly spared someone who'd kill again. He wondered who, Luster or a Greeber.

The voice, not far from him, brought him to his feet, his blood unthawing and circulating madly once more.

"Go git us a light, Buck," Luster said. "Hit's hard to see in the dark."

Buck felt his way along the wall to reach the door. He struck a match and discovered an oil lamp on a small claw and ball table. He lighted it and returned to the room. Cautiously he crossed to the mantel and set it down, and the pale yellow glow revealed the carnage about him and caused his stomach to somersault and almost empty itself through his throat. He had to swallow fast and hold himself very still.

In front of the bullet riddled coffin Sarl Greeber lay on his back, arms and legs outspread. His eyes stared wide like brownish white marbles and blood still trickled from his nostrils and the corners of his mouth. It looked like a red cravat tied around his neck to a crimson scarf thrown around his shoulders.

Fallen face down across his chest was the boy Clell, whose head rested on his folded arms, his long blue-black hair parted to his cheeks. Back near the door and over near the corner behind Luster, Seebey lay folded like a jack-knife. A double-barreled shotgun lay just behind him. Code and Corbin lay face-down, the latter still gripping a .45 Colt revolver.

Blood had run down the slanted floor and formed in a pool not far from the coffin. Buck looked up at Luster. The big hillman was wiping off his knife on a blue bandana handkerchief. If there was any change of expression in his bronzed face, the boy couldn't detect it. It was like something carved out of wood.

At a low whimpering moan, Buck whirled around. Clell Greeber was trying to get up. Luster stepped quickly forward, put an arm under Clell's stomach and lifted him off the dead Sarl and eased him on his back on the floor. The boy's eyes, like black glass, were watching Luster like a wounded animal that knows it is to be finished off right away. His black, mane-like hair fell around his bloodless cheeks.

Buck held his breath and closed his eyes. He couldn't watch it. He was about to cry and he wanted to run screaming from that house and keep running forever and forever.

"Go on and shoot, damn you," the boy moaned huskily, "you done got all the rest."

No sound came. No movement. Cautiously Buck opened his eyes just a fraction and slanted them toward Luster. The big hillman had a bottle to his mouth. He emptied it and tossed it over the coffin into the fireplace. He began rolling a cigarette.

Buck watched in fascination as he saw the boy start crawling slowly, painfully toward the rear of the room, leaving a trail of sticky blood. Just as he saw the red hand reach out tremblingly toward the gun, Luster strode past him unhurriedly and kicked the .45 far into a corner. He came back to the coffin.

"A...ain't you gonna...gonna kill him too, Luster?"

"I hain't never killed no tapper," the big Cherokee said coldly. "I figger ever'body orght to have a chanst to become a man."

"He's about dead anyways, Luster," Buck said, a great relief flooding over him.

"He hain't hurt none, Buck. Hit's Sarl's blood on him. I jest tapped him on the jaw with my knuck-hand."

The boy Clell was sitting up, watching Luster in bewilderment. He placed his palms against the floor and with a great push got to his feet. He stood swaying uncertainly before he staggered from the room.

Buck was amazed, "How could you tell which was him, Luster?"

"He was fool enough to keep a-cussin' and I guess hit hoped in his case. But hit's a wonder he didn't git plugged before him and Sarl come on me with the knife. I figger he musta been sorter behind the others."

It was the most he'd ever heard Luster say. Buck spoke fast now, for he heard people stirring. Talk recommencing, feet shuffling.

"I can't still understand why they didn't git you, Luster."

The big hillman drew deeply on the cigarette. "They must notta been used to shootin' or fightin' in the dark. They figgered I was squatting in a corner or behind the coffin. Actual I was laying flat in front of hit and faring from the floor. That ere Sarl and Clell was rushing toward the corner when I leapt up and crawled 'em."

Granny, Urfie Pearl and Clemmie came stumbling in, drawing a stream of people behind them. All had waited until they were sure the shooting had stopped before they ventured to converge on the death room.

Buck had seen enough. He met the incoming people, sieved between them and rushed out into the open air.

18

Just inside the door, Granny Blackburn leaned over on her stick and Urfie Pearl, Clemmie and two other women stopped just behind her, drawing in close together. Squire Kiler, Freel Goddard, Elmer Runnels and four or five men crowded around the walls. They were all that remained of the big crowd that had come to the sitting up over Ard Greeber.

Granny's old eyes moved at a snail's pace from one sprawled form to the other. She put her hands to her withered face, "I be goddamned if hit don't just look like the devil's done passed through and towed Hell after him. He shore-God's claimed his own, for you done sent the Greeber men-folks back to Missouri or some unknown place, Luster. You really clean't house."

The crowd gawked, mouths open and eyes opened wide.

"Hit's a sight now," Urfie Pearl said, eyes filled with a new light, "I count all of 'em 'ceptin' that boy Clell. Wher's his body at?"

Everybody looked around. Luster said nothing. He was taking another drink from an upturned pint of whisky.

Tessie Burress caught her breath. "They's somebody over in yon corner," she answered in a tone of discovery. She started tottering across the room when her feet flew out from under her and she hit heavily in the pool of blood, splashing drops of it on those behind her. She lay very still for a moment, then began to wail mournfully.

"He'p me, he'p me, for sweet Jesus Christes's sake, he'p me. I've done broke something bad," she hollered frantically.

Granny turned to Elmer Runnels and Fate Peacock. "Lift her gentle and git her outta here. I 'low she's busted a hip, but I hain't got no time to fiddle with no broken bones when they's so many prime corpses to see atter. They's no fool like an old fool." With shaking hands she took a dip of snuff. Her eyes danced with a weird anticipation, and her laugh sounded low in her guts like a "whur-whur-whur." She stated, "Old as she is, I figger we'un's'll be layin' her out 'fore first frost anyways," she added, chewing her toothless gums together. Granny was ruthless when it came to the business of a corpse.

As the two men carried the wailing Tessie out of the room, Granny edged slowly around the wall to the corner behind Luster. She took one look and grasped the big hillman by the arm.

"Who in the name of Satan is hit settin' back thar a-spoutin' blood like durned drinking fountain, Luster?" she pointed toward a headless corpse.

Luster walked closer and stooped over. He straightened up and turned back to the old woman.

"I hain't got no more idear than a new-borned calf, Granny. His head's done blowed clear off his shoulders. He musta got the full load of the shotgun close up when I got rushed," he said as he stared at the headless body.

Still holding his hat crushed in one hand, Squire Kiler slunk forward toward the corner. He hawked his throat twice before he began talking as he examined the situation. His voice was high and hoarse, "Hit sho-God ain't hain't no Greeber. Even Old Tank's mash barrel drownin' cain't katch up with this here. Hit's the first damb time I ever seen a body a-settin' up without one head on hit. 'y God, what's left looks like hit had been drownded in pure blood. You jest cain't make head nor tails of hit, 'ceptin they hain't no head to start with unless hits what's plastered up here like guts and feathers on the wall paper."

"Jest let hit be, Squire," Urfie Pearl answered the old Squire, "We may can tell more when we git the trunk warshed."

The Squire's grizzly face was a sandy white. He kept walking from one side of the room to the other, like he wasn't sure what to say or do next.

"Are they all gone?" a new voice asked, soft, bell-clear.

Every eye shot toward the doorway as Blanche Greeber, the mother entered. She wore a dark, taffeta silk dress and her honey-blonde hair was softly waved and drawn back over her ears by a narrow black velvet ribbon. Her eyes, a clear sky-blue, shone brightly from her slightly tinted face. She held shapely hands in front of her, fingers interwound. Few of those present had ever seen Blanche Greeber, for she never showed herself out of the home. They remembered that she hadn't even gone to Sobby for her husband's funeral. Few recalled ever having seen such a beautiful woman since Dossie Bell passed away. She moved gracefully in the midst of the terrible carnage.

At her entrance, the Squire had started forward with a springy step, then stopped shortly, arms falling at his sides. His cheeks were flushed and he was excited. Nervously, he put on his hat.

"Are they all gone?" she repeated in an anxious tone as she looked around at the death and slaughter lying at her feet.

"All but Clell," Luster drawled, "he's around the place some'rs or 'nother."

"It's good it's over," she sighed, her soft eyes now on Luster alone, and there was relief in her voice.

"I got to be going to my cabin to warsh up, Miss Greeber," Luster said in the same even voice. "Would you admire to go with me now? I'm well shut of my woman now. Sudie, she's taken out with Brother Lazenby. I figger they've went to Arkansas."

"Yes, Luster, I been waitin' a long time, and they ain't no further need of me here," Blanche said rather flatly, as if the carnage around her had just been a hog killing and she was just passing by the slaughter pen and looking forward to the scalding.

"You can live there with me," he said and started toward her. At the moment, it seemed the excitement was over and all would be calm again. Still looks can be deceiving. Just as Luster came up close to Blanche, he wheeled suddenly with a swiftness that can't be comprehended until all is past. During the course of that swift and smooth turn, Luster whipped out his .32-20 and shot Squire Kiler right between the eyes, a straight line measured neat between his now dead eyes. The already dead Squire made no sounds at all. Instead, the old fellow's hairy mouth had dropped open and the red-veined gray eyes bulged like a bullfrog as he caught the flash of steel as the gun came up at him. He died like that, swaying back and forth for an instant as if about to lunge forward before he seemed to come loose at the joints and every limb gave way at the same moment. He pitched face first toward Luster, and the big hillman shoved him backwards. He hit the floor with a big plop and spread out, limbs jerking spasmodically before he lay very still.

Paralyzed by the suddenness of the action, those present never budged from their tracks until the Squire ceased to move. They stared at the tall rangy corpse lying dead on the floor and seemed to be trying to comprehend the very fact that the Squire was dead. Then they started slowly moving back, fright-filled eyes on Luster Holder.

The big hillman blew in the barrel of the gun, replaced it under his belt beneath his unbuttoned shirt and stepped over to Blanche. He paid no mind to anyone else. Indeed, everyone else was too shocked to speak anyway.

He said solemnly, "Hit was him killed Tank. Wurner, he suspicioned him from something he overheard him sayin' to Birdie whilst Wurner was hid under their front porch that Saddiday morning. He trailed him through the woods when he left the house and seen the murder. He tole me and I closed hit up in his mind till I mulled over hit and got hit to all to come straight way."

Luster never looked around or broke his gaze from the now dead Squire but flatly added, "Damned old bastard shore 'nough tried to bushwhack me today on the back lane behind the barn."

After a long moment, someone blurted out, "How'd you suspicion hit was the Squire? What made you dead sure hit was him?"

Luster stared off into the wall beyond him and declared, "I minded his wet clothes, and he forgot and put his hat on and I seen the two holes I plugged through hit down on the lane whilst I was on my way up here."

Luster looked at Blanche Greeber and reiterated, "The Squire aimed to bushwhack me too if your stepsons didn't git me. I been layin' off to plug him for a long time. He was dead-set and determined to have you."

"I been a-knowin' it for over six months now, Luster. He tried to slip up here when the men folks was gone. I had to hide myself," Blanche admitted.

Then Blanche lowered her eyes to the spread-eagled form of the Squire. "It's good to see him dead," she mused, "because he was a wicked and dangerous man. Every time he was here he had to come to the kitchen for water. When I wasn't there, he'd pry through all the rooms looking for me. He never let me know what he was planning because he wanted to wait until he was sure. He just passed the time of day and told me what a pretty woman I was and how I'd sure make some man a good wife. And all the time his hungry old eyes were eating through me and filled with fire, and I just naturally wanted to crawl in a hole and drag it in after me. Him and my sons meant to force me to marry him. He'd been tryin' to shoot you, Mister Holder. He wanted you dead, just as you said, but he was scared my stepsons would never have the nerve to kill you or couldn't even if they tried. So he decided to do it himself."

She stopped abruptly and turned back to Luster, "I'm ready now, Luster. I want to git as far away from this house as I can."

"You wantin' to take yore young'uns with us?" he asked.

She shook her head. "I can't find hide nor hair of Tiddy, and I just figger she's run off to the woods and's hidin' out with Pistol and Tadpole. They can come to us when things settle down, if you ain't mindin.'"

"I hain't mindin' one floggin' bit, Miss Greeber. They can stay out there as long as they's wantin'. That ere Clell too."

"Clell was like his brothers, Luster," she said sadly. "They hated me because I tried to take their mammy's place, all but Ard. I figger Clell'll go on back to Missouri or on to Detroit, and git him a job jest like he's been a plannin' since his pappy's death. That tore him up like crazy."

Luster shook his head and declared, "We better start. I'm all tard out."

Everybody moved back to let them out. At the door Luster said, "Granny, I'll be back in the mornin' to he'p out. Miss Greeber, her and me'll drive up to Sobby for the buryings. I 'low you better send a runner out to Kiler's to let Birdie know her pappy's quit."

Granny shook her ancient head, "I'll durn well do hit, Luster. Hit'll take four wagons or two trucks to cart the boxes out from Melburg."

"I'll jest send Crip after them, Granny. Him and two or three others can dig the graves up to Sobby after they git back. I 'low hit'll dig easy since the soaking rain. Somebody needs to tell the High Shuriff they's been a little trouble out here."

Granny nodded her head in agreement, "I 'low hit would make hit more lawful, but, Luster, they hain't no hurry. They'll let things ride and cool off for a few days afore they venture out."

"I figger so," Luster replied to Granny and took one more look around. He turned back to Blanche and announced, "I'm ready, Miss Greeber."

With that, he took her arm and they were gone into the night.

Meanwhile, Urfie Pearl dropped into a chair and exclaimed, "That just about finished me, Granny. If anything else happens tonight, I'll have a conniption fit!"

A wistful smile crawled over Clemmie's thin face, "We really seen true love in this here room tonight, gals. She just pure worships him and I'm not to be last to say…she don't deserve him."

Granny snorted, "Please shet up, Clemmie, my stomach's awful weak for sech sluice of slush."

Free to turn her hands to her work, Granny became an aged dynamo of activity. "I never see'd the like in all my borned days," she said gutterly. "If

you'un shain't too tard, we can start in right now.
Oncet we git started we can work in shifts…I'll
decide later which is to sleep and how long. Norey,
you go git water started boiling on the range. Fill up
ever' empty vessel. Tell Granny Gates to far up the
warsh kettle in the yard. Some of you men folks can
draw water and keep the fars going. And you'd better jest leave the bodies in the hall till we can scour
this here room. We'uns'll haft to pull off barefoot so
we won't slip. And somebody bring in some more oil
for this here lamp and fetch the one outta the kitch-
en. We'll be a'needin' both of them. If Wurner's still
in there cleanin' up the scraps, jest leave him in the
dark. I figger he can still smell out the grub like a
durn she bear."

"Reckon I better wet the camphor rag and damp-
en Ard agin, Granny," Clemmie said.

"You let Ard be. He'll stay put till we can see to
him proper a'gin. These other dead boys need our
attention now. From the holes in that coffin, him
and hit must have ten pounds of lead in them, but
maybe the extry weight'll he'p hold the varmint down.
Don't waste no more of that camphor on him. We'll
be needin' hit bad fer the others. Freel, I figger you
better go open yore store and fetch us out about six
extry bottles."

While the men folk carried the six whole corpses and the headless unknown one into the hall, the
others scattered to their various tasks…all except
Granny Blackburn, Urfie Pearl and Clemmie.

Granny sighed and declared, "I feel like I'd been drug through Hell back'ards and beat to death with a soot bag."

"Draw up chairs, girls," Granny sighed as she sat down in a rocker. "I'm so tard I cain't tell which end's rightly up. I got to rest my carkiss so I can git me a fresh start and let's have a little time to git in a few words 'afore the battle begins. They hain't no quittin' now."

"Yes, we better rest our carkisses so we can gather stren'th for a fresh start," Urfie Pearl replied.

"I'm so tired I cain't tell which end's rightly up myself, Granny," Clemmie said in a whispery voice, before adding, "Granny, when did Luster and Blanche decide they was made for each other?"

The old woman scratched her chin and answered, "At the settin' up over Tank, I suspicioned hit there, but I wasn't shore. I shoulda knowed, the way they kept settin' with their eyes glued on theirselves. And then oncet when Luster went out behind the house, I plain seen a woman through the kitchen winder a-talkin' with him. At the time, I never thought of Blanche Greeber. I was a-thinkin' hit was that ere organ player, Trula Priddy, which ever'body knows has been horsin' bad fer him ever sinst she seen him at Dossie Bell's buryin.'"

"Well, I just do know into my time," Urfie Pearl said, "Reckon he'll wedlock her, Granny?"

Granny chuckled and smirked, "He may if she craves hit, but he hain't never married no woman before, not even Dossie Bell."

"Live and learn, die and rot it," Clemmie put in, "couldn't nobody never figger out that Indian's mind."

Granny thought that over and replied, "He sho' takened to her like a bear to honey and she was the same way. Hit's the first time I ever heard tell of a feller havin' to nigh clean out a whole family to git the woman he craved. Things worked out jest like God Hisself had planned hit. Sudie takened out at jest the right time."

"Clell, he's still breathin. Reckon he'll be out for revengeance?" Urfie Pearl asked.

Clemmie shook her head and sighed, "Not if he wants to keep still breathin.' I figger he's off somewhar now, stripped naked and pinchin' hisself all over to see if he is really alive. I jest cain't git it straight why Luster didn't finish him off with the others but I think hit's right Christian and neighborly of him to see that the widder woman's taken care of. Hit's downright touchin.'"

Granny sputtered her lips and said measuredly, "Was yore brains snuff, they wouldn't sneeze a hummingbird, Clemmie. I sometime honest think you oughta go over to Melburg and have good doctor examine yore brain. Hit may be dangerous for you to be runnin' 'round loose. Hit's not neighborly thoughts Luster's havin' fer her. He seen her as the purtiest woman since he lost Dossie Bell and what he sees and wants, he jest purely takes."

Clemmie declared to Granny, "Well, I know some things. I heard a body tell that oncet when she brung in a fresh jug of corn which Luster called her to fetch him, she come in like ghost and floated out the same way. How a beanpole of a woman like her, with skitterish eyes and looks like she's ready to jump whenever a body hollers, 'Frog!'...how she brung comfort to Luster Holder is more than my worm-eat brain can understand. Durn if you can figger that Cherokee. First, he lives and loves with a woman like Dossie Bell and then he turns to Sudie Lazenby and seems just as satisfied. Hit's funny to me he never taken Birdie Kiler long ago 'cause she's just solid built for the kind of service I 'low a pow'ful man like him is needin.'"

Granny stood and tried to straighten her back with palsied hands. "Enough chit chatchin.' Come on, girls, we'uns is the only ones not fainty at the sight of slaughtered bodies. I figger we can work more stiddy this way with that ere Pistol and his nigger twin outen' the house."

"They may be back, Granny," Urfie Pearl said uneasily. "I'd rather be bemessed a mile from water than to go through with all that a'gin."

Granny scoffed, "Not in a coon's age. That ere wild girl is deep in the woods now a-sleepin' with them at her side. I figger she sleeps sounder with no roof over her head." Granny cackled. "We'uns done got our work cut out for us and hit looks like for oncet in our lives, we done bit off almost more than we can chew comfortable but a body never knows till he's taken a holt. I'm shore I'll look back on it as the most glorious night of my long life."

"Well, I'll say this, Granny, things has shore rounded off."

"You just hain't throwin' notions to the breeze now, Urfie!"

"I still cain't see why Squire Kiler thought he could get Blanche Greeber," Clemmie said.

Granny had a ready answer, 'Why he thought he could git Luster Holder by hisself is what's pesticatin' me, unless his old blood was bilin' so for Blanche that his brains got addled. And like she told us tonight, after he seen her with Luster he went hog-wild and decided to act. And he musta figgered if he got rid of Luster by hisself, them boys wouldn't only rush through with the deal for their step-mammy, but would throw in a whackin' good piece of the Nation lands to boot. And hit's clear why Tessie Burrus seen him ridin' his stud out towards Humphries's place earlier tonight and why he was lookin' for Buck. Ain't no doubt, he was gonna kill that boy before he could tell Luster what happened at the fight. Buck…he musta dodged him someways. But the bastard made his big mistake in not tellin' the Greebers that Luster was on his way out here when that ere idiot told all of us in the kitchen tonight. All of 'em mighta been able to bushwhack him, since the Squire figgered right as to the short-cut Luster was takin'."

Granny took a breath and shook her old head and countered, "As for thinkin' he could get Blanche, that old bastard thought every woman in the county was horsin' and a-sizzlin' for him. And as I've said before, they say he could sure as rain satisfy a woman!"

With that, she slapped her thigh and laughed raucously, "The reason won't be no secret to us for long."

All of the old gals got a hearty laugh over that prediction.

"Well, Birdie's free at last," Clemmie said.

Urfie Pearl nodded, "Yes, she's got only herself though, poor pitiful thing."

"Poor pitiful thing, yore hind foot!" Granny snorted, "What more does she need? As long as she's whole and in good sound health, she'll never want for money. She's carrying a good livin' 'round with her on her two solid legs day and night. All that'll grieve her is not being able to git Luster for herself."

Wheezing heavily, Granny took still another breath and continued, "And had you thought about it? Luster's shot cut the cords on that ere preacher which the Squire had threatened to cut in an entarly diff'rent way. I figger he's well on his way to them parts the Old Squire tore him from. They say Brother Dipple's body had perished to practical nothing and he looked like he'd swapped tails with a killdeer and got cheated in the bargain. Come on. Git a hustle on. I've admired to lay out that ole Squire sinst the first time I ever see'd him."

"Me and you both, Granny," Urfie Pearl declared, "I'm on far coals to git my hands on him."

As Clemmie asked the question, she kept having to raise her chin higher and higher to hold in the accumulation of amber. Her words came in a bubbly mumble, "I wonder who the man with no head is?"

"I hain't got no more idea than a cut pig, but 'y God when we git him stripped and cleant off, then we may can tell."

Clemmie hurried to the fireplace and emptied her mouth over the coffin. She turned back, wiping it on her raised skirt before asking in earnest, "Whur'd they take Tessie to, Granny?

"Out under the hickories or home or some'rs or 'nother. Like I done said, I hain't got no time for broke bones when they's corpses to tend to," Granny declared.

She turned to Freel Goddard and informed him, "Freel, they's gonna be one more setting up tomorrow night and some folks will bring grub but most'll be here to eat it. Hit'll be a disgrace if we'uns don't have enough to feed 'em. SoI 'low we better send word to Cobey Yates to barbecue some hogs. Luster... he'll foot the bill, I'm sure, him sorter being kin to the dead ones now on account of Blanche. Six hogs orghta be plenty. They orghta put them hogs over the coals by daylight anyways so to be ready by full night."

Freel nodded, "I'll see to it, Granny."

"Hit's gonna be a sight up to Sobby too. Reckon they'll hole Ard over till they're ready to bury the others?" Clemmie asked.

"I 'low if hit's left up to me, I'll do hit. I'm thinkin' if we keep camphor in him steady he'll keep, and hit'll be more sensible to git hit all over at one settin'," Granny answered.

"Blanche...she didn't say," Urfie said.

Granny pulled thoughtfully at the flaccid skin of her turtlish neck. "Blanche...she's got other things on her mind and they ain't got nothin' to do with dead bodies. If I see that Clell I may can git a decision from him. Anyways you take hit, everybody betwixt here and the Mississippi River'll flock to that church house."

Granny looked past the other women and declared, "Here comes the men folks with the scourin' water and the brooms. Hit's time to start humpin' hit."

19

TIDDY DREAMED she was swimming with Buck in a golden river. While he watched from a sandbar, she dove far down to the bottom and lay on the smooth river floor smiling up at him. She could see his brown body plain as day and he was as beautiful as the picture of a statue she'd seen in an old story book. She opened her arms and cried for him to come to her. She saw his head split the crystal water and come toward her, growing bigger and bigger. Their slick bodies wound together, and just as their hips clove tightly, the river disappeared. It wasn't sand at her back. It was cottonseed and she was the girl of the shed once more. She began squirming and pushing to escape his vice-like encircling arms, whimpering, "I'm…I'm…I'm…" She tried three choking times before she raised her voice in a scream.

She sat up in the close darkness, still trying to free herself from the encircling arms, whispering, "I'm afraid, Buck, I'm afraid."

The lips were small and warm as they mumbled ticklish at her ear, "It ain't Buck, Tiddy. It's me, Pistol. What you a'faid of, huh?"

She dropped back down, squeezing the little boy to her, while her love went out to him and the boy she'd run away from earlier in the night. And at that moment, she knew she'd never be afraid of Buck Humphries again. He was the one that would fear her. Like a fool, she'd ruined herself with him forever. She'd wanted him then the same way he'd wanted her. Her fright had tricked her into losing a moment she'd always regret.

As she fought the ache deep in her body, the stillness of the night was broken. It sounded like somebody bursting a box in the front room. She sat up and listened, wide awake now. She could sense Pistol's alertness by his tightening arms.

Whoever was working on the boxes took his time. There'd be the crack of a plank, silence, then another crack.

"Reckon they's messin' with Ard, Tiddy," the boy whispered breathlessly.

"I don't rightly know, Pistol," Tiddy admitted.

Then a thousand boxes burst right together and now it wasn't boxes at all. Buck was right. Luster was in there.

She sprang from the bed, new fright chills lacing her naked body, and rushed to the washstand in the corner. She found a match and lighted a candle in a cracked saucer. Hastily she began dressing.

"Something went bad wrong," she cried to the wide-eyed boy sitting straight and stiff in the bed. She said to the boy, "Wake Tadpole."

The white boy began shaking his Negro pal, "Dood Dod, Taddy! Dit up! All hell done b'oke loose and you s'eep frough it!"

Tadpole raised up, dabbing his eyes with ebony fists. He looked about him in bewilderment, his eyes all whites.

"Whar you bin, Pist?" Tadpole asked.

"We can't talk now, Tadpole," Tiddy said weakly, "you two pull on your pants and let's git out a here fast. Somebody's shootin' up the place!"

The three of them left the room by the low window and huddled near the death room behind an althea bush. All was very quiet from inside the house. But in the yard several dark forms were visible among the pine and hickories. She could plainly hear a woman taking on something dreadful.

Tiddy got up and crept to the side window, Pistol and Tadpole holding to her hands. The window was closed against the cats and the small square panes were cloudy. She could hear voices, but couldn't tell what was being said.

Another shot cracked, followed after an interval by a falling body. Tiddy sprang back, squatting

behind the damp bush, the two little boys clinging
fiercely to her.

"O Dod, I tared, Tiddy!"

"I is too!"

"Shhhh…"

After what seemed like an interminable time,
they heard some folks leaving the house. As they
descended the porch steps, someone followed, holding a lamp. Tiddy's heart jumped. Her mother was
leaving with Luster Holder. She opened her mouth
to cry out, then choked off the words, both realiza-
tion and indignation coming to her like a sudden jolt.
She remembered the day after her father's burying,
her mother talking with her in the kitchen. It flashed
back through her mind now, clear and revealing.

"What do you think of Luster Holder, Tiddy?"
her mammy had asked her.

"He killed off Pappy," she'd replied then.

Mammy had replied, "I ain't so sure. It don't sound
like what I've heard about him."

"Somebody killed him, mammy," Tiddy had
retorted.

She continued to reminisce about their long ago
conversation, that of mother and daughter. It seemed
like yesterday still.

"They say he don't kill underhand-like," Mammy
had reasoned.

"Maybe not."

"What do you think of him?"

"I don't even know him, Mammy."

"He was at the setting up last night."

"What do you think of him, Mammy?"

Her eyes were over-bright as she said, whispery, "I don't want to think. I'm mortal scared to think too deep."

Tiddy had thought it was hate, but it wasn't.

Now her eyes misted as she watched her mother disappear under the trees with Luster Holder. She heard the car start. She had been deserted, but she knew her mother loved her. She just loved Luster more and badly needed him now. She thought of Buck and couldn't blame her. She'd caught just this one glimpse of Luster. It was enough. He was a man any woman could be proud to go anywhere with.

She knew that her brothers were dead. A lump pressed against the walls of her windpipe. She hadn't liked the older ones, but she hadn't wanted them killed. She'd have to go to the funeral now to see Clell. He'd always been short off to her and tried to act like he was her pappy instead of her half-brother, but he was a right comely boy. She liked the way he wore his hair long and silky black and spearing into his hollow cheeks. She liked to run her fingers through it because it sent pleasure tingles all over her. But usually he slapped her hands away, except that time when her pappy lay a corpse. She'd played with his hair as he sat, eyes grief-swollen, on the back porch and he'd taken her on his lap and kissed her on the cheek, his lips soft and sweet then and not snarly like they usually were. His voice was tender, hoarse and unlike his usual one as he said, "I do love you, Little Sis, sinst pappy's went now, I'm gonna see nothin' ever harms you." A week later he beat up the sharecropper boy.

Her breath hitched in a sob. Clell couldn't have been anything but tough, the way he grew up. He was a good boy and really kind-hearted if they had first let him live his life like he admired to live it. He was her best half-brother next to Ard, and she'd loved both of them.

She heard the little fellows against her sucking in their breath and sniffing their noses. She had to take them somewhere because they couldn't stay in that death house. She never wished to come around it again. She knew where she'd like to go, but after what happened tonight she just couldn't. He wouldn't like to have her there anyway and his old pappy would turn her back at the door. She would take Pistol and Tadpole to the barn loft or the cottonseed shed if the very sight of those places wouldn't bring back sick and awful memories to her.

She knew. They'd go down in the woodlot and sleep on the bed of moss in the holly clump, where she'd napped on many a hot afternoon. She could get a quilt against the chill of early morning and, snuggled up close, they would sleep cozy.

"We'll go sleep in the woods," she whispered, "Will you be afraid?"

"Doodness, naw, Tid, me and Taddy, us ain't 'cared with you. Ere you, Taddy?"

"Nuh uh, Pist, I ain't."

"Stay here till I fetch a quilt." She ran toward the rear window with them tearing in close behind her. She vaulted over the sill like a boy and was back, out almost instantly with the folded quilt under one arm.

As they passed the kitchen door, it was flung back and a square of light cut out the three of them distinctly and an old and cracked voice called, "Who's thar?"

Tiddy could just make out the dark silhouette of the old woman framed in the door. She recognized the owner of the question...that Buckner woman, and wasn't upset.

"It's me, Tiddy," she said low toned.

"Whur you goin' off to, chile?"

"I...I was a-goin'...Mammy said come over to Luster Holder's cabin."

"That's a fur ways, chile. You'd never make hit. Whyn't you come on in and sleep here? You 'orght to know me, I'm Miss Buckner."

"I mind you well, Miss Buckner," Tiddy replied.

"Ere them little tappers with you?" the old lady inquired.

"Yes, Miss Buckner. We'uns don't crave sleepin' where they's so many bodies."

"Is they more corpses, Tid?" Pistol interjected.

"I ain't knowing, Pistol," Tiddy explained.

"Have you saw that 'ere Buck Humphries around anywheres?" Urfie Pearl said urgently.

Tiddy's flesh crawled around her bones. "No, I ain't, Miss Buckner. Why you askin'…askin' me?"

The old woman speculated, "I figgered you knowed him. Anyways, if you see him any time early tomorrow tell him his pappy needs him bad."

"Where is Mister Humphries at, Miss Buckner?"Tiddy inquired figuring Miss Buckner would know.

The old gal cackled, "He's a layin' right in the front room without no head on."

Tiddy was puzzled. "You mean he's sick?"

Urfie Pearl Buckner shook her head and began emphatically, "I mean he got his head blowed right clean offen his durned shoulders in the fracas which killed yo're brothers. The way they figger hit, he was a settin' in a corner jest whur Luster stood at and being practical stone deaf didn't know no more'n a blind weasel what was taking place. Yo're brother Sarl…he lunged forward and emptied the shotgun whur he thought Luster was and instid a gettin' him, he unheaded Old Henley. Anyways, they shouldn't be much grief or regret even from Buck, 'cause the old Toot had sho-God lived out his time anyways and was jest bobbin' 'round in the way and as can-tankerous as a ole blue hen and with about as much sense as a last year's bird's nest. He was jest a-usin' up good air some healthy body coulda used handy."

Tiddy gulped, "Miss Buckner, how do you know it's Mister Humphries, if he ain't got no head on him?"

The old lady cackled, "Granny Blackburn recognized him after we got the body cleaned off."

She stopped and spat to one side in the darkness.

She continued, "I jest meandered out to snatch me a fresh breath of air. I got to git back to my labors. You go on to yo're room and catch you a good night's rest. Tomorrow's gonna be a big day."

The door closed and old Miss Buckner was gone.

The girl stood in her tracks like a statue. Her blood sang and pounded and roared in her ears. The glorious feeling began at her toes and eased up her legs and thighs and middle and breasts to reach her burning, enflamed face.

Tiddy jumped as Pistol punched her and asked, "Is they more dead bodies in there besides Ard, Tiddy?"

"I ain't knowing, Pistol," she said vacantly.

Tadpole tugged at her belt, "I'se getting' cole, Tid."

"Come on," she said in a high voice, which sang clear and far into the dense, star-dotted night.

She took each by the hand and rushed them to the lot gate. They were halfway to the barn before she stopped and pulled them behind the lone hickory in the center of the enclosure. A horse broke from the barn hallway and raced toward the wire fence. As it leaped over in a high arc, she heard, "On your way, Rebel!" in the husky boy-voice of Clell himself. Someone else seemed to cry for her, "He's alive, Clell's alive. Sweet Jesus, be praised!"

Something soft rubbed against her leg and meowed in distress. Tiddy reached down and began rubbing the cat's skinny back. There was a painful howl as Pistol yelled at the cat, "I tick the livin' guts outta you, you damn ole sneak!" Pistol kicked him hard. The cat squalled loudly and Pistol raised his head saying flatly, "I think I done kilt Ard's old tom. I kicked the sonna bitch right tare betwixt the eyes."

"Was it Muddyspring, Pistol?"

Tiddy chuckled, "I'm sure glad you did. Muddyspring's an old snake in the grass. He's the kinda cat that'd eat his master. After Ard fed and tended him so good, he'd eat Ard."

"Yeah, I till him tomorrow. Le's find Noble Preen. She's a dood ole pussy tat. I want to feed her..."

"We'll find her when daylight comes on," she explained.

She entered the dark hallway of the old barn and, leaving the boys, felt along the wall for a rope. She opened a stall gate and stepped in, feeling in front of her until she touched a soft velvety nose. She looped the rope around the mule's neck and called, "Ho, Pansy, easy now, girl." She pulled on the rope, backing out of the stall, the mule tramping after her.

Outside she led it over to an oak stump, threw the folded quilt over Pansy's middle and climbed astride. "Come on, kids," she said, "Tadpole hold on behind me, you in front, Pistol." She pulled them up one at a time.

"Where we headin' to, Tid?"

"A house a far piece. Hold on tight 'cause I'm going fast as Pansy can gallop."

"A ways off in the woods, Tiddy?" Pistol asked.

She absently but dreamily replied, "Yeah, in the prettiest woods in the whole wide world."

"Is we goin' to a house?" Tadpole asked.

Tiddy answered the boy with a simple, "Yes."

Tadpole was curious and asked, "Whose house we goin' to?"

"Buck Humphries hisself, boys. I got to tell him his pappy ain't no more," she cried in a wild glee she could no longer hold back.

"Dood! I like ole Buck somethin' terrible."

"Bofe of us, Tid."

After a brief silence, Pistol, curious and worried, asked, "Are we comin' back to bury Ard?"

'Sure as shootin', my little Wiggletail," she reassured him.

Tiddy held on to Pansy, and Pistol and Tadpole held on to Tiddy and all that was heard was the hollow plump-plump of the mule's hoofs as she galloped through the night. Low in the east, the moon was shrouded in folds of silver mist and was just hanging there and not lighting upon the earth one single bit. Night and woods and fields flew by them, and the air had the wet, musty smell of early morning. Overhead the birds were beginning to stir, chirping to each other about their good sound night's rest, impatient for the dawn.

Pansy climbed the last steep clay hill and came up to the cornfield behind the Humphries place. Tiddy pulled her up and slid off and helped the kids to the ground. She pulled off the quilt and put it under her arm.

"Keep good and quiet. We don't wanna wake Buck."

"We'll be 'twiet," Pistol whispered quietly.

The three of them crept through the high corn and came out just behind the back porch. Tiddy knew where his room was, because she'd caught sight of Buck watching for her from the upper attic window when she used to hide in the corn.

With the little fellows close in her wake, she walked up the hallway. In the grayish light of approaching dawn, she couldn't see any stairway. She opened a front-room door and found the four steps which led to the door to the upper story. Gently she pulled back the door and found the main flight of steps. When she reached the upper floor she was near the shingled roof.

She stopped and listened. Above the short, excited breathing of Pistol and Tadpole she heard the steady breathing through an open door in front of her. She knelt down and whispered, "I'll fix a pallet on the floor with the quilt. You and Tadpole and Dink can sleep there."

"Dink?" Pistol asked.

"Yeah, he's living with Buck now," she answered Pistol.

Pistol smiled, "I glad. Is we 'donna live wif' Buck too?"

Tiddy smiled and put her finger softly to her lips, "Shhhh…both of you wiggle tails go to sleep now."

Pistol hugged Tiddy and his small cheek was hot against hers. The little fellow breathed long and hard for a minute, the lungs rising and falling like tiny bellows, before his head jerked up again.

"Tiddy, how do you think Ard's soul left outta the house?" Pistol asked innocently.

She smiled and answered him reassuringly, "It went up the chimney hole, Pistol. They always do."

"It's a million tillion mile off by now, huh?" the boy asked.

She pointed skywards, "Way up in the stars. Now quit squirming, Wiggletail, and go to sleep."

She tiptoed into the room and with the boys in tow, she spread the quilt out in the middle of the floor. She could just make out the dark bed in the corner.

"Lie down and go to sleep," she said again to the boys very softly. "I'll throw something else over you in just a bit."

"Ain't you 'donna s'eep with us, Tiddy?" Pistol asked.

She shook her head, "No, there won't be room. Hush now and sleep."

The boys drifted off to sleep in just second and Tiddy moved softly and quietly to the corner and held her eyes on the bed for a long time until her eyes made out the smaller ridge under the covers. Slowly she slid her hand along the wet sheet and under the sleeping boy. She pulled him out gently and for a moment pressed him close to her breast. Then she walked back to the pallet and, still feeling, eased the naked little fellow down between Pistol and Tadpole, who were now sound asleep.

She fumbled around in a corner, found a cotton blanket, and spread it over the boys. She straightened up and with shaking hands began unbuckling her belt. Her breath was hot and dry on her lips. She stepped out of her pants and began unbuttoning her shirt. A button hung and, impatient to the point of nausea, she ripped off the shirt and threw it at her feet.

She heard the springs creak as Buck sat up.

"Is that you, Pappy?" Buck asked.

The breathless Tiddy replied, "No, Buck."

Startled, Buck inquired, "Who is it then?"

"Light a lamp and you'll see," Tiddy answered.

Buck shook his head in the dark, "I cain't...I ain't got no clothes on."

In a sultry manner, Tiddy replied, "I ain't neither, Buck. I'm in the skin God give me."

"What? Tiddy, it's you!" he gasped.

"Big as life and twicet as natural, Buck. I'm gonna crawl in bed with you."

She heard the springs ting loudly and knew he was getting up on the other side. "You cain't git in here with me, Tiddy. It's a sin to bed up with a boy you ain't married to. The bed's all soaked anyways."

She was firm in her response, "I ain't mindin' none, Buck. A body'll warm it so quick he won't know the difference."

With that she crossed the room in one happy, heart-throbbing leap. It took less than another moment to slide over the wet sheets pulling to her middle. Then her arms were around his waist and she pulled him back down, burying her face in the soft fuzz of his warm breast.

At first, he lay very still, arms by his sides, then shaking so that the springs hummed. When he spoke the words were hoarse and blended together in a distant mumble.

"You hadn't orght to be here like this, Tiddy. Your folks won't like it."

She raised up on her elbows, her mouth near his face as she whispered, "It ain't just in their power to know, Buck, and where they's bidin' now they ain't carin' none. They're all dead but Clell and he's going off to Detroit or back to Missouri, I'm sure, just not which one. And Mammy...she's went to be Luster's woman and Pistol and Tadpole and me's come to live with you and Dink. They's all down there on the floor palleted up, and sleeping like little fresh-hatched chicks."

He turned a little toward her. He tried to speak tenderly but his words were somewhat frantic, "It'd pleasure me gloriously to have all you'uns here with me, Tiddy. It'd break the lonesomeness of this place all to flinders but you cain't stay here in bed nekkid with me, Tiddy. Pappy...he won't like it, we may of already woke him."

Tiddy giggled nervously and snuggling closer said, "It'll take Gabriel's mighty horn to wake him now, Buck."

"He ain't that deaf, Tiddy. He'll crop up on us 'fore we've know it," Buck warned her, his pappy's death still unbeknownst to him.

Tiddy said nothing more. She lay very still against him while time threaded hastily by. Something like chimes and beautiful bells rang in her ears, in the far distance, then music from a sacred choir up in the far sky. Her lips were wet when they pressed into his cheek. Her breath was wet too, and hot like heat waves. She held herself very stiff for a moment before she turned her body loose. As all her flesh melted together, in one sudden spring, she turned over on top of him, found his lips and lowered her mouth to them lightly. Even as she felt them leap to life and start drawing her own between them, the hard arms pinioned her whole quivering body. They released her and the sigh was long and painful as he panted, "Forgive me, Tiddy, for what I tried back yonder."

She whispered tremulously back, "They just ain't nothing to forgive, Buck. I ain't no longer afraid."

"Pappy may..." The rest was lost as he made one last weak effort to untangle himself from her before she felt his whole worried mind release him and shout to his body to claim her that was truly made by his God for him. At that point, she also knew at last that she was safe forever. Then she was riding away on a golden moon beam high in the silver sky...up where no sound of bullets could ever disturb her again.

THE END

ABOUT THE AUTHOR

J ACK HAPPEL BOONE (1903–1966) was born in Gibson County, Tennessee. He spent his youth in Chester County and attended public schools in Henderson. Educated at Memphis State College and Vanderbilt University, he began writing professionally as early as 1932. Between 1932 and 1944, he was published in such publications as *Prairie Schooner, Household Magazine, Southern Review, A Vanderbilt Miscellany*, and *Story*. He taught at such prestigious universities as Clemson, Vanderbilt, Georgia Tech, Mississippi State, and Rensselaer Polytechnic Institute, as well as lectured at the University of Iowa.

Boone wrote regularly from 1932 until the mid-1950s. His novel *Dossie Bell is Dead* received critical acclaim after its publication in 1939. *Woods Girl* is the long-buried sequel to that novel. He wrote most of his works in a manner that would reflect the language, speech and tradition of his subjects. His works provide a glimpse of backwoods and rural life in West Tennessee in the 1930s and 1940s including many archaic customs held over from far earlier times. The majority of his works are set in rural West Tennessee in the area commonly known as The Nation. Boone remained primarily in Chester County until his death in 1966.

ABOUT THE EDITOR

 JOHN E. TALBOTT is a native of the area about which Boone wrote. He was raised within miles of the Nation area that was fictionalized as the Tolby Nation. Raised in Finger, Tennessee, Talbott was educated in McNairy and Chester County, Tennessee, schools as well as Freed-Hardeman University and the University of Memphis. He and Boone share two alma maters in common: Chester County High School and the University of Memphis (formerly known as Memphis State College). Talbott practices law within a block of where Boone wrote many of his novels and short stories. He has actively written and lectured on subjects of local and regional interest during the last

twenty-five years. He had previously written five works of local and regional history or biography and edited four works of history and fiction, including *Woods Girl.*

As the Administrator of Jack Boone's Estate, Talbott is actively engaged in the curation, editing, and publication of Boone's long archived works. Having dedicated some twenty-five years to the search for the story of the man and his works, Talbott is himself a collector of original works and papers of Boone. A practicing attorney in Henderson, he is also a former educator, having taught and lectured on both secondary and university levels.

Talbott has both promoted and discussed Boone and his works in print and lectures as well as on radio and in podcasts. His goal is to see all of Boone's long-hidden works published so that Boone may finally be evaluated and his legacy both explored and established.